THE
OF D

A Minnesota Book Award Finalist
A *Parents* Magazine Best Book
A *Kirkus Reviews* Best Book
A RISE: A Feminist Book Project Selection

"Through Ursu's hallmark thoughtful and inspiring
writing, readers delve into a story that seamlessly combines
intriguing world building that is full of magic with a
feminist perspective that interrogates the systemic oppression
at society's core."—*Kirkus Reviews*, starred review

"*The Troubled Girls of Dragomir Academy* manages the particular
magic of being both a true fantasy novel and a clear-eyed
reflection of the here-and-now. Bighearted, generous, and
outstandingly original, this is a story only Anne Ursu could
write."—Elana K. Arnold, author of *The House That Wasn't There*

"Readers present for the tale's magical trappings and
interwoven intrigue won't be disappointed, and they'll
welcome Marya's determination to assert herself as
powerful in her own right."—ALA *Booklist*

"Via a winningly curious protagonist who has a keen interest in
the truth, Ursu weaves a layered tapestry—filled with close-knit
relationships and a well-explained, intriguing world—that questions
authority, misogyny, and whom a story serves."—*Publishers Weekly*

"A thoughtful and incisive story of lies told to control people and the complicated girls who ask questions, push back, and keep fighting."—Tui Sutherland, *New York Times* bestselling author of the Wings of Fire series

"An accessible, timely school story with a rather Transylvanian flavor to its fantasy setting. Ursu explores girls' conditioning in timidity and shame in a male-dominated world and, ultimately, envisions a hopeful, female-determined future of magical ability."—*The Horn Book*

"It's no secret that Anne Ursu is a gifted storyteller. *The Troubled Girls of Dragomir Academy* is intricately plotted and compulsively readable, with characters who will stay with you long after you stop reading. I could not put it down."—Aisha Saeed, *New York Times* bestselling author of *Amal Unbound*

"Anne Ursu practices her own brand of sorcery—the ability to craft wondrous, magical stories that are unlike anything you've ever read. Another extraordinary tale from a remarkably talented author."—Erin Entrada Kelly, Newbery Medal–winning author of *Hello, Universe*

"A suspenseful tale woven with secrets and magic, with a gasp-worthy twist at the end, *The Troubled Girls of Dragomir Academy* is everything I love about fantasy. Spell-binding."—Christina Soontornvat, Newbery Honor–winning author of *A Wish in the Dark*

Library of Congress Cataloging-in-Publication Data

Names: Ursu, Anne, author.
Title: The troubled girls of Dragomir Academy / Anne Ursu.
Description: First edition. | New York : Walden Pond Press, an imprint of HarperCollins Publishers, 2021. |
  Audience: Ages 8-12. | Audience: Grades 4-6. | Summary: Marya Lupu's parents have always believed that
  her older brother, Luka, is destined to be a sorcerer and make the family's fortune, so when the day he is tested
  turns into a disaster, and the Guild declares that he has no magical talent, they find it easier to blame Marya
  for upsetting the test than admit the truth, and she is sent to the Dragomir Academy, a school for wayward
  girls—a school where she finds friendship and ultimately discovers her own talents.
Identifiers: LCCN 2021005562 | ISBN 978-0-06-227513-4 (pbk.)
Subjects: LCSH: Magic—Juvenile fiction. | Wizards—Juvenile fiction. | Brothers and sisters—Juvenile fiction.
  | Families—Juvenile fiction. | Schools—Juvenile fiction. | CYAC: Magic—Fiction. | Wizards—Fiction. |
  Brothers and sisters—Fiction. | Family life—Fiction. | Schools—Fiction.
Classification: LCC PZ7.U692 Tr 2021 | DDC 813.6 [Fic]—dc23

LC record available at https://lccn.loc.gov/2021005562

Typography by David DeWitt
22 23 24 25 26  PC/CWR  10 9 8 7 6 5 4 3 2 1

First paperback edition, 2022

# THE TROUBLED GIRLS OF DRAGOMIR ACADEMY

## ANNE URSU

**WALDEN POND PRESS**

*An Imprint of HarperCollinsPublishers*

To Debbie Kovacs

THE CONTINENT OF
DOVIA

ILVANIA

BEZNA FOREST

FANTOMA FOREST

ILLYRIA

MERUBE

TORAK

DONAU RIVER

KEL

MUNTELAND

ROSA MOUNTAINS

DRAGOMIR
ACADEMY

SARABET

LACSAT

SATMARE

COLT DE LUP

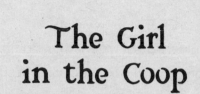

# The Girl
# in the Coop

There were few women pictured in the great tapestries of Illyria—besides the witches, of course. The tapestries depicted moments of heroism, epic battles of good and evil, of powerful sorcerers and brave noblemen protecting the kingdom from the monsters that had threatened it throughout its history.

That is not to say that girls and women did not matter to Illyria: behind every great tapestry was a woman who wove it, just as behind every great sorcerer was a wife to tend to his domestic affairs, a governess to teach his children, a cook to warm his gullet, a maid to keep his fires lit.

And behind every boy who dreamed of being a sorcerer was a mother who raised him to be brave, noble, and kind. And perhaps that boy even had a sister, who, right before the Council for the Magical Protection of Illyria finally visited his humble home to test him for a magical gift, made sure the chicken coop was spotless.

If some master weaver were to immortalize the scene at the Lupu house on the day this story begins—the day before the council would come to find out if Luka Lupu was, indeed, a sorcerer—maybe somewhere on the edges of the tapestry you would find an image of Marya Lupu doing just that, while her father and her brother sat at the dining room table reciting the names of the Illyrian kings and the years of their reigns, and her mother scanned the family library, making sure it demonstrated that theirs was a household of superior quality, with books full of the best information, and void of any dubious predilections or philosophies.

The Lupus had been waiting for this day since Luka had come into the world thirteen years earlier, bright-eyed and somehow already sage-looking, as if he had absorbed enough wisdom in utero to declaim on some of the weightier issues facing a baby, if only he could speak.

Of course, with every male birth in the entire kingdom of Illyria came the hope of a magical gift, of a letter from the council appearing one day early in the boy's second decade, of the council itself appearing at the door, of the eventual pronouncement that the boy was, indeed, gifted and Illyria had a new sorcerer to protect the realm. For most this dream was not realized. But everyone could tell that there was something special about Luka, so when the letter arrived saying he was one of the few boys every year who had been identified as having magical potential, it felt more like a happy inevitability than a dream come true.

What was it about Luka that made him such an obvious sorcerer? Was it his good looks? His quick wit? His strength? His comportment? His ready smile? If you asked his parents, it was all these things, plus something else, something you couldn't put into words. So, naturally, they talked about it all the time. If you asked his sister, though . . . well, you would learn quickly not to ask his sister. Anyway, people never seemed to care what Marya thought about such matters.

For instance: Marya thought that scrubbing out the chicken coop a second time this week was ridiculous. The council would be here to evaluate her brother, not the chicken coop. They would not look in the chicken coop, and even if for some reason they did look in the chicken coop and find it not to their naturally exalted chicken-coop standards, it would hardly affect their evaluation of Luka. They were not going to say, *Gracious, what a powerful sorcerer that boy will be—too bad about the chicken coop, though.* Either he was a sorcerer or he wasn't. Right?

Nonetheless, there she was, scrubbing out the chicken coop.

It was hot, and the coop was even more foul than usual. Marya's apron was filthy, there was something sticky woven into her long brown braids, and feathers had taken up residence in her mouth. Her nostrils tickled. A fly buzzed around her head in a manner that seemed deliberate.

But at this moment Marya wasn't worried about stickiness, nostril tickling, or deliberate flies. Because yesterday she had put honey in Luka's undergarments, and today she could expect retribution.

Why had she put honey in his underthings? Two reasons: First, her older brother had spent his entire life being told by everyone that he had a great destiny; someone had to put honey in his underwear.

Second, he had started it.

When Marya was nine, Luka had filled her boots with dung. She had responded by making him oatmeal with sour goat milk, causing him to spend the entire night locked in the bathroom. Any normal person would have considered it done then, but Luka had felt he had to get revenge on her, and so she'd had to pay him back, again. And on and on it had gone.

And so, this morning, when he appeared behind her as she was scrubbing some unspecified goo off of the front of the coop, she jumped up and stood an arm's length away from him, just in case.

"Aren't you supposed to be studying?" she asked.

Luka stared down at her. He'd always been taller than she was, but over the course of the last year he'd stretched upward toward the sky, and now he could look down upon her literally as well as figuratively.

They did not look much alike. Luka had straight, nearly black hair that lay neatly on his head, while she fought to keep her indistinctly brown hair settled into braids every day. He had golden-brown skin that radiated health and vitality, while Marya's was pale and did not radiate anything. He was tall and sturdy, Marya short and bony. But still, the way he stood over her and spoke down to her, it would be obvious to anyone that he was her big brother.

"I told Papa I needed some fresh air for a moment," he said. "To help me take in everything we're studying."

She should have known. Their father was a tutor and a great believer in the educational benefits of fresh air.

"There's fresh air over there," she said, pointing off in the distance. "On the other side of the river."

Ignoring her, he nodded toward the coop. "That doesn't look very clean."

"Maybe you should use your magic," she said, crossing her arms.

His eyes darkened. "That's not funny."

It was funny, at least to Marya. Luka had shown no sign of being able to do magic yet. And while this was to be expected—magic usually didn't manifest in boys born with the gift until they were fourteen or fifteen—she could tell he was anxious about it.

"Just try," she said. "Before the council comes. Maybe it will work! That way when they admire how clean the coop is you can tell them you did it with"—she flung her arms out—"magic."

"I don't have to prove myself to you."

"But you have to prove yourself to the council! What if they ask you to do something and you can't?"

"That's not how it works," Luka said.

"You don't know that."

"I do know! The council tests you before your magic

comes in so an experienced sorcerer can mentor you through the process. They don't need to see magic. They can just tell."

Marya pressed her lips together. She couldn't argue. After all, everything always worked out exactly the way Luka wanted.

Which was a kind of magic, really.

"Anyway," he said, straightening, "you better be nice to me for once. When they give me my own estate, I can just leave you here. I can order you to an asylum. Or banish you to Munteland to be bait for the giants."

"That's all you care about, isn't it?" Marya spat back. "You just want to be rich and important. You want servants to boss around and do the work while you lie around wondering if your slippers are comfortable enough."

Luka drew up, as if this were the most offensive thing he'd ever heard. "That's not what it's about. Being a sorcerer is a heavy responsibility. They need places to live! And people to manage their affairs." He sighed portentously. "I can't be worrying about the household when I'm supposed to be protecting the kingdom from the Dread."

*The household.* Like it was already his. Like he was already in his office at the center of some grand estate, giving orders, eating plums, letting someone else clean up the pits.

This, Marya could imagine him doing. As for doing a sorcerer's actual job of battling the Dread, the monstrous force that lived in the forest and roamed to nearby towns to devour them whole, it was impossible for Marya to picture. Luka could barely handle the goats.

"And," Luka added with a sniff, "we need to know our families are safe and taken care of."

At this she crossed her arms. "So you'd start worrying about your family, then?"

Luka narrowed his eyes. "I always worry about my family. I'm the one everyone is counting on. Just because you don't think of anything but yourself . . ."

Marya's fists clenched.

It had not always been like this between them. There had been a time when Marya and Luka shared a room, and at night they'd lie in bed and whisper scary stories about giants and witches and Dread, and then neither of them could sleep. There was a time when they'd played sorcerers in the backyard, waving their hands in the air and pretending to enchant the chickens.

Marya had her mouth open, ready to fire an insult back, when her mother's voice boomed across the yard.

"There you are, darling!" She was, of course, speaking to Luka. "Aren't you supposed to be studying?"

Marya whirled around, brushed her apron off, and stood tall, like she was having a normal conversation with her beloved brother and they hadn't just been hissing at each other like warring barn cats.

Luka turned toward her, his eyes bright, his face now noble, innocent, and stalwart. "I needed to get some fresh air," he said.

Her mother turned to her. "Marya, you're not arguing with your brother instead of working, are you?"

"No, Mama," Marya said.

Mama eyed her suspiciously. "Your body looks angry, Marya."

Yes. It likely did. Probably because she was angry. But anger, she had learned, was not an emotion she was supposed to feel or—even worse—look like she felt. With an exhale, Marya tried to make her body look as un-angry as possible.

"Better. He doesn't need distractions right now. We have so much to do! I am off to the dressmaker's. Our new clothes are ready!"

Marya didn't need to be told where her mother was going; her eyes were sparkling in the particular way they always did when she was about to acquire something far too expensive for the family to afford.

This was the way things were at the Lupu household. Though magic was not about lineage, not about wealth or class, though magic could appear anywhere—in boys from the royal and noble classes, yes, but also in the sons of tradesmen, farmers, servants, and laborers—Marya's parents had always believed that it could not hurt to act like you had a sorcerer in the family already. It could not hurt to dress well.

And now, with the council coming to Torak for the first time in a generation, they needed even better clothes, so they would look like a good family, the sort of family that would produce a sorcerer of the realm, the sort of family that, even if they were not born into nobility, would slide into it effortlessly.

"It may take some time in town," Madame Lupu continued, "so I won't be home to supervise you, Marya. Remember—"

"So clean even the king could live in it. I know."

"Marya, I do not want any attitude from you, not today of all days."

"I'm sorry, Mama," she said, clasping her hands together and casting her eyes down. Luka and Marya both had their roles in the family: his was to make them proud; hers was to disappoint them. Someone had to do it. And while she was not always good at keeping the words in her mouth from flying out, at least she knew how to act afterward.

"That's better."

"May I still go to the Bandus' when I'm done? Madame is expecting me." Marya spent every day at the neighbors' house, watching over the young children; this, especially, seemed like a good day not to be home.

"Today!" Mama exclaimed. "A sorcerer is coming to this house tomorrow! Aren't you taking this seriously?"

Marya kept her eyes down and her mouth shut. As if she didn't know to *take this seriously*. She had been hearing about *this* her entire life. *This* meant that their family fortune would change. *This* meant that they would be given a title, an estate, servants, clothing to befit their station. They would be given horses. Imagine, Marya—horses!

There was a look her parents got when they talked about such things—their eyes grew bright and distant, focused on something above Marya's right shoulder, as if their dream future were always something just above and beyond where she was, something they had to look past her to see.

"And I'm sure Madame Bandu understands what's at stake here," her mother added. "She can certainly watch her own children for one day."

"But—" Marya started to say, though nothing good ever came from arguing with her mother.

"I think she should go, Mama," interrupted Luka, voice bouncy and bold. "The coop is almost clean, and we're ready. It will be good for Marya." He beamed at her beneficently, sagely, paternally, as if he cared very much for her well-being and had not spent the previous day stuck to his underwear.

And that did it. Mama's face relaxed, brightened. "All right," she said. "After you are done and the coop is impeccable. Impeccable!"

Marya swallowed. "Thank you."

"There you go, Marya!" said Luka. "Aren't you happy now?

Marya snuck a glance at her brother, who was still beaming at her with the happiest almost-sorcerer smile the world had ever seen, like someone who was really delighted that his sister would be gone all afternoon and he would have free rein over her things.

This was not good.

Marya did as her mother said. She spent the rest of the morning making the chicken coop look like it had never held even the tiniest chick before. *Mind the details, Marya!*

Then she checked on the goats again—the five nanny goats in the big pen, and Anton, the skittish billy goat, in the pen on the other side of the grounds. Marya was in charge of taking care of the animals—especially Anton, who liked to charge any member of the family who was not Marya. He liked her because she understood him: Anton did not like being in a pen; he did not like being told what he could or couldn't do; he just wanted to run around the grounds and destroy things.

"I'm going over to the Bandus'," she told Anton, scratching his ear. "Try not to mess up the chicken coop."

Anton bleated.

"No, no, it's extremely important," she said. "The whole fate of Illyria rests on that coop! Now, I am going to be very careful to latch the pen gate. Nothing personal."

Once inside, she washed herself off and rinsed the goop out of her right braid, then changed into a fresh dress and apron and tied a clean kerchief around her head, doing everything she could to neither look nor smell like a girl who'd spent the morning cleaning out the chicken coop. Downstairs, her father was throwing geography questions at her brother—*where can you find the Alb Mountains? How many miles from the capital to the border of Kel?*—and Luka was parroting back the answers like the good trained animal that he was.

As Marya crept down the stairs, she tried to make as little noise as possible. Papa was generally happiest when he didn't remember she existed, and least happy when he was forced to recognize the reality that she did. He wouldn't hesitate to order her to go up to her room and sit still until suppertime. Of course, her leaving the house for the rest of the day would be the best possible outcome for him, but he wasn't logical about these things.

It had always been her father and her brother in the library with a stack of books, Papa telling Luka all about the mysteries of the big, wide world around them. When Marya was little, she sat outside and listened to them, waiting for the day she'd be invited inside.

That was before she understood that she did not have a place in that room, that the mysteries of the big, wide world were not hers to ponder. Whatever her place was, it was not there.

# The Bandus

The village of Torak was in the southern part of Illyria—far enough from the border to Kel to avoid the skirmishes that had been happening since the Witching Wars ended, and far enough from any of Illyria's thick forests to be safe from the Dread. Though the nearest kingdom was constantly trying to invade, though Illyria was menaced by a terrible monstrous force, Torak was the sort of place where a twelve-year-old girl could walk down a dirt road without any fear.

The wide-open skies and green rolling plains of Torak

were all Marya had ever known. But if Luka became a sorcerer, they would leave. They could be sent anywhere in Illyria—to the sea, to the mountains in the north, to the edge of one of the vast, dense forests that ranged across the kingdom.

She could not fathom what it would be like to be somewhere else. In her mind, the rest of Illyria was beset with battles and monsters, still ravaged from the wars two centuries before. But it was not losing the safety from the armies of Kel or from the Dread that Marya feared, but losing the safety of the place she was heading right now.

The Bandus lived about a mile from the Lupus. Dr. Bandu was the village physician, and Madame Bandu was a master weaver, and thus they had enough social status to satisfy Marya's parents that they would not be reinforcing any of her *less refined* instincts. They had two young sons, though they were older than parents of young children typically were, a fact that Marya's mother often noted. "It must be so hard to have little ones at such an advanced age," she would say.

The two boys were now eight and six, and Marya had been watching over them for four years. She had already had experience with young boys when she started; when her little brother was born, the job of taking care of him had been given entirely over to her, as was only a proper duty for the eldest (and only) daughter. For almost two years, her life was Baby Pieter—his meals, his naps, his diapers, his soft curls, his little arms wrapped around her neck, his warm body pressed against hers at night.

The fever came during the day and he died during the night. She was eight, then. It happened while she was sleeping. She'd tried to stay up to watch him, but she was so tired from a day of trying to get the fever down.

"Nothing to be done," Dr. Bandu had said, clutching his medical bag in his hand. "This fever takes our little ones away; it steals their breath in the dark."

After the burial, her parents never mentioned Pieter again.

Marya could not be in the house. She'd felt like she was being slowly compressed. She spent her days by the river, talking to foxes, climbing trees, as if she were looking for something hidden in their tallest branches. She did not come home until dark.

"Do something," her father said to her mother one night. "Control your daughter."

"You cannot run around like a wild girl," her mother told her. "We have a household to run. You have responsibilities here."

*Responsibilities.* She did her best, but what did it matter how clean a pot was when Pieter was dead?

"Why is she so slow?" her father asked her mother. "Why can't she do the things she's supposed to do?"

*Smash!*

The plate that had been in her hand was in pieces on the floor. She seemed to have thrown it. Her parents gaped at her. She could say nothing, just turned and ran upstairs to her room.

After that, she did her chores and otherwise stayed inside the house, letting the shadows cloak her like blankets until she was all covered up.

That's where she had been when Dr. Bandu came to check on the family one month after Pieter's death. Her parents' faces stretched into smiles as they assured him that they were all well, thank you for your concern, but it was unnecessary.

Then one day she came downstairs to find Madame Bandu there, talking to her parents over tea. "I wonder," Madame was saying, "if I might take Marya off your hands during the days. I could use some help with the boys while I am weaving."

The steam from the tea rose into the air and dissipated. Her parents did not answer.

"Josef and I can only imagine," Madame continued, "how demanding it is to have a son as gifted as Luka. We would like to assist you in any way we can."

At that, Mama lowered her eyes. "It is," she said. "It is demanding. Yes, I think that would be very helpful. It would be good for Marya to be of some use. It is just that she can be . . ." Her eyes fell on her daughter.

Marya looked at the floor.

"She can be of excellent help to your fine family," her mother finished, not taking her eyes off Marya. Her gaze pressed at her.

Madame Bandu nodded solemnly. "Of course she will be."

"Don't gawp, Marya," her mother muttered to her. "You look like a fish."

Marya did her best to relax her face. She did not want to look like a fish. No one wanted a fish to help watch their boys.

It must have worked; the next day, after she was done with the animals, Marya walked to their house and spent the morning with the little boys down by the river, talking to foxes and climbing trees, and Madame Bandu never told her that she shouldn't be running around like some kind of wild girl.

Today the boys rushed to greet her as soon as she got to the door, Mika trailing just behind Sebastian as he always did, with their thick waves of dark brown hair, round faces, light brown skin, and big eyes, both miniature versions of their mother.

"Is the council here yet?" Sebastian breathed.

"Not yet," said Marya. "Tomorrow."

Of course, they knew that already. The whole village knew exactly when the council was arriving—it was the most exciting thing that had happened to Torak in years—but Sebastian never let facts interfere with his hopes.

"Do you think we could come over and watch when they come?" asked Mika. "We could hide in a closet. We wouldn't make a noise."

She grinned. All of Torak would hide in their closet if they could, for the chance to see a real live sorcerer.

"What if the council thought you were spies from Kel?" she said. "Hiding in our closet? And they turned you into weasels?"

Mika's eyes grew wide. "Weasels?"

"Yes," she said. "That is the standard fate for Kellian spies hiding in closets. If you hid in the barn, you would be turned into a goose."

"I don't want to be a goose," Mika said solemnly.

"Well, then. You'd better not hide in our barn."

They spent the rest of the morning outside, Mika and Sebastian playing spies while Marya hunted them down and pretended to turn them into various animals. Sebastian made a particularly fine goat.

During lunch, the boys peppered her with more questions about the upcoming council visit, as if she had any answers at all, and when she had nothing new to tell them, they reverted to asking her about things she'd already told them.

"Tell us about the letter again."

She had told them about the letter almost every day for the last two weeks—how the knock on the door had sounded, how tall the green-cloaked messenger had been, how still the black horse behind him had stood, how the messenger had handed over the rolled parchment as if he were bestowing the entire realm onto their family.

And the letter itself, communicating just what it had to and no more:

> *Dear Monsieur and Madame Lupu—*
>
> *Representatives from the Council for the Magical Protection of Illyria, serving the Sorcerers' Guild, will be at your home in fifteen days, at noon, to evaluate your son, Luka Lupu, for potential giftedness in the art of sorcery.*

*Long live the king!*

*Count Vasiliy Florescu*

"'Potential giftedness in the art of sorcery,'" Sebastian repeated, voice full of awe, as he had every day.

Both boys were always full of awe about Luka. She'd heard it her whole life—the men who urged their sons to be more like Luka, the woman at the bakery stall who said he just seemed to *glow*, the girls in town who told her how handsome her brother was, which made Marya want to gag eternally.

Marya could not fathom any of it. Everyone assumed he was going to be a sorcerer because he was so admired. And everyone admired him because they assumed he was going to be a sorcerer.

"Someday," proclaimed Mika, sitting back in his chair, "the council will come for me."

"No, they won't," said Sebastian. "They'll come for *me*."

"They'll come for both of you," Marya said smoothly. "You'll be the first brother sorcerers. You'll make Torak famous! The Dread will have no chance against you!"

"We'll take you with us!" Mika said. "You can live on our estate!"

Sebastian stopped, his face suddenly twisted. "She can't."

"Why not?"

"She's going to live on Luka's."

Mika turned to her. "You'll leave? Here?"

Marya swallowed. She'd been trying to talk about the visit as much as they wanted without ever opening the door to what would happen after.

The boys were looking at her, Sebastian's face challenging, Mika's hurt, both wanting something from her that she could not give.

Madame Bandu appeared in the kitchen then, waving the brothers toward her. "All right, boys. It's time to practice your sums. Marya, come sit in the workroom with me?"

One day, a few months after Marya had started working there, Madame had sent the boys to their room, led her into her workroom, and put a book in front of her. "I would like to teach you to read," she said firmly. "I imagine your parents have not done so?"

Marya had gaped at the book, then at Madame Bandu, probably looking much like a fish. No, they hadn't taught her. Her mother could read, yes, but never seemed to think Marya needed to.

Madame Bandu nodded, even though Marya hadn't spoken. "Reading is power," she said, her voice soft. "I would ask you not to tell your parents—since they did not teach you, I can only assume they would not like it. Do you understand?"

Marya did not understand. But she did not ask. She just held the conversation in her hand, warm and bright.

Now in the late afternoons she sat in Madame Bandu's workroom and read everything she could. The Bandus had so many books, they seemed to be stacked everywhere. Marya knew where the Alb Mountains were, and how far it was to the border of Kel, and how big the Fantoma Forest was. And when her father was asking Luka these questions this morning, and he did not know the answers and she did, there was indeed a kind of power in that.

While Marya read, Madame Bandu worked at her loom. There were not many trades open to women in Illyria, but weaving was a feminine art, and the job of recording Illyria's history was considered well suited to women's natures. Madame Bandu was one of just a few of Illyria's master weavers—weavers of such skill and renown that the nobility came to them to make tapestries that would record their family's deeds for posterity.

This afternoon, like every afternoon, Madame Bandu perched on her adjustable stool, posture perfect, facing the back side of the tapestry. This particular tapestry was of a man in a red-and-black cloak riding a galloping white horse into a forest, poised to shoot an arrow. In the forest lurked a pack of ghost-like dreadlings, while wisps of purple Dread floated in from the depths of the forest. Two dreadlings lay slain on the forest floor, arrows sticking out of their chests.

Madame Bandu always sang softly to herself as she wove, old Illyrian folk songs about the time before the Sorcerers' Guild, when monsters freely roamed Illyria and villages were left to fend for themselves. The sort of songs people in the village sang during festivals, the sort Marya never heard around the house because her mother felt they were "common." Marya learned about the world from books, but she also learned from the songs—from the words, yes, but there was something in the melodies, too, something yearning, something sorrowful, something always breaking but never quite broken.

Today Marya did not read, just watched Madame's hands fly along the loom—weaving in and out, tamping the new weave down so there was no gap between the lines, picking up another of the dozens of thread-laden bobbins that hung behind the tapestry and starting again with the new color.

"How are things at home?" Madame asked, after a time. "A bit frantic?"

"You could say that."

"And Luka? How is he doing?"

Marya shifted. Right now, Luka might be smearing goat dung all over her bed. But she'd never told Madame Bandu about their private war; how did you tell the only person in the world who believed in you that you spent most of your time fantasizing about retribution?

"I suppose he is nervous."

"I imagine that you are correct. He knows that no one expects him to perform any magic yet, right?"

"Right," Marya said.

"And you? Are you nervous?"

"No. I don't have to do anything. Except not mess it up, I suppose."

Madame stopped weaving and gazed at her. "Now, how would you do that?"

Marya shrugged. "If you ask my mother, by not cleaning the chicken coop well enough."

"Oh yes, that's the most important part of the visit," Madame Bandu said.

It took Marya a moment to realize she was kidding.

"I understand that your parents must be very nervous,"

she continued, "but I promise you that the council is only interested in whether Luka might be a sorcerer, and the state of your chicken coop has nothing to do with it. The Dread is too great a threat for the council to care about trivialities."

Madame Bandu knew things like this. Her work meant she knew noblemen, royalty, even sorcerers. The man who had commissioned the tapestry she was working on now was a count with one of the biggest estates in all of Illyria.

"Do you know how many people they take?" Marya asked. "I mean, out of how many potential sorcerers there are, and . . ."

Madame shook her head. "The Sorcerers' Guild has always been able to detect potential sorcerers through some kind of spell. It used to be that all of those boys would go to estates so they could be mentored when their magic did come in. It's only in the last few decades that they developed a test that could—with reasonable accuracy—predict which boys would actually become able to wield magic. I know that that meant a sizable difference in how many boys were taken in by the Guild, but what exactly the numbers are, I do not know." The weaver's eyes rested on Marya. "Are you hoping he will be chosen?" she asked, gently. "Or hoping he won't?"

"I don't know," Marya said. It was hard to have an opinion on something when your opinion mattered so little to the outcome.

"If he is chosen," she said carefully, "what do you think you will do?"

"What will I do?" Marya repeated.

Well.

If a boy was chosen, the family was immediately taken to live on a sorcerer's estate, where the boy would serve as an apprentice for the next decade, studying sorcery. Eventually he would be given an estate of his own. His parents would live on a cottage on the estate, and his sister—well, his sister would sit around until she came of age and was married off to another sorcerer's brother or cousin or nephew or lonely uncle with fish-breath, where she could become someone else's problem.

That was what she'd do.

"We would miss you here," she continued. "And, well . . . I wondered if you might be interesting in being my apprentice."

Marya stared up at her.

"It would have to be an untraditional arrangement, of course, as there is not much of a chance you will be living close enough to be here every day. But we could send our carriage for you and you could stay here, perhaps for a few days every month."

Marya could not speak.

"I am being selfish, I should admit. With another pair of hands I could make bigger tapestries—the larger ones are in demand now, and it would take me too long to do them by myself."

It was like she was eight again, trying to hide in the shadows, afraid that if she moved, everything that was being so delicately built would fall apart.

"You could become a weaver yourself someday, if you wanted. Perhaps even a master weaver, if you were willing to train. There is a lot of study involved—not like being a sorcerer, of course, but study nonetheless. We would love to have you here. The boys are so fond of you."

*Don't gape, Marya.*

"As are Josef and I."

*You look like a fish.*

"I understand that perhaps that might not interest you. A sorcerer's sister need not be concerned with her future. When you are of age, you will marry well, and before that you will have everything."

"No," Marya said, the word tumbling out of her mouth.

Madame nodded swiftly. "I understand."

"No! No. I mean"—*deep breath*—"no, I wouldn't have everything."

Threads of words flew around in the air, and Marya tried to catch the right ones, to weave together some sense. A melody played in Marya's head, something yearning, something breaking but not quite broken. "I would like to be your apprentice," she said finally. "I would like to stay with you as often as I can."

And there. A small smile. "Good. Your parents would need to agree, of course. I could not take you on without their permission."

Marya swallowed. "I think my mother would be glad to have me go away."

"Marya, that's not true."

She looked up. "I think it might be."

"Oh, my girl," Madame Bandu said, picking up Marya's hands and squeezing them, "your mother is trying to make a good life for you. There are so few options for girls, and so many rules governing their conduct. I do not have a daughter, but if I did, I would do everything I could to ensure she could have security. I did not like all the lessons my mother taught me, but now I am glad for them." She stopped, pressing her lips together and gazing softly at Marya. "Your mother is trying, in her own way, to give you the world."

Her voice was kind, impossibly kind, but her face looked so sad.

Marya looked down. Maybe she was right, but did that world her mother held in her hands have to feel so small?

# Folk Songs

There was a reason the folk songs of Illyria sounded the way they did. Certainly, the kingdom's history was one of conflict, chaos, and disaster. Certainly, in its early centuries distant invaders had come as if drawn there. Certainly, the kingdom was constantly under threat, always breaking but never broken.

But Illyria was no ordinary kingdom.

There was a fault running under Dovia, Illyria's mother continent—not just in the land, but in the forces that bound the world together. Unnatural creatures roamed

Dovia: giants stalked the northern mountains; in the eastern forests prowled the pricolici, enormous, bloodthirsty wolves risen from the dead; while the two-headed ogres known as capcaun lurked in the caves by the western sea.

In Kel, the kingdom to the south of Illyria, the queen reached into the fault and found chaos, and then discovered she had the ability to manipulate that chaos to her own ends. Witchcraft then spread through Kel, and the witches turned their attention to their enemy in the north.

But, over the centuries, men in Illyria found in themselves an ability to reach into the fault, pull out the chaos, and tame it, make it orderly, make it a force that could be used for good. The sorcerers banished the monsters, protected the kingdom from Kel and her witches, and when the witches unleashed their last, greatest curse on Illyria in the form of the Dread, the sorcerers kept the kingdom from being destroyed.

For the last two hundred years, the sorcerers have honed their magic, have kept the ever-growing curse of the Dread at bay. To be a sorcerer is to be among the most revered and noble people in all of Dovia.

For a village girl, being the sister of a sorcerer meant a whole new life.

It was supposed to be a dream come true.

But not for Marya. For Marya, the dream was the life Madame Bandu had offered her, the promise she held tight in her hands as she walked home.

She turned the conversation over and over in her head.

*Your parents would need to agree.*

They would, wouldn't they? Wouldn't they be glad to get rid of Marya for a week every month? Wouldn't they be glad that she was getting trained in some kind of trade?

Could she be a master weaver?

Marya flushed thinking of it. Yes, it was a lot of study, but it was the sort of study you did hunched over books in a library. It was the sort of study that opened the world to you. She could do that—or at least she could try.

The truth was, it was hard to imagine the rest of it: sitting in a chair all day, your hands making music across a loom. Marya was confident that her hands could not make music, could not make tiny, perfect stitch after tiny perfect stitch that would somehow transform into art. Then there was the meeting with the nobility, where you had to dress and act like someone worthy of associating with them or else they wanted nothing to do with you.

Maybe that was the sort of thing that happened when you grew up. Maybe you became a person who could sit still, who could make elegant things, who understood how to talk to people who thought they were better than you.

No, she could not imagine being a master weaver. She could not imagine being a weaver at all. Nor could she imagine being a wife, or a shopgirl, or a servant. None of her possible futures felt like they could really be hers—they all belonged to some other girl, some girl who knew how she fit in the world.

No, she could not imagine any of it.

But she could, now, imagine being at a place where she was wanted. She would like to be at that place.

Maybe the rest would come.

*I could not take you on without their permission.*

She could ask her parents at supper tonight, when they were so distracted they might just agree without even thinking about it.

Or would it be better to do it right after the council rendered its verdict on Luka, just when her parents were handed their dreams?

So occupied was she thinking about Madame Bandu's offer that it was not until she got home that she remembered that Luka owed her some mischief.

Luka had never failed to retaliate, and he certainly would not fail now, would he? He had been home without her for hours now, plenty of time to enact any kind of revenge. So when she got home, she opened the front door trepidatiously, as if she might walk into the house to find it covered in chicken feathers or swarming with angry bees.

But there were no feathers, no bees. Just Luka, sitting at the table surrounded by books, looking as if he had spent the day trying to stuff as much knowledge as possible into his brain and now had regrets.

And maybe that was what he had done. Maybe he had been too busy to think about her. Maybe now that the council was coming, now that his fate was here, he was done with trying to punish her for existing.

There were so many Lukas. There was the boy her parents saw: the gifted boy, the genius, the dutiful son, the one who did everything right. Then there was the one only she saw: the cruel one, the one who saw her as an opportunity to act out his worst instincts so he could keep his best ones for the world at large. Then there was the imperious Luka, the one who acted like he was already wearing a sorcerer's cloak, already felt its privileges and, of course, its burdens.

But there was one more Luka, one Marya saw so seldom she mostly forgot it existed, so incongruous was it with every other Luka.

This Luka appeared when their parents talked about the future—the title, the estate, the wealth—that they believed in their bones Luka would earn. And, she saw it in him now, a kingdom's worth of knowledge spread on the table around him: this Luka was scared.

Without even really realizing what she was doing, she stepped toward him.

When he noticed her, the fear slipped back beneath the surface, and his face took on an expression of great wisdom. He nodded at her, and then proceeded to turn his attention solemnly, sagely, back to the thick tome open in front of him. "You know," he proclaimed, gesturing toward his book, "the Gnostic Wars could have been avoided entirely if the sorcerers had been organized earlier. The Ilvanians would never have tried to invade us."

"Uh-huh," Marya said. She'd read all about the Gnostic Wars at the Bandus'. Technically, it was Illyria who had struck first by raiding Ilvania's underground libraries, and it seemed to her that the best way to have avoided the wars would have been for King Boris to respect the treaties. But she didn't think Luka would appreciate hearing facts that interfered with his opinions.

"Really," he went on, "I don't understand why the king didn't see it. It's such a simple solution."

"If only he'd had you around," Marya said.

He harrumphed in agreement.

Was it more or less fun when he didn't get that she was being sarcastic?

*No, Marya. Be good, Marya. Just one more day.*

Mama came in then, carrying a large, paper-wrapped bundle, smile as wide as the sky.

"Our clothes look magnificent," she declared. "Monsieur Tomas really outdid himself this time. The whole village is coming together to support us! Though"—she beamed at Luka—"I suppose it is an honor for all of Torak, really."

In a moment, the new clothing was spread over the sofa. For Mama, a green velvet long-sleeve dress with puffed sleeves, with glistening gold embroidery on the chest and a high collar made of layers of lace. For her father and Luka, black velvet suits with two rows of gold buttons down the front and new white shirts with collars that stood up like flowers.

And for Marya, a shiny blue dress, made out of the most elegant-looking fabric Marya had ever seen, trimmed with thick white ribbon.

Marya gasped.

"That's for you," Mama said.

"It's beautiful," Marya said.

"Would you like to try it on?"

Marya looked up at her mother. Did she mean it?

Her mother nodded, a smile on her face. "Be ever so careful, though!"

So Marya ducked up to her room and changed—carefully, carefully—and then came back downstairs and looked in the mirror.

A grin spread across her face, warm and bright.

She saw her mother in the mirror, standing right behind her looking at her reflection, just as Marya was. They were like a tapestry, daughter dressed in finery, with her proud mother behind her, eyes shining.

"You look like a lady," she breathed. "A beautiful lady."

The words wrapped around Marya like a cloak. She closed her eyes, and opened them again.

*Your mother is trying,* Madame Bandu had said, *to make a good life for you.*

"How should I wear my hair tomorrow?" Marya whispered, tugging at a braid.

Her mother's smile spread, as if it was the sort of question she'd been waiting for Marya to ask her whole life. "I'll pin it up myself," she said. "Just like the capital girls wear, in the latest style." Her hands fell on Marya's shoulders, warming them. "And soon you'll be just like them. Can you imagine, Marya? Our lives are going to change. Let's see a curtsy."

Marya inhaled, then picked up the sides of the soft skirt, placed one foot in front of the other, and dipped her body down as she'd been taught: *Back straight! Chest forward! Bow your head!*

Mama beamed at her.

Of course she could curtsy. She felt so light now. She knew how to move; she knew what it was like to feel like the forces of the world were working with you instead of against you.

"Now," Mama whispered, "take it off and don't put it on again until just before the council comes." She squeezed her shoulders again.

Up in her room, Marya took the dress—carefully, carefully—and spread it out on the chair in her room, petting it slightly. These would be the sort of clothes she would wear all the time on a sorcerer's estate, and maybe they would help her fit there.

The dress had given Marya clarity: now she had a plan. She could not ask her parents about apprenticing with Madame Bandu tonight. They were full of excitement, full of Luka. Everything they'd ever hoped for was about to be handed to them; they'd spent the last thirteen years preparing for this moment, and it must go exactly as planned, step by step, one foot in front of the other, ending with the golden key clutched in their hands. She would wait. And then, later, Madame Bandu would come over, just as she had before, full of congratulations and admiration and gratitude on behalf of the whole village. *I wonder if I might take Marya off your hands here and there,* she would say, and her parents, generous in their new wealth, would say yes.

And, as supper progressed that evening, it became apparent that this was the right choice. Her mother fretted over Luka's food consumption, her father fired history questions at him, and Marya quietly ate her stew.

While on the surface Luka seemed to be sitting right there at the table, answering questions tersely and cutting his turnips into easily digestible pieces, it was clear he'd vacated his body somehow, gone for fresh air or tucked himself into bed and fallen fast asleep. But Mama and Papa kept at him.

After supper, Marya and Mama cleaned up—*not a drop of stew, not a crumb of bread anywhere, Marya!*—while Luka still sat at the dining room table, a shell.

As Marya went up to her room, she cast one last glance at Luka, who did not look back at her, who had perhaps forgotten all about her; perhaps the council would come tomorrow, and anoint him, and whisk him off, and he would forget all about the honey in his underthings. These were childish games, and tomorrow he would not be a child anymore.

Before she went to sleep, she looked at the dress draped over the chair. Tomorrow she would wear it, and she would look like a sorcerer's sister. She would *be careful* and *not stare* and *mind her manners* and *be soft* and her parents would be happy with her and glad to say yes to her—finally, she was the girl they wanted her to be, and thus they could let her be happy.

She would look like a lady, and she would feel like a lady too. For one day. And maybe, perhaps, her mother would let her take the dress with her, and she could wear it when she and Madame Bandu met with clients. And her inside would match her outside.

But when she woke up, the dress was gone.

# The Council Visit

Marya sat straight up in bed, gaping at the empty chair, panic coursing through her body.

Luka.

She should have known. She should have acted like the dress was scratchy, ill-fitting, as if she hated it, as if she'd like nothing more than to have Luka hide it from her.

No—she realized—it still wouldn't have mattered. It wasn't that Marya liked the dress. It was that Marya's mother wanted her to wear that dress for the council visit.

Which was today.

She burst out of her room and pounded on Luka's door, and then flung it open without waiting for a response. Luka was fast asleep in his bed, just a lump of boy under his blankets.

"Where did you put it?"

No response.

She stormed over to him and shook his arm. "Where is it?" she demanded.

His eyes flew open. "What?" he snapped, wrenching his arm away from her.

"You took my dress."

"Why would I want *your* dress?" he said, rubbing the sleep from his eyes. "It wouldn't even fit me!"

"You did something to it. You did."

He looked at her now, innocent. "You mean the dress Mama bought? You lost that?" He shook his head. "Oh, she's going to be very upset with you."

"Tell me where you put it, or I'll rub goat manure on your head for the council visit."

A grin spread across his face. "I don't think you want to do anything to disrupt the council visit, now, would you? Mama and Papa would not like that at all."

Her cheeks burned. He was right.

"Don't you have chores to do?" he asked silkily.

Her eyes narrowed. If she could have shot fire from them, she would have. Not enough to scar him, just enough to hurt.

"Do you really think I wanted you there today? After everything you've done? You think I trust you not to do something to ruin everything?"

"What are you talking about?" she spat.

"What am I talking about? All you do is try to sabotage me! I'm supposed to be trying to master ancient Ginian so Papa isn't mad at me, and instead I'm trying to get my boots down from a tree!"

She couldn't even take in what he was saying. So she pushed him as hard as she could, then ran down the stairs and straight out the back door in her nightgown and bare feet.

It was unseasonably cold out, and the morning wind bit at her arms and toes as she stood in the doorway surveying the grounds, while dire possibilities fled through her mind.

*Don't you have chores to do?*

The goats.

She ran to the big pen where the nanny goats were, and they all trotted up to her expectantly. "I'll feed you later," she said, scanning the pen for her dress—or remnants of it.

But there was no sign.

She darted across the field to the billy goat pen. As soon as he saw her, Anton let out a happy bleat and bounded up to greet her.

But she saw no sign of the dress, or scraps of the dress, which would be all that remained if Luka had put the dress in the goat pen.

At least, *this* goat pen. Anton could do the damage of four goats in one. Maybe eight.

She let herself into the pen, Anton bounding up to meet her.

"Did Luka come in here?" she asked him, as if Anton might answer. He did not, so she went into the pen and peeked inside the shelter where Anton slept; she had once put Luka's bedding out here and then remade the bed with it, and Luka smelled like goat for a week. But no dress. Of course Luka hadn't come in here. Luka was terrified of Anton after the incident with the shiny pants.

There was only one place left to look.

And somehow, as she approached the chicken coop, she knew.

The chickens were hopping around their pen, squawking at each other, irritable. Irritated.

The chickens were very particular about the state of the

coop, and if there was any kind of disruption, they tended to register their displeasure by pooping with great alacrity.

And there had been a disruption. For Luka had come in and spread her beautiful new dress on the floor of the coop. And the chickens had, apparently, responded by pooping with great alacrity all over it.

Marya's whole body went cold. She could only stare.

And that was when she heard her mother calling to her.

She whirled around, just as her mother appeared in the coop doorway, the morning light shining right behind her so she seemed to glow.

"Marya! You left the back door open again! What if we got flies in the house, today of all days! You have to pay attention, Mar—"

She stopped. Marya swallowed. There was no escape for her.

"Is that . . . ? That can't be." She took a step forward, and then gasped. "What did you do? Marya!"

Marya squeezed her eyes shut, willing the tears not to come. "Luka was mad at me, and—"

"Is that what this is about? Did you ruin your dress in order to get your brother in trouble?"

"No!"

"I don't understand you, Marya!" Her mother's voice

sounded squeezed, like she herself was being strangled. "Are you so envious of your brother that you want to ruin the most important day of our family's life?"

"No! No!" She could feel her hands clenched into tight little fists, her nails digging into her skin.

"Then what is it? Why? Do you just hate us? Is that it?"

"No!" Her voice cracked. Tears were streaming down her face now.

"I've done my best with you, Marya! I've tried everything! And this is how you repay me?" Mama was crying now, too. "What are you going to be like on a sorcerer's estate? You'll humiliate us!"

"Fine, then I'll stay with the Bandus!"

Mama drew up. "Pardon me?"

She could not help it. She just kept talking. "Madame Bandu wants me to be her apprentice. I could be a weaver. She wants to make bigger tapestries, you see, and she needs another pair of hands, and—she says I can come stay with them and she'll train me."

"I see," her mother said, unreadable emotions flashing through her eyes.

"I don't mean—I won't stay with them for good or anything. Just come to Torak once a month and stay a few days and apprentice—"

"So. We've worked your whole life for this moment, for the sort of security that people like us can scarcely hope for. And now that that moment is finally here, you tell me you want to learn a *trade*?

"It's not that, I—"

"What? Want to get away from us?"

*Yes. No. Yes.* Marya's mouth hung open.

Mama clasped her hands together so tightly her knuckles were white. "I've been hard on you, I know. But I didn't have anything, growing up. We were so poor. Your father's parents didn't want him to marry me because of who my family was. It was only because I knew how to act properly that they didn't disown us entirely. If they had, we'd have nothing."

Marya could only stare. She had never heard any of this before.

Mama shook her head despairingly. "And here you are, destroying your beautiful dress and telling me you don't want any of it."

Still, Marya could not speak. It felt like Anton was chewing on her stomach.

A moment. Mama kept staring at her, eyes red. She'd started wringing her hands so hard it looked like she was going to break them. Then suddenly her shoulders slumped. She exhaled.

"Well," she said, voice flat. "Maybe it would be better. You clearly cannot cope with your brother being gifted. You won't learn propriety, I dare say you'll never learn to keep a house." She closed her eyes a moment, as if gathering her strength. "All right, Marya. If the visit goes perfectly today, we will *consider* it. But if anything goes wrong, *anything*, you will never see the Bandus again. Do you understand?"

"Yes," she whispered. She felt so, so small.

Her mother drew herself up. "Now, I want you to go up to your room. Do not come down for the rest of the day; do not make a noise. As far as the council is concerned, you do not exist, do you understand me?"

Marya looked up at her mother, feeling the tears run hot down her cheeks. There was absolutely nothing she could say. She did not exist.

"I haven't fed the chickens yet," Marya whispered.

"I'll do it," hissed her mother. "Now go. Go!"

So Marya ran back into the house and up to her room, and then fell onto her bed and cried.

She slept for a bit, and dreamed strange dreams of giant mice scrabbling at her door, bursting inside her room, and chewing up her fingers, her hands, her arms. Soon they would eat her all up.

The noises of the house drifted in and out of her mind as she slept—her parents calling to each other, someone banging around in the kitchen, doors opening and shutting, chairs being rearranged, and rearranged again. She did not hear Luka at all—perhaps he was sitting in his room, thinking great thoughts about the kingdom and his destiny in it.

And then a sharp knocking at the front door seemed to shake the walls. Her mother's call rang through the house. Luka's footsteps came bounding down the stairs. A moment of quiet, the whole house holding its breath.

Then the door opened, and her father's cheerful voice boomed, "Welcome!"

The council was here.

Marya threw on a robe and snuck into the hallway, moving as slowly and softly as she could. There was a place behind the railing where she could crouch and see most of what was happening in the front hall while being barely visible herself, and it was here that she perched.

Her family was right below her, facing the front door— her mother and father standing like two columns and Luka slightly off to the side, as if he were incidental to the architecture. And in front of them stood two men: the first was one of the regular noblemen who sat on the council, dressed like royalty in a lush red coat with gold roping; the other, well . . . the other was clearly a sorcerer. Marya inhaled sharply. All this time, she'd known that there would be a sorcerer in the house, but knowing that and actually seeing a sorcerer in your front hall were two entirely different things.

He was tall and extremely thin, as if he had been lengthened somehow, with sharp cheekbones and wise eyes. His brown face was etched with deep, perfectly sculpted lines. He wore a long black robe intricately embroidered with gold thread, with wide sleeves that covered his hands, which he held in front of his chest so the sleeves hung down like a banner, their shiny gold cuffs sparkling when they hit the light.

It looked so strange to see the rest of her family in their finery, the house sparkling, and these two otherworldly men standing in the front hall; it was like she'd fallen out of her life for a moment and come back to find everything had changed.

The man in the red coat was called Count Barbu, and the sorcerer was High Count Georgescu, so Count Barbu told them. The sorcerer did not speak.

"Monsieur Florian Lupu," said her father with a bow.

"And my wife, Alina." She curtsied in one fluid motion. "And this," he said, his voice polished, "is Luka."

Luka bowed deeply, as if he'd been practicing for years, which of course he had.

The count looked around. "Is there anyone else?"

"We have no other children," her mother said quickly.

Luka blinked. Her father's face was steady. Marya's hand tightened around the banister.

"Would you like tea?" Mama asked quickly. "I'm afraid our maid is sick today—what terrible timing!"

They did not have a maid.

"Or would you like a tour of the premises?" her mother continued brightly.

"We don't really—"

"It will just take a minute," she said. "Let me show you the library. I'm sure you'll be interested in our collection of historical volumes; Florian is a tutor, after all, and requires an extensive library."

"That will not be necessary," Count Barbu said, voice firm. "Now . . ." He motioned toward the sorcerer, who stepped forward.

This was it.

Despite everything, excitement crackled in Marya's chest.

Her parents stood on either side of Luka, both looking

as if they had swallowed the sun but were trying not to let on.

Luka's eyes were wide, and his face was white.

"Now," said the count, "as I'm sure you know, the council's methods are confidential. And we must ask that you all swear that you will not share anything with anyone about the process, only our verdict."

"Oh, we swear!" interjected her mother. Luka and her father nodded in agreement.

"Perhaps I was not clear." Count Barbu nodded toward the sorcerer, who put his palm in the air gracefully, face stern. Her parents' eyes widened, and even from her perch on the second story she felt some kind of murmuring in the air below, as if it was whispering secrets.

Magic.

Marya's heart quickened. She'd never seen magic done before—though really she didn't see the magic now as much as she felt it, and maybe heard it too. Her parents and her brother were blinking, as if they had momentarily forgotten where they were but were trying not to show it.

Was it a spell to make sure they didn't talk? Or a curse if they did? Or something that would notify the council either way?

Marya clutched the banister. Whatever it was, it was

the most interesting thing that had ever happened to her.

And that was when she noticed the other disturbance in the air, some misfit kind of noise, coming not from the front hall, but from behind her. The skin on her neck prickled. It seemed like a strange kind of magic that could creep behind her this way, a strange kind of magic that made shuffling and smacking sounds—neither of which should have been coming from inside their house right now, or ever.

A sense of wrongness flooded Marya, as did an all-too-familiar smell, one that also didn't belong in the house. She turned around cautiously, as though if she moved slowly enough the sound would stop and everything would go back to normal, and then peeked into the spare room.

Anton.

Eating the draperies.

*Smack, shuffle, smack.*

Marya stifled a yelp, then sprang up and into the room, heart in her stomach.

Of course Anton was in the house. Of course he was eating the draperies. He had to, for he'd already eaten the pillows, the chair cushion, and the crocheted throw that Aunt Isabelle had made. Bits of fabric and fluff were scattered around the room, the remains of his morning work.

After all, he was hungry. She'd forgotten to feed him, she realized now. And he'd decided that after he was so cruelly neglected for breakfast, he should get to eat his favorite meal—human possessions.

And she'd left the pen open. And the back door. And so he'd just trotted up the back staircase and helped himself.

*Details, Marya.*

Anton perked up when he saw her and hopped on the bed—or what was left of it—in way of greeting. "Anton," she whispered, "I'm going to shut the door now, and we are going to stay in here and be so quiet, you understand? You can eat whatever you want as long as you stay—"

He bleated.

"Quiet," she hissed. He pranced up to her and licked her face. Another strange rumbling from below, a shifting in the air, and Anton started suddenly.

"Shhh, it's okay, it's okay."

It was not okay. Anton sprang through the doorway, and Marya hurled herself after him. *Stop, stop, stop, stop.*

He had stopped. He was pressed against the wall of the hallway, body tensed, eyes fixed on the hall below. Marya wrapped her arms around his neck and hugged herself against him. "It's all right, Anton," she murmured. "You just stay still. It's all right. It will be over soon, and I will give you so much hay to eat, and all of Luka's underwear, too."

She could hear her father's voice droning on below her, something about Luka's research into the initial formation of the council. Whether or not the council members cared, the sound seemed to soothe Anton, and his body relaxed slightly.

"Good job, Anton. That's a good boy. It's all right." Her curiosity about the visit had completely disappeared now—all that mattered was keeping Anton still and calm.

"Very interesting," said Count Barbu, clearly not at all interested. "Now we must continue."

"Of course," said Papa. "Ask Luka anything you'd like. His knowledge of llvarian history is also—"

"That won't be necessary." Marya could hear the count's impatience from where she knelt. It did not much surprise her that, for all of her family's efforts, all the council cared about was whether or not Luka could work magic.

Anton bleated quietly.

"I know," Marya said, stroking his chin. "I know."

"Now," continued Count Barbu, his voice suddenly commanding, "if we may have silence. . . ."

Marya let out a sudden, involuntary exhalation. It was as if someone had grabbed the breath in her lungs and yanked it out. The air around her seemed to swirl toward the front hall like the sorcerer was commanding it toward him. Anton shuddered in her arms, and Marya held him tighter.

"It's okay," she whispered.

The sorcerer was holding both his palms in the air now. Marya watched, frozen. Then, in one quick motion, he reached into his robe, pulled out a small glass orb with some kind of silver fog inside, and held it out toward Luka. The orb seemed to shimmer, as if it wasn't quite sure it wanted to stay in this world.

"You are Luka Lupu," he intoned, his voice a low rumble.

A moment. Count Barbu looked over to Luka and nodded, a prompt.

Luka blinked. Marya could feel words rising up in both her parents' mouths. Luka, answer him! Luka, what are you doing? Luka—

"I am Luka Lupu," Luka said. His voice cracked.

The sorcerer gave a curt nod, held his hand up, and then turned his palm toward Luka.

And then Marya's stomach lurched. Or maybe it was

the floor. Or the house. Anton lurched too, and let out something that sounded more like a howl than a bleat.

He exploded out of her arms, knocking her to the floor. Marya yelped. Anton didn't notice—all he wanted to do was get out of the house as quickly as he could. So he put his head down and jumped through the railing, wood shattering everywhere, dropping perfectly right in the middle of the group. Everyone fell backward, avoiding the falling pieces of railing, not to mention the panicked goat. Then Mama and Papa started yelling, which further scared Anton, and he sprang wildly around the hall, while Marya's parents grabbed for him.

They would never be able to control him. She was the only one who could. So Marya dashed down the stairs, trying to swallow the panic in her throat. Meanwhile, High Count Georgescu wiped some bits of wood out of his beard, then stepped toward Anton, palm out. The goat bleated, put his head down, and charged.

For being one of the most powerful people in all of Illyria, tasked with keeping it safe from the Dread, the Ilvanians, the Kellians, the creatures of the Fantoma Forest, and all the other innumerable threats to the kingdom, the High Count Georgescu proved surprisingly ill-equipped to deal with a panicked billy goat.

He tried to sidestep Anton, but seemed to get caught in his robes, and Anton clipped his hip as he charged at him. The sorcerer stumbled, and the glass orb fell from his hands and shattered as it hit the ground. Marya's mother screamed, the sound apocalyptically high-pitched; her father yelled and grabbed at Anton's horns; Count Barbu stood completely frozen; and Anton bounded around the room, dodging Monsieur Lupu and all sorts of imaginary terrors.

Luka was standing a few steps back from the chaos, watching the proceedings with an odd, blank expression, as if he were observing a pantomime that had taken an unexpectedly surreal turn.

"Anton!" Marya shouted. She was still in her nightgown and robe, still in bare feet, still with her hair wild. She was not even supposed to exist—*we have no other children*—but here she was, running into the hall amid the chaos, the felled sorcerer, the shattered orb, the shocked count, the frantic goat, her apoplectic parents, because she was the only one who understood Anton.

"Marya!" her mother exclaimed, voice cracking. "What did you do?"

Her father kept lunging for Anton, but he knew nothing about goats.

"You're scaring him!" Marya cried. "Everyone be still!"

"Quiet, Marya!" snapped Papa.

"Listen to Marya."

These unprecedented words came from Luka. That stopped Marya still. She looked at him, and in response Luka threw up his hands, as if to say, *What can you do?*

Nothing, apparently. Nobody else paid attention. Her father shooed her and went back to trying to grab Anton, and her mother took a step toward her, looking murderous.

But the sorcerer put up a hand again, ready to cast a spell on the goat, which was the worst possible idea given that was what had panicked Anton in the first place, and Marya yelled, in as commanding a voice as possible, "Stop! Don't!"

Everyone froze.

Village girls were not supposed to yell at sorcerers.

Marya turned to ice.

Count Barbu gaped at her; Mama gasped; Papa raised his hand to slap her.

As for the high count, he turned his attention to her, thick eyebrows knotted, dark eyes peering at her, as if wondering whether she herself might be a rampaging goat in a girl's skin.

"Marya," Papa growled, a bear about to attack. Marya flinched.

"I am so sorry!" Mama said to the council representatives, words tumbling over each other. "She doesn't know what she's saying! She is not well, she—"

Whatever she was, Marya would not hear, for Anton decided he had had enough and ran straight toward the window, put his head down, and jumped right through.

He could keep running and running, straight on to Satmare, and they would never find him again. He could run all the way into the Bezna Forest and get eaten by a bear. And no one was moving; no one was doing anything. So, with one last look at the ludicrous scene before her, Marya ran out the back door to chase down Anton.

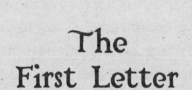

# The
# First Letter

After Marya caught up with Anton and coaxed him back to his pen, after she fed him some more, and scratched his chin, and sat with him as long as she could, and even longer than that, she went back into her house, though every part of her wanted to run all the way to the Eastern Forest, and maybe get eaten by a bear.

And the whole time all she could think was:

She had yelled at a sorcerer.

She'd yelled at a sorcerer, a high count, one of the most important people in all of Illyria. She might as well have screamed at the king.

Marya walked into the house carefully, as if maybe, if she moved softly enough, everyone would forget she existed. But no one was there. The council was gone, and all that was left of their visit was the broken railing and shattered window. Her parents and Luka were all in their rooms with the doors shut. So, moving like a girl who did not exist, she crept up to her room and did the same.

It wasn't until suppertime that she saw her family. When she appeared in the dining room to set the table, a ball of fear burning in her chest, her parents' gazes slid past her like a blight on the landscape.

This was the way it was going to be, then: If Luka was chosen, they would pretend none of it had ever happened. And if he wasn't, well, they would blame her.

During supper, her father kept repeating that all the council cared about was whether Luka had magic, and a little goat-related mayhem would not affect their decision, especially as Luka had nothing to do with the incident. Finally, her mother snapped, "They won't give a title and an estate to a boy who has maniacal goats running around his house!"

At this, her gaze landed on Marya, and then snapped away.

Marya's heart burned. She clenched her hand around her fork and kept her eyes down.

The letter arrived three days later.

> *Dear Monsieur and Madame Lupu,*
> *The Council for the Magical Protection of Illyria thanks you for the opportunity to evaluate your son, Luka. We have determined that Luka does not possess magical ability, and thus we will not be extending an invitation for him to be trained in sorcery.*
> *You will remember that the proceedings of the council are confidential, and any disclosure of the details of yesterday's test will be considered treason.*
> *Long live the king!*
> *Count Vasiliy Florescu*

"It's a mistake," Papa said. "That orb must have been broken. Or it didn't have a chance to work before Anton—"

"Papa, it's not a mistake," Luka said, voice quiet and flat.

"The council isn't always right," Papa added. "There have been stories of boys who didn't pass the initial test and still came to manifest magic later."

"That's not going to happen," Luka said. "It's not."

And he went up to his room and closed the door.

All that day, Marya lay on her bed, holding her pillow tight, hoping that by some miracle her father was right, that it was a mistake, that the council would come back. After spending her whole life completely ambivalent about whether Luka was a sorcerer, now it was all she wanted in the entire world.

*They won't give a title and an estate to a boy who has maniacal goats running around his house!*

What Mama had meant was: *They won't give a title and an estate to a boy whose sister behaves like a maniacal goat.*

But it couldn't be true, really. Either Luka had magic, or he did not.

Right?

They needed sorcerers to fight the Dread. It was that simple. The armies could keep Kel from invading, but the only chance Illyria had against the Dread was the sorcerers.

The Dread was Kel's last stand in the Witching Wars, a curse laid down by the witches that took root in Illyria's forests. It rose from these forests like a sickly fog, moved from one village to the next, leaving the population slain in their beds, all the blood drained from their bodies. And though the sorcerers had wiped out the witches, the product of their curse lived on.

While it had been years since the Dread had taken a town, it was only because the Sorcerers' Guild worked constantly to contain the threat, to stop the clouds and to evacuate people when they could not.

Illyria needed sorcerers in order to survive.

You would think, then, that a goat could not interfere with finding a new sorcerer.

You would think, then, that a sister could not interfere with finding a new sorcerer.

You would think it could not be her fault, no matter how ill-bred she seemed.

But still.

But still.

Marya stayed in her room all day, lying on her bed watching shadows move across the ceiling. At some point the door opened, and her mother appeared in the doorway. Marya sat up with a start, clutching the pillow to her chest like a shield, but Mama just stood there in the doorway, not saying anything, her face oddly blank.

"It wasn't my fault!" Marya exclaimed.

"Really, Marya." Mama took a step in. Her face was no longer blank. "You know that? You, Marya Lupu of

Torak, have special insight into the workings of the king's council?"

"No, but—"

"Marya, don't be so naive. The sorcerers are the most accomplished people in all of Illyria. You saw the high count. Did he act like some farm boy?"

". . . No."

"No, he did not. The king needs the people to have faith that the sorcerers can contain the Dread. It's not enough to simply have ability; sorcerers must be the best of men, come from the best of families, or else no one will believe in them. Don't you see?"

"But—" Marya said.

Mama slapped the wall, the bang echoing through the room. "Marya, for once, do not interrupt me. Perhaps if you listened more instead of arguing all the time, we wouldn't be in this mess. Think about it: What if some sorcerer acted in a vulgar fashion? What if his sister caused some scandal? And everyone was talking about that? What would happen?"

"I don't know," Marya said, voice cracking.

"Really, Marya? You don't? And you don't see the consequences of displaying yourself to be a girl with no breeding to the king's council?"

Marya flushed.

Mama shook her head. "I don't know what I'm going to do with you, Marya. If you could not behave yourself on Saturday, of all days. If you could not hold your tongue in front of a sorcerer, of all people!"

"I was just—"

Her mother put up her hands. "I know what you were *just* trying to do, Marya. Do you think that makes up for what you did? Talking to a sorcerer like that?"

"No, I—"

"I've done everything I can to teach you how to behave. You will not listen; you will not try. This was your chance for a secure life. Now what will become of you? You have shown you cannot keep a house. We have no fortune; you have nothing to offer in marriage to make up for your . . . deficits. It is my job to ensure your future, Marya, and I have failed!"

"But you haven't!" Marya exclaimed. "Madame Bandu said that—"

Her mother's eyes narrowed. "Madame Bandu. A woman blessed with two sons, and no daughters to be concerned with. If you cannot find a place for yourself, what is it to her?"

Marya flinched. *A woman blessed with two sons.*

Mama had also been so blessed, once.

"I told you," Mama continued, "that if anything went wrong, you would never be able to go over to the Bandus again. And something went very, very wrong, wouldn't you say?" She raised her eyebrows pointedly. "I would not be doing my job as your mother if I went back on my word. Actions have consequences, Marya." Her mother's words slithered around her like a snake, and Marya could do nothing but wait for it to squeeze.

"Besides," Mama continued, "I do not believe that woman is a good influence on you. I think she has given you ideas."

Marya swallowed. Mama was right. Madame Bandu had given her ideas; she'd made Marya feel like there might be a place for her, somewhere.

"Can I go see them one last time?" Marya whispered.

"Marya, you heard me."

"But they're expecting me! I can't just not show up." Marya pressed her hand to her heart, as if that might keep it from breaking. "They think Luka is a sorcerer now, and they won't know that—"

"Oh, they know, Marya. The whole village knows! Do you know how many notes I've gotten today? Our humiliation is the talk of the entire town. They're *laughing* at us.

The only thing more exciting for this town than having Luka be chosen is having Luka *not* be chosen!"

Mama's voice broke, and Marya looked to the floor, trying so hard not to cry.

Her mother began to walk out of the room, and then stopped.

"I might have failed you to this point, Marya," she said, voice low and determined, "but I will not fail you again. That is my promise to you. It is my job. You don't understand what could happen to a girl like you."

With that, she stalked out.

Marya lay back on the bed, clenching her pillow to her chest. Her mother blamed her, and there was nothing she could do. And the voice that had been lurking deep inside her for four years whispered, *That is not all she blames you for.*

Marya squeezed her eyes shut and pushed the voice away.

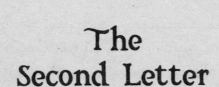

# The
# Second Letter

The next morning, after doing her chores, Marya slipped away to the Bandus. It wasn't like she could be in any more trouble than she already was. And she needed to tell them goodbye.

Madame Bandu opened the door, and when she saw Marya, she knelt down and put her arms out. Marya collapsed into them, letting herself dissolve into the embrace—one moment, two, three. Then she stepped back and brushed off her apron.

"Are you all right?" Madame asked gently.

"The council rejected Luka."

"I know."

"I can't come back here anymore."

She blinked. "I understand."

"I can't be your apprentice. I want to be. But my mother—"

"I know. I know. I understand." Madame stood and held her hand out, and Marya took it like she was a little girl. "Come inside with me for a while."

"Are the boys here?"

"They're visiting their grandmother today. It's just me."

Marya swallowed and nodded. In a way, it was a relief. She did not know how she would say goodbye to them.

Soon Marya was sitting in Madame Bandu's workroom, a mug of hot tea in her hands. She did not realize until she drank it how very cold she felt, how part of her, it seemed, had frozen over.

"Do you want to talk about it?" Madame asked, after a bit.

Marya watched the steam rise from her mug. She was not supposed to say anything, according to the council. But she was pretty sure that that was about the test itself, not about the goat part.

"I left the back door open and Anton got in," Marya said

quietly. "He went up the back stairs. The sorcerer started casting spells and it made the air in the room funny and Anton panicked and jumped through the railing."

"Oh my," Madame said, putting her cup down.

"He knocked the sorcerer over."

"Goodness."

"And then jumped out the window."

Madame's face was a mask of concern, but there was something else there, something twitching in the corner of her mouth. Marya stared at her, and the twitching quickly stopped.

And then Marya cracked up.

The mask on Madame Bandu's face dropped, and she burst into laughter. This made Marya laugh harder, and soon tears were streaming down her face.

Yes, it was absurd. Yes, it was hilarious—Anton leaping around, the count gaping like a cow, the sorcerer felled, her father lunging for the goat and missing so terribly, every time.

"I daresay that has never happened during a council visit before!" Madame Bandu said.

"The sorcerer did seem to be quite surprised."

"I bet!"

Marya stopped herself. "You can't tell anyone, though.

We're not supposed to say anything."

"Well, I can see why they might not want this getting out. If the Kellians heard, they might just send an army of billy goats."

And then Marya cracked up again.

It was so good to laugh, to feel warm, to have someone look at her with something other than anger, disdain, or indifference. And suddenly Marya found herself confessing.

"There's something else," she said quietly. "When Anton was running around, the high count tried to cast a spell on him, and . . . I yelled at him to stop."

"Oh," Madame said, tilting her head.

"I was trying to calm Anton down, and I thought it would make things worse. And . . . I didn't think . . ."

Madame put a gentle hand on her arm. "I understand, Marya. You thought you were doing the right thing in the moment."

Marya nodded. It was true; that was always true. She always thought she was doing the right thing in the moment. It was just that in the next moment, she usually discovered that it was the wrong thing.

"Mama thinks that that was enough to make them not pick Luka," she said quietly. "She thinks they'd never pick someone who acted low-class because people would lose faith in the sorcerers." She glanced up at the weaver. "Do you think that's true?"

Madame Bandu leaned in and grabbed Marya's hands. "Marya, I don't know the answer to that. But I do know that Illyria needs sorcerers. I believe that if Luka had the ability to work magic, they would have taken him into the Guild. It's not like there are enough magic wielders in Illyria for them to be picky."

Marya looked at the floor and nodded.

Another moment. "When you hear a story powerful people tell about themselves, and you're wondering if it's true," Madame said, "ask yourself, who does the story serve? If it serves the people telling it, well, maybe you want to consider the possibility that it is false somehow. If the story were that a terrible curse would be unleashed upon the land if the royal family lost their power, well, the royal family certainly benefits from that story, and maybe we want to question it. The council tells us that any boy can potentially be a sorcerer—rich or poor, highborn or low, from the capital or from right here in Torak—and I don't see a way that that story really serves powerful people. So no, I don't think that manners or breeding can keep a boy from being accepted into the Guild. But, it is never a bad idea to question the stories the world tells you." She gave Marya's hand another quick squeeze and said, "Here, let me show you something. Come look at the tapestry."

Marya blinked. She did not understand anything Madame Bandu was saying—except that she'd said she thought it wasn't Marya's fault. And maybe she was just saying that to make Marya feel better—but Marya would take it.

Madame Bandu motioned Marya around to the front of the tapestry and pointed toward the small initials woven just above the bottom right corner. "You see my signature here, right?"

Marya nodded. Madame always signed the tapestry that way—an L joined with a *B*.

"And this," she said, pointing to a small symbol next to the signature. It was the shape of a crescent. "Do you see this mark here? It's a moon. That is weaver code."

"Code? For what?"

Madame looked at her levelly. "You have to promise me you'll never tell anyone. I am trusting you."

Marya's eyes widened. "I swear, I promise."

"All right. This tapestry tells a story, yes? Of Count Andrei single-handedly taking down a pack of dreadlings?"

"Yes!"

"And he told me the whole story and asked me to make a tapestry recording his great deed?"

"Yes."

"Do you find that story believable?"

Marya blinked rapidly. ". . . I don't understand."

"Count Andrei may be a skilled swordsman, but he's not a sorcerer. And even a sorcerer likely couldn't battle this many dreadlings on his own."

"I . . . guess not? But—"

"Weavers are asked to record history, and in recording history we are creating history, you understand? So we have this symbol we add to tapestries when we think the story it tells is false."

Marya simply stared.

"Count Andrei," she continued, "wants people to believe he is brave and a warrior. And he has money. So he can pay me to put this story in a tapestry, and make it look like it actually happened. Then it reads like history, and history will say he was brave and unusually powerful and somehow fought off the Dread. After all, it's in a tapestry."

Marya gaped. It was like she was holding her hand above a flame, daring herself to touch it.

"But people don't know about that symbol. . . ."

"No. Only the weavers. It is a small rebellion. But we

are the ones who record history. And we know."

"But . . . what if he finds out?"

"Then I suppose I would be executed," she said matter-of-factly. "But he will not find out. They never do. It would never occur to these men that we might not believe them. Now"—she motioned to the chair—"sit. I have something for you. I made it in case you were going away."

The something proved to be a small, wrapped package that Madame Bandu pulled from a drawer. As Madame watched, dark eyes warm, Marya unwrapped the tissue, and then gasped.

It was an intricately embroidered apron, the most beautiful Marya had ever seen—covered in flowers and vines and birds, all done in purple, turquoise, green, and pink thread. Breath caught, Marya ran her hand down the front slowly, tracing the rhythm of the stitching with her fingers.

"You made this," Marya said, looking up.

"I still do a little embroidery here and there," Madame said, with a soft smile.

"It's so beautiful!" It was the second time in a week she'd been presented with the most beautiful item of clothing she'd ever seen.

"This must have taken forever," Marya breathed.

"I wanted you to have something special. Now"—Madame pulled her chair next to Marya's—"speaking of symbols, there's meaning here. Village women used to put symbols in their embroidery, their meaning passed down from mother to daughter. The language is dying out, but it does not mean it doesn't still have value. See here? This vine? What does that look like to you?"

Marya studied the batlike leaves. "Dreadbane?"

"That's right. The dreadbane is for protection. This border here? See how it looks like fire? It's for light in the darkness. And the diamonds here?" She pointed to another border. "They are for courage."

"And the flowers?" Marya said, voice still an awed whisper.

"They're just pretty," Madame said with a laugh. "I'd wanted you to have something so you knew we were still watching over you, even if we were far away."

Tears flooded Marya's eyes. She would still be just down the road, but it might as well be all the way across Illyria.

And this. It was the most beautiful thing she'd ever seen. And she'd never be allowed to wear it.

"I love it," Marya said, voice thick. "But I . . ." She couldn't complete the sentence.

Madame understood. "You don't need to wear it for it to have power, Marya. Keep it in a drawer. It will still be there for you."

Before Marya could say anything else, there was a flurry of knocks at the front door. Marya froze. She knew that knock.

"That's Mama," she whispered. "I'm not supposed to be here."

Madame Bandu nodded and stood up, brushing off her apron. She strode out of the room and closed the door behind her.

Marya waited, completely still.

"Madame Lupu!" she exclaimed cheerfully. "How nice to see you."

Mama's voice floated into the workroom. "Is my daughter here?"

"I have not seen her," Madame Bandu said.

Marya swallowed.

She sighed. "I can't find her. We need her home urgently."

"Is everything all right?"

"Yes. Yes. We have some news," Mama said.

At this, Marya straightened. Had it happened? Had the council written to say they'd made a mistake?

"I see. Perhaps you might try by the river? Marya does love it down there."

"I am aware of what my daughter loves. But if she does appear here—"

"I will send her straight home."

"Thank you."

"And Madame Lupu? I'm sorry about the sorcerer's visit. If I can do anything . . ."

"Just send my daughter home if you see her."

And the door shut.

Marya counted to ten, not daring to move. Madame Bandu may have done the same, for she opened her studio door exactly when Marya got to ten.

"You should go home," she said.

"What do you think that was about?" Marya whispered.

"I don't know."

"Did she seem excited?"

"I can't tell. I'm sorry. Perhaps you can tell me later."

Marya cast a look at the tapestry, at the signature and the small, rebellious mark next to it.

"I have to go. Tell the boys . . ."

Madame Bandu squeezed her arm. "I will. Here, take this. For the apron." She handed Marya a simple cloth sack, the sort that would attract no notice at all.

"Thank you."

Marya ran all the way home. For the first time in her life she was excited to get closer to her house. She imagined her whole family sitting in the parlor, celebrating.

Though . . .

If they were, why did they need Marya?

And when she walked in, she did not find her family gathered in the parlor, or anywhere else. The house was quiet.

But there was an official-looking letter on the mail table. With a quick glance around to see if anyone was watching, Marya picked it up and read:

> Dear Monsieur and Madame Lupu,
> The Council for the Betterment of Illyrian Youth would like to invite you to send your daughter, Marya Lupu, to Dragomir Academy, a school dedicated to the reform of troubled girl near Sarabet. At Dragomir, Mademoiselle Lupu will receive a first-class education, as well as the discipline, guidance, and purpose she needs to become a contributing member of Illyrian society. Because the king is devoted to ensuring all Illyrian youth grow to be good citizens, Madame Lupu's attendance at the academy is compulsory, and

at no cost to your family.

A coach will be coming for her at nine o'clock tomorrow morning.

Long live the king!

Count Sergei Stan

# Trouble

Marya stared at the words in front of her, hand shaking.

For a moment, she thought that perhaps she didn't know how to read after all, as the words on the paper couldn't possibly say what she thought they said. So strange, that she'd been reading things incorrectly all this time, that everything she thought she'd learned from all the books at the Bandus' was actually completely wrong, and had caused her not just to read badly, but to read things that were not there.

"You can read?" came Luka's voice from above her. "How did you learn how to read?"

Marya jumped, nearly dropping the letter. Luka was standing on the second floor where the railing used to be, eyeing her curiously.

She stared up at him, frozen. She should deny it, make something up, but at the moment she could do nothing but gape at him, while the words from the letter swam around in her head.

Without waiting for an answer, Luka headed down the stairs toward her. "It was delivered this morning," he said, motioning to the letter. "Carried by a messenger on a grand horse, just like my letter. You can imagine what Mama thought."

Yes, she could imagine.

"She's out looking for you," he continued. "Papa's still teaching. He has to work more, you see, as he wasn't expecting to pay for"—he motioned around him—"unexpected house repairs."

"Is this real?" Marya asked, clutching the letter.

"It seems to be."

She still stood there, trying to understand.

She knew about schools, of course. There was a school in Torak for village boys; Marya passed it every Wednesday when she went to the market. And she knew, too, about boarding schools. Mama and Papa had once considered sending Luka to one—some fancy boys' academy near the capital that wore its reputation like a crown—until they ultimately decided that if Luka were far away it would be difficult to control every aspect of his education and upbringing.

What was a school for troubled girls?

*Troubled* could mean a few different things. It could mean that the girls were all worried. As in, kings in Illyrian history were *troubled* by an increase in the number of witches in Kel. And, certainly, Marya was troubled in this way.

Or it could mean that they were having problems. As in, the King Coston era was *troubled* by insurrections. Marya was troubled in this way as well.

Or it could mean that there was something wrong with the girls. As in, before King Danut organized the sorcerers, the times were *troubled*. Meaning difficult. Meaning full of problems. Meaning, in need of fixing.

Marya did not feel troubled in this way. But everyone else in her family seemed to think that she was. And this was surely the kind of troubled that the Council for the Betterment of Illyrian Youth meant.

"I don't understand," she whispered, holding the letter out.

"Well," said Luka, taking the letter from her, "I don't know for sure, but I'm guessing that the council thought a village girl who screamed at a sorcerer might have some problems that needed to be addressed."

"But . . . what is this place?"

"A school for troubled girls. Like, to rehabilitate you, I guess." He said this so flatly, like it meant nothing.

"What did Mama say? Are they really going to send me away?"

"It doesn't look like they have a choice."

It didn't, no. The letter invited her parents to send her, and then told them it was compulsory. "They're coming tomorrow?" she asked. It wasn't what she wanted to ask, not really. But she was too scared to put words to the question she really wanted to ask. "How can they come tomorrow?"

Luka shrugged. "I mean, it's the end of the summer. The school year is starting up."

*The school year.* Marya had never even heard the phrase before. "And they're letting me know now? That's weird— isn't that weird? And where is Sarabet? I've never heard of it!" Marya could feel her gestures getting bigger and bigger as she fired questions at her brother; there was not enough room in the house for the questions she still had.

"In the north," Luka said. "In the Rosa Mountains."

At this, Marya straightened. "Where the giants are!" she exclaimed.

He sighed wearily. "There are no giants in Illyria anymore, Marya."

But she was already on to the next thing. "I don't understand. How long will I be gone for?"

"It's a boarding school in the north," he said, looking at her levelly. "Probably until you turn eighteen."

Now her hands dropped to her sides with a *thwap*. "What?"

Luka crossed his arms and raised his eyebrows. "Really, this is good news, isn't it?"

"Wha . . . what do you mean?"

"Well, you're leaving," he said with a shrug. "Everything works out for you, as usual."

Marya's eyes narrowed. "Pardon me?"

He took a step closer to her. "Oh, come on. You do whatever you want. You do a few chores and then you run off to the Bandus'. Mama and Papa don't care what you do."

"How can you—what?"

"And you don't even care," he said. His voice was still so

calm, so flat, the way he'd been saying everything since the council visit. "You act like your life is *so hard*, but nobody counts on you for anything. All you have to do is feed the chickens and keep Ánton from attacking anyone." He raised his eyebrows at her, as if to say that he knew how good she was at *that*. "And now you get to leave for good."

Marya clenched her fists. She was neither calm nor flat. "I'm being ordered to some academy for troubled girls! So I can learn *discipline*!"

He shrugged again, apparently now his answer for everything. "Would you rather be here every day, knowing you failed the whole family?"

"I'd rather—" she began, then as his words settled over her she fell silent.

Just then their mother came in, out of breath.

Marya whirled around to face her, panic coursing through her body. This was it.

"Where did you get to, Marya?" she exclaimed breathlessly. "I've been looking for you everywhere. Is this really a time to go running wild?" Her eyes fell on the letter in Luka's hand. "Well, that is what I wanted to talk to you about. Did you tell her, Luka?"

"No, Mama, I didn't."

Marya's head snapped to her brother, waiting for him to

tell their mother that he hadn't needed to, that Marya had read it herself, that she'd learned to read behind Mama's back.

But he did not.

Mama snatched the letter from his hand, giving Marya a tight smile. "Marya," she proclaimed, "you will be going away to school. A carriage will be picking you up tomorrow."

Marya just stared. Since she was still in shock, she had no trouble pretending that these words were shocking to her.

"It appears that your behavior at your brother's council visit had repercussions," Mama added. "You are going to a school for troubled girls, by order of the king. Perhaps they will know what to do with you, since I do not."

Marya swallowed. Out of the corner of her eye, she saw Luka's face twitch slightly.

"Apparently, the council found your behavior so egregious that they notified the proper authorities immediately. Goodness, I do not know what we will tell people! First Luka, and now this!"

As her mother talked, Marya had the distinct impression that she was actually shrinking, that by the time Mama finished she might be the size of an ant, and that this school would need a whole separate extremely tiny wing to accommodate their new ant-size student.

The question she'd been afraid to ask before rose up in her mind. It was: *Did Mama seem upset that I'd be leaving?*

And the answer, apparently, was no.

"But, Mama!" she said finally. Her voice sounded like it was being squeezed out of her. "What is this school?"

"Well," her mother said, drawing herself up, "it is called Dragomir Academy, and it's in Sarabet, which I believe is in the east."

"Sarabet is in the north, Mama," Luka said.

"And," she continued, "it is run by one of the king's councils. They will give you discipline, guidance, and purpose."

Marya wrapped her arms around herself and squeezed tight, as if that might keep her together. Mama was just reciting what was in the letter. She knew nothing else. Was she really going to let Marya go off to some school she'd never heard of before? Way up near Munteland? Where the *giants* were? When she was the size of an *ant*?

Maybe that was what they did with troubled girls—sent them up north into the mountains to be giant bait, and the few who survived would be considered well educated, possessing *discipline, guidance, purpose*. Maybe that was how the sorcerers got the giants to stop attacking in the first place—*oh, we'll send you some girls every year. They're troubled, which makes them more delicious.*

Marya found her eyes filling. "I don't want to go, Mama," she whispered.

Mama straightened. "Well, I am afraid what you want is not particularly relevant here, Marya. You do not have a choice. Just as we had no choice about your behavior at the council visit."

Marya winced. That was it, then.

"What's in that bag, Marya?" Mama asked suddenly.

"I—" She'd completely forgotten about the bag she was carrying with the apron from Madame Bandu. Her hand flew to it, as if to protect it.

"Oh," Luka said, "that's mine, Mama. Thanks, Marya. I'll take it now."

Marya stared at him. Luka held his hand out to her.

It was just a few days ago that she'd been picking her beautiful velvet dress off the poop-covered floor of the chicken coop, thanks to Luka. But a lot had happened in those few days, and even though her brother had just gotten done explaining to her exactly why and how he resented her so much, she handed him the bag holding the most precious thing she'd ever been given.

And when she'd done her chores and was finally able to go up to her room that afternoon, the bag was on the bed, untouched.

Marya spent the rest of the afternoon there cloaked in the shadows.

They had no choice but to send her, she reminded herself. It was by order of the king. Count Barbu had clearly reported her to this Council for the Betterment of Illyrian Youth, whatever that was, which had ordered her to this school. So how her mother felt about it didn't matter, really. It wasn't like she could do anything about it.

Except it felt like it mattered.

And . . . was it really true that there was nothing they could do about it?

Her father was up in Merube today, tutoring the son of the count who lived there. Whenever he came back from there, he was full of news about the kingdom, because the count had friends at court. So maybe the count could intervene with this council if her father asked.

And maybe Mama's anger would pass.

Maybe something would change.

It was this hope that Marya held on to as she set the table for dinner, because she needed something to hold on to. And for a moment it seemed like something might actually change.

Because Papa was, indeed, full of news.

The Dread had appeared near a village that was a hundred miles from a forest, without any warning. This was not supposed to happen; the witches' curse had originated in the forests that ran between Illyria and Kel, and the Dread always emerged above a forest before it headed toward the nearest village, toward its prey. The sorcerers had been able to keep the Dread from consuming villages by watching the forests.

But no one had seen this cloud coming; no one knew where it came from.

Fortunately, there was a sorcerer living close to this village who was able to slow the Dread while the townsfolk evacuated, and eventually enough sorcerers arrived to disperse the cloud. But as for how the Dread could arrive near the village without the Guild knowing where it originated, no one seemed to know.

"It's getting worse, isn't it?" Mama asked.

Papa nodded.

"How is that possible?"

"I suppose that's what the sorcerers are asking themselves right now," Papa said solemnly.

At this, Marya looked up at her parents. Maybe it wasn't time to be sending your daughter off to the other side of the kingdom. Maybe it was time to keep her at home.

"Well," Mama said. "You'd think they'd need all the sorcerers they could get." Her eyes fell on Luka, and then on Marya. "Perhaps the men from the council will come back. Perhaps things will be different now."

Marya's hand clenched around her fork.

*Perhaps things will be different now, with you gone.*

Marya threw her fork down and ran out of the room. No one stopped her.

She was someone else's problem now.

# 8

# Goodbye

In the morning Marya went out to tend to the animals for the last time. She told the chickens to be good, and to try not to make too much of a mess, and to take care of each other, if that was a thing chickens did. She gave the nanny goats some extra hay, and petted them and whispered to them.

And then there was Anton.

"Don't let anyone tell you it was your fault," she said to him, scratching under his chin the way he liked. "You were just being a goat. That's exactly what you're supposed to be."

He nudged her gently in response. Was it better or worse that he couldn't understand that she was leaving? Is it worse to hurt because you know what's happening, or because you don't?

"I could write you letters," she murmured to him, "and then you could eat them. Would you like that?"

He nudged her again. She took that as a yes.

Suddenly, Anton's head shot up. Marya turned around to follow his gaze, and there, standing behind the pen and looking uncertain, was Luka.

"Hi," he said.

"Hi."

"You're good with him," he said, gesturing to Anton.

She nodded. It was true.

"I'll probably be taking care of him now. Mama and Papa won't."

Yes, that was also certainly true. She gave Anton an extra scratch, lest his feelings be hurt.

". . . So,"—he kicked at a clump of dirt—"do you have any advice?"

"Oh." She tried not to stare at her brother, who had certainly never asked for her advice before. "Well . . ." She looked at Anton and considered. There were so many things she could say. *Don't be too loud. Don't wear shiny things. Don't let any sorcerers perform spells near him.*

"Don't treat him like he's bad."

"Okay."

"If you treat him like he's bad, then he'll act bad. But if you say nice things to him, if you take care of him, if you treat him like he's worth taking care of, well . . . then he'll be good."

"Okay."

"And scratch him under the chin. And maybe bring apples."

"Okay."

"You'll do that?" she asked, trying to keep her voice from breaking.

He nodded.

"You know," she said, still looking at Anton, "Mama and Papa not caring what you do, that's not great either."

A pause. "I understand," he said.

"You should go over to the Bandus' sometime. Play with the boys. They love you."

"Still?" Luka asked quietly.

"I'm sure," Marya said. "Tell them where I went, okay?"

He nodded. "There aren't any giants up there anymore," he said. "I'm pretty sure."

"I suppose we'll find out," she grumbled.

The edge of his mouth twitched up, just for a moment. "Anyway, Mama wants you. She says it's time to pack."

Her eyes widened. "Luka," she said, "I don't know what to pack!"

Up in her room, Marya surveyed her belongings.

Luka had told her she would probably just need a few changes of clothes, her hairbrush, that sort of thing, that a boarding school would have everything else. Which was fine, but presumably she would grow over the next six years. How would she get new clothes?

Luka had said he did not know.

So she packed what clothes she had, her nightgowns and robe, her extra pairs of boots, ties for her hair. Luka had said they'd have bedding, but what if he was wrong? So she took a pillow and folded up her quilt, too, and put it on top. A neighbor had given them that quilt when Baby Pieter was born, and when he was out of his crib they'd used it for the bed they shared.

She had to keep it. She was the one whose job it was to keep Pieter's memory. No one else would.

Then, after peeking out of the hallway to make sure no one was looking, she took Madame Bandu's apron out from the bag.

She could not help but unwrap it to look at it again. The dreadbane for protection, the fire for light in the darkness, the diamonds for courage. And the flowers, because they were pretty.

This she would need.

She gave it a little pat, and then folded it up again and slipped it under the quilt.

The coach arrived exactly at nine a.m., as promised. The driver was dressed formally and bowed stiffly at them, as if he had been sent by the king himself.

He brought the trunk out to the coach while her mother supervised and Luka hung back in the shadows of the porch. Her father had gone off to see students while she was with the animals. He hadn't even said goodbye.

And then it was time to go. Marya's mother escorted her to the carriage, and then stepped backward and paused. Marya's breath caught. She might not see her mother again for years.

Mama reached out a hand and squeezed Marya's arm, tight.

"I don't know what to do with you, Marya. But perhaps they will."

And then she turned and walked back into the house.

Something rose in Marya, and she turned away and

pushed it down, down, down.

Before Marya climbed into the coach, she looked back. Luka was still there. He caught her eyes and raised his hand as if to wave, but his hand just stopped, as if he did not quite know how to proceed. And as the coach drove away, Marya saw him stand in the doorway, watching the coach drive off, hand up—a goodbye wave, caught in time.

As the coach rumbled down the road away from the only home she'd ever known, Marya's emotions were whirling around one another until they blended into a great churning mass. It would have been nice to have space to figure out exactly how to cope with the things swirling around inside her, not to mention try to catch hold of some of the thoughts zooming around in her head. But she was not alone.

There was a woman in the carriage who introduced herself as Madame Rosetti, the deputy headmistress of Dragomir Academy.

She looked exactly like that title might suggest—gray hair pulled back severely into a well-contained bun, a black dress with a black apron, and her olive face was made of angles and edges. She sat perfectly straight, as if it were the most natural way in the world to sit. She seemed like the sort of person who would say, *I will brook no nonsense*, and all the nonsense would run scared.

*Posture, Marya.*

"I'm Marya Lupu," she said, trying to pull together all her manners, trying to look like the least troubled girl possible. As if maybe this severe, no-nonsense-brooking woman would say, *Why, there has been a terrible mistake! This girl is not troubled! Turn the carriage right around!*

"Indeed," said Madame Rosetti. She eyed Marya. "Don't you have anything for the journey?"

"Pardon me?"

"It is a two-day ride to Dragomir. We will be stopping overnight at an inn. I assume you have on overnight bag prepared?" She patted a small suitcase next to her.

"No," Marya exclaimed. "I didn't know."

"Well, someone should have known," Madame Rosetti said.

Like her parents.

Marya's jaw tightened.

Madame Rosetti let out a sigh. "We can stop at inns for meals. Do you have any clothes in your trunk?"

"I do," Marya said, trying to keep the question out of her voice. Did the deputy headmistress think she was so ignorant that she wouldn't bring any clothes with her?

"Good," she said. "Now, if you don't mind . . ." She picked up a book and turned her attention to it.

"Wait!" Marya exclaimed.

Madame Rosetti looked up, gray eyebrows twining in disapproval.

Marya had a thousand questions, maybe a million questions about the journey and the school and whether they were going to leave her out for the giants. And perhaps because some voice was whispering to her that that still might happen, that the reason the deputy headmistress seemed surprised that she had any changes of clothes was that she was riding to her doom and one did not need clothes for one's doom, she asked, "This place, is it really a school?"

Now Madame Rosetti's eyebrows went straight up. She gazed at Marya coldly. "Dragomir Academy is a reputable institution," she said, "where you can expect the same quality education as at any other academy in Illyria."

"Oh! I didn't mean—"

"I believe your letter addressed that very question. Did it not tell you that you would be receiving a fine education?"

"It did!"

"Do you have reason to doubt the king's councils?"

"No!"

"Good. Then you may trust the letter."

Marya bounced in her seat. This was not going well. "I didn't mean—I just—I—"

"Mademoiselle Marya, as I'm sure you read in the handbook—"

"I didn't get a handbook!"

Madame Rosetti looked at her sternly. "This is what happens when we invite a girl in without giving her time to prepare," she muttered.

At this, Marya leaned forward.

"Far be it from me to criticize Headmaster Iagar, though," said Madame Rosetti, holding a hand up. "And you will be caught up. Fortunately," she added, opening her suitcase, "I carry a copy of the handbook with me." She moved to hand a thin volume to Marya, then pulled it back. "You do read, yes?"

Marya nodded.

Madame Rosetti's mouth twitched in clear relief. "Excellent. This should answer some of your questions."

While the deputy headmistress turned her attention back to her book, Marya eyed the booklet in her hands, breath caught.

The front page of the handbook read:

# DRAGOMIR ACADEMY
## Established 740
## CHARACTER ABOVE ALL

And here is what she learned:

First: Dragomir Academy was named after Count Dragomir, a nobleman who donated his estate to establish the school and was its first headmaster. Count Dragomir founded the school two hundred years ago, just at the end of the Witching Wars, as a sort of social experiment, to see if *a positive educational environment* could turn Illyria's *most troubled girls* into *fine young ladies*.

Second: Even though they were not yet fine young ladies, Dragomir girls were supposed to do their best to act like fine young ladies from the moment they crossed the threshold into the school. If they were confused on how to act like fine young ladies, they needed only follow the school motto: CHARACTER ABOVE ALL.

This seemed to Marya to be quite unhelpful.

Third: There were a lot of principles they were to follow. For instance, *Punctuality*, which the handbook defined as being at your desk, ready to learn, with *appropriate posture*.

Also, *Participation*, which meant *maintaining an eager countenance* and approaching every challenge with *grace*, *humility, and a willing spirit.*

Also, *Propriety*, which meant behaving in a respectable manner at all times, minding rules of etiquette, *following the core virtues (see pages 13–14)*, and showing deference to authority. If authority figures were not around, the girls were supposed to *ennoble each other* by being *exemplars of good character.*

Also, *Positivity*, which meant focusing on Dragomir and the future. That meant that girls were asked not to discuss their pasts but rather to *imagine themselves anew*, as Dragomir girls, ready to learn to *serve the kingdom* and *participate in her protection.*

Whatever that meant. How Marya was supposed to help protect Illyria was beyond her. It seemed like they were more afraid she would single-handedly destroy it.

Fourth: The reason Madame Rosetti was relieved she had clothes in her trunk was that most girls didn't bring any—the reason being that all students are provided with a school uniform. This uniform promoted a sense of unity, discouraged class-based divisions, and evidenced *the desirable willing spirit* in each Dragomir girl. Not to mention, it helped them to act like fine young ladies, which built *character*, which you may remember was *above all.*

There was more, too. Mealtimes and class times and

curfew and lights-out. There were procedures to be followed, protocols and policies to respect. And so, so many rules.

Marya shut the book. It was too much. And too familiar. It was like everything her mother had ever tried to teach her. Which she had never really been able to learn, which was why she had been condemned to this school in the first place.

In other words, she would be even more disappointing there than she was at home.

Her mother's last words ran through her head again:

*I don't know what to do with you, Marya. But perhaps they will.*

Marya had never left Torak before—the rest of Illyria had always existed to her only in books, songs, and tapestry stitches—so the view outside the window provided plenty to distract her. As the sun began to set on the first day of the journey, the coach approached the Donau, the vast river that bisected the continent. There were many Illyrian stories about the Donau: in the fourth century, marauders came all the way from Gutland, intending to take Illyria's capital, but as the army amassed on the river's banks, the river rose up and swept them away.

And of course the Donau featured heavily in the folk songs, and as the carriage began to cross the great river, one in particular took up residence in Marya's mind, something she'd heard Madame Bandu sing to herself on more than one afternoon:

*My village lies beyond the river*
*Keep it well*
*Keep it well*
*My home lies beyond the river*
*Keep it well*
*Keep it well*
*My heart lies beyond the river*
*Keep it well*
*Keep it well*
*I cross the river, where the armies wait*
*Keep me well*
*Keep me well*

Then, unwittingly, she found another song replacing that one in her head:

*Oh, Mother, why are you waiting there?*
*I am waiting for my daughter*

*Oh, Mother, where did your daughter go?*

*She went over the river*

*Oh, Mother, when will your daughter return?*

*She will not return*

*Oh, Mother, why won't your daughter return?*

*She went into the river*

*Oh, Mother, why are you waiting there?*

*I am waiting for my daughter*

She closed her eyes and tried to push all the songs away.

They spent the night in an inn, Marya on a small itchy cot in the corner of the room she shared with her new deputy headmistress.

She did not sleep well.

Marya started the second day of the coach ride feeling like a piece of thread that had been gnawed on. It didn't help that Madame Rosetti told her that there would be no time to stop for lunch that day, as they did not want to be on the road too late.

Marya nodded off for a few hours, and when she awoke, she looked out the window to see mountains off in the distance. Wide-eyed, she looked to Madame Rosetti, who said, "Yes, those are the Rosas. We'll be there by sunset."

Marya had seen illustrations of mountains before, but never the mountains themselves. They looked like gods against the sky.

Afternoon was turning slowly over into evening when the carriage ascended the path up the foothills of the Rosa Mountains. Dragomir Academy loomed above them, a mammoth stone estate framed with red-capped towers. The school sat high enough in the hills to be visible from several miles away—were there anything or anyone to see it. But Dragomir was completely isolated from the rest of Illyria, hidden away like a secret.

For the rest of the journey, Marya looked out the window, watching as the coach approached the school. She should not have worried that they were just going to be dumped in the mountains somewhere. If this had once been Count Dragomir's estate, as the handbook had said, Count Dragomir had been unimaginably wealthy. The manor was made of gray stone, with decorative accents everywhere. Marya had never seen so many windows— big stately ones in front, arched ones going up the towers, circular windows lining the top story. There were towers reaching upward off the wings, with yet more towers growing out of them. Marya had seen illustrations of estates before; this one looked like several manors put together.

"It's so big," Marya said, because she could not help herself.

Madame Rosetti looked out the window and nodded. "Dragomir is one of the finest estates in all of Illyria, grander even than sorcerers' estates, if quite a bit more private. You'll find you'll want for nothing while you're here."

The Dragomir estate was surrounded by a vine-covered fence with tall iron gates. As they got closer, Marya saw the familiar bat-shaped leaves on the vines.

"Dreadbane," she whispered. *For protection.*

"Yes," said Madame Rosetti. "The Dragomirs planted it. Though in their day it would have been called witchbane."

They stopped in front of the gate, and before Marya could wonder if maybe they'd be trapped out here in the dark, an attendant appeared and the gates opened. The coach rolled forward, up the hill, and to the front entrance of the school.

The gates closed behind them with a *clank.*

# 9

# Dragomir Academy

W hen the coach stopped in front of the school, Madame Rosetti motioned for Marya to wait while the attendants brought her trunk in. This was fine with Marya. The expanse of Dragomir Academy loomed over the coach like a nightmare. Plus she could still feel her body vibrating from two days in the coach.

"Now, Mademoiselle Lupu," Madame Rosetti said, drawing herself up. "The rest of the first-year girls have already been here for a few days getting acclimated to the school and its rules."

At this, she started. *The rest of the first-year girls.* It was obvious, of course. It was a school for troubled girls, plural, but with all the things Marya had been anxious about, she'd completely forgotten to be anxious about the other students.

Marya barely knew any other girls her age; there were a few she saw in town, but her mother did not approve of her interacting with village girls. Not that Marya would have had much of an idea how to do that.

"Therefore," Madame Rosetti continued, "it is even more important that you show us you are ready for this opportunity. There will be eyes on you. You have read the handbook and there is no excuse for not following the rules, do you understand?"

"Yes, Madame," Marya said. She had only read as much of the handbook as she could bear, but she didn't tell the deputy headmistress that.

The sun was setting now, and it was time to go in. Madame Rosetti led Marya up the wide stairway up to the front entrance of Dragomir Academy. The front doors were ridiculously large, as if people might be going into the house on their horses. Maybe that was what noblemen did: maybe they trotted around their massive manors on horseback just because they could. And maybe coming in this way was supposed to make her feel like nobility her-self, like the sort of person who might trot into an elegant manor on horseback. But she was not royalty, she was just Marya, and all it did was make her feel very, very small.

If the main doors were impossibly grand, the front hall was even more so. It was bigger than Marya's entire house, which seemed excessive for a room that no one even used for anything. The hall had scarlet walls laden with gold-framed portraits of stern-looking men, all of whom seemed to be gazing suspiciously at Marya. A grand, gold-trimmed staircase rose up in front of her, and on the landing wall loomed a tapestry with the school's crest that read:

## DRAGOMIR ACADEMY
### Established 740

And, lest she forget:

## CHARACTER ABOVE ALL

It was one thing to understand that mansions like this existed, and another to be standing in the great hall of one, craning your neck at the ceiling while paintings of great men gazed down at you.

"Yes, it is very impressive," Madame Rosetti said. "As I mentioned, Count Dragomir was one of Illyria's most prominent nobles in King Danut's time, and this estate was his great pride."

As strange as it was that this was a school, it was even stranger to think that this had been someone's home once, that anyone could feel they belonged in a place like this. But, Marya thought, casting her eyes again on the gold-framed portraits staring down at her, it was built for men like them, not for her.

She slowly realized that while she was busy being intimidated, Madame Rosetti had been talking to her, likely about things she would want to know. At the moment she was explaining to Marya something about the next day's schedule.

"Madame," Marya said suddenly. "Is there supper?"

"Pardon me?"

"We couldn't stop for lunch, and it's late. I'm . . . hungry."

Madame Rosetti's eyebrows knit together, and suddenly Marya felt even smaller.

"Supper is over. If you have any questions regarding mealtimes, please consult the handbook. Now come with me and I'll show you your dormitory."

Four flights of stairs later, Madame Rosetti was opening the doorway to Rose Hall, where, she explained, Marya would be living with her classmates during her time at Dragomir. And before Marya could ask more questions, an older girl emerged into the hallway and beamed at Marya as if she'd been waiting to meet her all her life.

"This is Simona," Madame Rosetti said, "your hall adviser."

Simona was the most beautiful girl Marya had ever seen, with thick, black, wavy hair in a long braid down her back, deep brown eyes, a heart-shaped face, golden-brown skin, and a wide smile.

"A pleasure to meet you," she said, with all the manners and grace that Marya's mother had been trying to instill in her for years.

"Hi?" Marya said.

Simona took Marya's hand in hers and squeezed it. "I'm here to give guidance, to answer questions, to enforce rules—though of course that will not be necessary, as you won't have any trouble there, now, right?" She grinned. "And please do not hesitate to come find me whenever you need anything. I know how hard it can be to settle in; after all, I was in your place once."

Marya blinked. "You were a student . . . here?"

Madame Rosetti raised her eyebrows. "Simona is a sixth-year girl. The top girl in the senior class is selected to be the hall adviser for the new class every year." She turned to Simona. "I trust you can handle things from here?"

Then Madame Rosetti gave them both a curt nod and was heading back down the long hallway, and Simona's face broke into a smile—not a *character above all* smile, but an actual smile—and Marya almost gasped in relief.

"It's all right," Simona whispered, tightening her grip on Marya's hand. "The other girls only got here a few days ago, so you haven't missed that much. We just found out about you coming yesterday; fortunately, there was an extra bed in one of the rooms. I've never seen them add anyone so close to the beginning of term, but I guess since we just got started, they thought it would be okay. When did you get your letter?"

"Um, the day before yesterday."

Simona's eyes widened. "Really? Then they just came to pick you up?"

Marya nodded.

"That's . . . interesting." She stared at Marya, as if Marya needed a reminder that her transgression during the king's council visit was so extraordinary that it required the rewriting of the school's own rules.

"Well, anyway, this place isn't so awful ," Simona continued. She began to walk down a hallway lined with doors, and Marya followed. "As long as you follow the rules and don't get on anyone's bad side, that is. Madame Rosetti isn't much of a charmer, but Madame Szabo makes her look like Auntie Sunshine, if you know what I mean. Speaking of rules, it's after eight o'clock, which means first-years need to be in their rooms. I'll introduce you to the other new girls tomorrow, but for now, let's meet your new roommates, shall we?" And with that, she knocked on the door in front of her, and pushed it open.

*Roommates.* All Marya wanted to do was flop on the bed or maybe crawl underneath it, but that seemed to be out of the question, because she would not be alone. Maybe she would never be alone again.

Once more, Marya took everything inside her and pressed it down, down. Then she eyed the two girls who had turned at her entrance.

They eyed her back. Both of them were wearing identical white nightgowns. The first was tall and angular, with sharp, dark eyes, brown skin, and a curtain of long curly hair. The second was smaller and rounder, with skin even paler than Marya's, and vivid red hair pinned up in some elaborate fashion on her head.

Both seemed controlled, confident, as if they belonged in places with front halls as big as Marya's house.

"Girls," Simona said, "this is Marya Lupu, your new roommate. Introduce yourselves, please."

"My name is Ana-Maria Bulova," said the girl with the red hair. She spoke in a clipped, precise fashion, and lingered over her last name like it might mean something to Marya. Then she turned her attention back to her book. Someone whose mother didn't mind if she learned to read, apparently.

"I'm Elana," said the sharp-eyed girl, regarding Marya curiously.

Marya shifted. Her trunk was already in the room, sitting right in front of the empty bed. There was a small bureau next to the bed with a lamp on top, and a wardrobe on the other side. Each girl had the exact same setup, with identical white bedding.

The room looked big enough to house many more troubled girls, should they announce themselves, and house them in style. The wallpaper was a light green, with parallel vertical lines of small pink flowers; an intricate woven rug filled nearly the entire floor, and thick green curtains hung around each window. There was a massive fireplace with a brass clock on the mantel, and a large light fixture hung from the ceiling, with glass flowers blooming out of brass vines.

"It's gas lighting," Simona told her. "Only the best estates have it. All the sorcerers do now."

Marya nodded, as if she had any idea what Simona was talking about.

"Now, Marya," said Simona, "tomorrow's the first day of school, so there will be an assembly. Right now what you need to know is that lights-out is at nine o'clock. After that, you must be in your bed until seven a.m.—bathroom trips are an exception, of course. And in an emergency, you can come get me. But I am responsible for making sure you girls are safe, and you follow the rules." At that, her eyes seemed to fall on Elana. "If you can do that, we'll all get along just wonderfully."

Marya took a deep breath. "Do you . . . think I might have something to eat? Could I go down to the kitchen and ask?"

"Oh, I'm afraid not. Eight o'clock is curfew for first-year students."

"It's just, I haven't eaten since breakfast, and—"

Simona tilted her head sympathetically. "I'm sorry, that must be really hard! Okay, anyway, I bet you want to get settled before we turn the lights off on you! You'll find toiletries in the bathroom, your nightgowns in the dresser. If they don't fit, let me know. In the morning we'll get you your Dragomir uniform. Sleep tight!"

Simona shut the door behind her, and suddenly Marya was alone with her new roommates.

Ana-Maria looked up at her, patted her red braids, and said, "My parents are getting gas lighting this year. It's not just the sorcerers."

"What Ana-Maria is trying to tell you," said Elana dryly, "is that her father is a count, and she has a big estate."

"Well, it's true," Ana-Maria said.

"But—" Marya started. And then stopped.

Ana-Maria knew what she was going to ask. "No, I am not and have never been troubled," she said. "I had a mis-understanding with my parents, but it will be settled, and as soon as they return from their summer holiday, they will decide that I have learned my lesson and will come get me." She gazed at both of them pointedly, and then looked back down at her book.

Elana raised her eyebrows at Marya, as if to say, *Can you believe her?* What she said out loud, though, was, "You're hungry?"

Marya's eyes widened. "Do you have food?"

She shrugged. "No food allowed in the dorms. It's a rule."

"Oh." That had certainly been in the handbook somewhere.

"But I know where there is food."

"Where?"

"In the larders."

Now, Ana-Maria looked up from her book. "Elana," she said, voice full of warning.

"But we can't go, right?" Marya said. "It's against the rules."

Elana raised her eyebrows, not taking her eyes off Marya. "It is against the rules, you're right."

"Wouldn't we get caught?"

Elana shrugged. "All the staff is in their rooms by ten."

"Elana snuck out the last two nights and explored," Ana-Maria said, "even though we're not supposed to do that."

"I'm not asking you to come, Ana-Maria."

"I'm not asking to come."

Marya looked from one girl to the other. "Thank you, but I'm not that hungry," she said. This was a lie. But she was not going to break the rules on her first night.

"Someone has sense," said Ana-Maria.

"Suit yourself," said Elana. "But if you change your mind . . ."

"Lights-out in ten minutes," Ana-Maria said warningly. "You might change, unless you want to sleep in your clothes."

Marya opened up the small dresser next to her bed. A white nightgown, a robe, and slippers were there, ready for her. There were no other clothes, but Simona had said she wouldn't have her uniform until tomorrow. Marya didn't mind the idea of a uniform, though it did mean that she would not be able to wear the apron Madame Bandu had given her. But she would still have it, and when she needed it, she could take it out and run her fingers over the embroidery—dreadbane for protection, fire for light in the darkness, diamonds for courage.

But when she opened her trunk, all that was in it was her underthings. Had they unpacked it for her? Marya went over to the wardrobe. Empty.

She looked around. Elana was still watching her.

"What happened to my things?" Marya asked.

"They will be likely donated to the less fortunate," Elana said.

At this, Ana-Maria scoffed. "Can you imagine? As if the less fortunate need puffed sleeves." She clucked, then stuck her nose in her book again.

"They just . . . took everything?" Marya said.

Elana nodded slowly. "You're a Dragomir girl now. We look forward to our lives to come, not the troubled lives behind us." She said this with a completely straight face, but Marya could hear the eye roll in her voice.

"But I had . . . some important things in there!"

"Not anymore, you don't," muttered Ana-Maria.

Marya couldn't answer, couldn't open her mouth lest everything she was feeling pour out. So she stared at her trunk. The apron. The quilt she'd shared with Baby Pieter.

The maelstrom churned inside her.

*Bam!* Marya slammed the trunk closed. Without saying another word, she took off her boots and apron, crawled into bed, and turned toward the wall, arms wrapped around her chest tightly, as if to keep herself from exploding.

She awoke in the middle of the night to someone tapping her shoulder. She sat up abruptly. The moonlight was creeping in behind the curtains, enough to show her Elana climbing into her own bed. Marya blinked. Elana nodded at the little dresser next to Marya, where two dinner rolls sat underneath her lamp.

Elana grinned at her, and then turned over and went to sleep.

# The Girls
# of Rose Hall

The next morning, Simona took Marya to find a uniform, and soon she was dressed in what was to be her daily outfit for the next six years—a white dress that went to her ankles, black boots, black stockings, green hair ribbons, and a green apron that went all the way around her skirt.

When she got back to her room, Ana-Maria and Elana were both doing their hair silently. Elana had tucked her black braids into loops, while Ana-Maria was pinning her red ones up again. With her bright red hair and full pink cheeks, she reminded Marya of an apple. Ana-Maria's apron and hair ribbons were a rich blue, and Elana's were red, but the rest of their uniforms were identical to Marya's. Together they looked like paper dolls cut from the same book.

Then Simona brought Marya to meet the rest of the paper dolls.

There were three girls in the other room at Rose Hall. Katya was quite small, with a round face, wide-set eyes, light brown skin, and thick black hair that she wore pinned into buns on either side of her head, like cat ears. She stared straight at the floor and held her arms around herself as if for protection. Daria was her opposite: as tall as Simona, bony and pale, with narrow features and light brown hair in a high braid that couldn't quite keep little curls from frizzing out. She eyed Marya suspiciously. As for the third, her name was Elisabet, and she was looking at everything but the other girls. She had olive skin and dark hair in two braids like Marya's, and she was chewing on her thumbnail. They all stood slightly apart from each other, as if each of them were trying to pretend they were all alone.

And there they were, the troubled girls of Rose Hall, all lined up in their white dresses and a rainbow of aprons. The uniforms worked—Marya could not tell who was a village girl, who was from the city, who had a count and countess for parents. One of them could have been a sorcerer's daughter and she wouldn't have known.

She wanted to know, desperately, what they'd all done to be sent there. And they were surely thinking that about her. Marya could feel their curious looks, the questions bouncing around in their heads.

She felt it even as they walked in a line to breakfast, Simona in front like a mother duckling. Marya kept her eyes on the floor ahead of her as they went down four flights of stairs into the great hall, and into the dining hall.

Now Marya looked up and beheld the scene in front of her.

The dining hall was set up with six rows of tables, one for each class. There were about forty girls in the room—so many girls—and a soft hum of noise, just the clinking of silverware on plates and an undercurrent of quiet conversations here and there.

All the older girls sat up straight, shoulders back, heads erect. They sipped their tea without slurping and loaded precisely calibrated amounts of porridge onto their spoons so none would drip over. At the sixth-year table, the girls moved impeccably, precisely, balletically: they ate soundlessly, almost as if they were not eating at all.

But when the Rose Hall girls sat down, there was a change in the air, some kind of murmuring. Marya looked up to find that a good half of the room was glancing furtively at her. Everybody seemed to know about the girl who'd come late.

Marya sat down with her back to the rest of the room, cheeks burning.

Simona settled at the head of the table with the grace and propriety of a sorcerer's wife, putting her napkin delicately on her lap. "To review for Marya," she said, "mealtimes at Dragomir are an opportunity to practice being a lady. Perhaps you girls have not been instructed in true etiquette before"—a scoff from Ana-Maria—"but here you will have the opportunity to learn to behave in a way that would have you welcome on the finest estate in Illyria."

As Simona talked, Marya could feel her hands swelling into mitts, could imagine lumps of porridge slipping off her spoon and attaching themselves to various places on her body.

*Sit up straight, Marya. Speak softly, Marya. Small bites, Marya. Do not hold your knife like you are going to stab your food, Marya.*

"Remember," Simona was saying, "whatever happened in your lives before is in the past. This is a fresh start. You are Dragomir girls now, and if you let the school help you, there is nothing you cannot do. Now, let's learn about properly holding spoons, shall we?"

Holding spoons. This, apparently, was what school for troubled girls was. Luka got to learn history, philosophy, languages, and literature at his father's side; Marya would become an expert on cutlery-holding. Maybe that was what all her classes would be—mornings for knives, afternoons devoted to fork theory. And somehow Marya was supposed to care about this? The handbook had said that girls would learn to serve and protect Illyria. Apparently that was done through the care and handling of silverware.

Katya, the girl with the cat-ear buns, was sitting directly across from Marya, holding her spoon so tightly her hand was shaking. Marya swallowed and looked back down at her own bowl of sticky porridge.

As Marya was nearing the end of her breakfast, Madame Rosetti appeared in the dining hall in her long, high-necked black dress, gray hair once again in its perfect bun. She seemed to float into the room, as if the air itself bore her from place to place. Her gaze fell on the Rose Hall girls, and she glided right over to them.

Simona said to her, "Good morning, Madame Rosetti." Then she looked at all her charges pointedly.

"Good morning, Madame Rosetti," Marya said loudly, as if she had been startled. The rest of the girls followed suit. Madame Rosetti eyed them all, distinctly unimpressed, and then raised her eyebrows at Simona.

Over the course of their carriage ride, Marya had noticed that Madame Rosetti's range of expressions began and ended with stern. She could be pleasant-stern or irritated-stern or even bored-stern. But on one thing she was always consistent.

"We're just discussing how mealtimes are an essential part of a Dragomir education," Simona said brightly. "An opportunity to practice etiquette and conversation."

"I see. It seems some more practice might be in order."

"Yes, Madame. It's only the first week, Madame."

"I am aware of the school calendar. And, Marya, I trust you're settling in?"

All of the other girls' eyes went to her.

"I am," Marya squeaked.

"I'm glad to hear it," she said.

With that, Madame Rosetti strode into the center of the dining hall and rang a small bell. Every girl stood up at once, before Marya had a chance to catch on. Simona shot her a look and Marya sprang up, knocking her chair over in the process. The sound echoed through the dining hall, followed by a titter of laughter from one of the second-years. Marya's classmates looked horrified, all but Ana-Maria, who had one eyebrow arched in an amused fashion, as if to say, *When I am freed from this place, I shall regale all the society girls with tales of your ineptitude.*

Madame Rosetti rang the bell again, and each girl folded her napkin next to her bowl. Then the sixth-year girls filed out in a perfect line, followed by each subsequent class, Marya falling into her place without any major breaches of form. That, at least, was a win.

While the other classes headed back to the grand staircase, Simona led Marya and the rest of the first years to a large classroom right next to the dining hall, with six rows of dark wooden benches set up facing the front, where a lectern stood, along with three wooden chairs. The room was lined with enormous tapestries of the sort it would have taken Madame Bandu a year to make. They seemed to be battle scenes from various historical conflicts in Illyria's bloody history, stretching back in time, all with the Rosa Mountains as a backdrop.

Madame Rosetti floated in, followed by another woman, and a man who could only be the headmaster.

Marya did not know exactly what she'd expected from the headmaster, but it was not what she saw—a tall, broad-framed, square-jawed man of about her father's age, whose thick, dark brown hair didn't have even a trace of gray. He had smooth tanned skin and wide brown eyes, and he dressed like a gentleman. There was something unusually polished about him, and Marya wondered if maybe when he was growing up, people thought he was going to be a sorcerer someday.

While Madame Rosetti and the other woman sat on the stage, the headmaster stood at the lectern, regarding the girls of Rose Hall: Katya, awkward; Daria, suspicious; Elisabet, anxious; Ana-Maria, haughty; Elana, controlled; and Marya—well, Marya had no idea how she looked, but inside she felt like an ant-girl. No, she was not going to be eaten by giants at Dragomir Academy—instead she was going to be nibbled at by protocols, policies, and procedures; etiquette, decorum, and mores; not to mention the teachers, the headmaster, and all the other girls, all of whom seemed to suspect there was something very troubled about her indeed.

"Young ladies," the headmaster said, voice filling the room, "I am Headmaster Iagar, and it is my great pleasure to welcome you to Dragomir Academy. Most of you have met Madame Rosetti, the deputy headmistress"—here, she floated upward and nodded in greeting—"and next to her is the woman who will be the primary Rose Hall instructor this year: Madame Szabo."

Madame Szabo stood up and gave the girls a small bow. She was the shortest woman Marya had ever seen—about Marya's height, though she added several inches with the hair gathered on the precise top of her head. With her white face, dark hair, and bun positioned where it was, she reminded Marya vaguely of a turnip.

"Now," the headmaster said, turning back to the girls, "I want to begin by acknowledging the truth of this place. You were sent here, to a school for troubled girls, by order of the king. I won't try to pretend that this all mustn't be very unsettling and difficult for you."

Marya's mouth twitched. She seriously doubted that this square-jawed man had any idea how she felt.

"I understand that attendance at this school can feel like a punishment, but I am here to tell you that it is an *opportunity*. This is an opportunity to make a new life for yourself, and by the end of your six years here, you will not even remember the girl you once were."

Around her, the people on the tapestries went on about their business, indifferent.

"Whatever your transgressions, whatever your history, it is all forgiven now. This is a fresh start. And whether you come from the poorest of villages or the grandest of estates, you are on equal footing here. One of our most foundational rules is that Dragomir girls do not talk about their pasts, because it is the future that matters now."

As he talked, the bench seemed to press harder against Marya's back, as if it, too, were made of rules.

"When Dragomir Academy was founded," he continued, "Illyria had just survived the Witching Wars. At the time, the only option for girls who had strayed from the virtuous path was an asylum."

At this, Marya nearly gasped. Asylums were like dungeons for people who went completely, dangerously mad. He couldn't mean that.

"But"—he held up a hand—"Count and Countess Dragomir believed that there was another way. What if we gave these girls a chance? What if, instead of locking them away, we gave them the best possible education? What if, when given discipline, guidance, and purpose, these girls could be not just rehabilitated, but transformed into active participants in the kingdom?"

She was just staring at him, waiting for him to say that he didn't really mean an *asylum*, that no one thought that there was something so wrong with *these girls* that they should be locked up.

"Of course," the headmaster continued, "their ideas were controversial. Some think education is a waste of time for girls. And some think it can even be dangerous. After all, look at Kel!"

He laughed, as if he had told a grand joke. Madame Szabo smirked. Marya blinked. Did people think education would somehow turn *these girls* into witches?

"At Dragomir, we do not believe that *ideas* themselves can lead a girl astray, as long as she has the tools to make proper decisions. And it is our job to give you these tools—values, morality, and perhaps most of all, a sense of Illyrian duty. In the meantime, all you need to do is apply yourself. The system we've devised will guide you when you cannot guide yourself. This is the Dragomir way."

He seemed to really believe in what he was saying; he seemed to believe *they* believed in what he was saying, that he was giving them a gift that they must be so grateful for.

But Marya felt like she was being gifted boots that were three sizes too small and ordered to walk back to Torak in them.

The headmaster lifted his hands from the lectern, and seemed to relax, just a bit. "That's my speech," he said, then, with a laugh. "But there's something else I'd like to say to you all. Those of us here at Dragomir, we understand that it is difficult to be a girl in Illyria. There are not many places for you. It is easy to feel as if you are not valued."

Marya stiffened. The words hit her like a punch.

Next to her, Katya gasped.

"But you do have value," he continued, "and we will prove it to you. If you do well here, each of you will go on to live and work on a sorcerer's estate."

At this, the air in the room seemed to shift suddenly, as if they'd all reacted at once. This was definitely not in the handbook. Katya turned to look at Marya, as if to ask if she'd heard it too.

"It is important that you learn to display good manners, that you learn how to conduct yourselves in the finest society. The Sorcerers' Guild works with us because they know Dragomir girls will serve our sorcerers well and act with the utmost propriety. Everything you do reflects upon us, and on one another. That is another of our principles: we stand and fall as a community."

His arms were out wide, as if to embrace them.

"So, yes, we will train you to be fine, accomplished ladies, ones who can stand proudly behind Illyria's most important people. And we will train you, also, to help them. When we say we will educate you here, we mean it. This is not simply a finishing school. You will learn history, philosophy, diplomacy, and mathematics, with the help of our fine faculty."

He nodded again at Madame Szabo, who nodded back.

"That is the purpose of a Dragomir education. Discipline, guidance, and *purpose*. You are here because you have been going down a dangerous path. But that is over now. You needn't worry about what you've done, the girl you have been. Let go of the past. You are Dragomir girls now. Value each other, the community, and the school name. Work hard, study hard. And remember, we're all in this together."

As the girls were filing out, Marya felt a hand on her shoulder. Headmaster Iagar was standing behind her.

"You're our late arrival," he said.

A surprised squeak got trapped in Marya's throat. She swallowed it down. "I am," she said, as if he needed confirmation.

He looked down at her, What was he thinking? What did he see? Did he think she must be very troubled indeed to be a last-minute addition to Rose Hall?

All these thoughts were pressing against her skull, ready to burst out. But before they could, the headmaster nodded and said, "Welcome to your new life, Mademoiselle Lupu."

# The
# Dragomir Way

As Madame Szabo led them up the grand staircase and down the hallway to her classroom, Marya turned over the headmaster's words.

They sounded so pretty. She'd get an education, something she'd never had a chance at otherwise. She'd have work on a sorcerers' estate—though Marya could not imagine what she could possibly do on an estate that she wouldn't be terrible at. She was no cook, no artisan; she did not have the attention to detail to be a maid, the patience to be a governess. She was good with animals, but men usually worked in stables, and she doubted most estates had a designated goat girl.

They sounded so pretty, but there were words underneath his words. No matter how he dressed it up, this was still a school for troubled girls.

Their new classroom was as pretty as the headmaster's words—bright, with large, white-trimmed windows and yellow-and-white wallpaper that seemed to shine in the sun. It looked like it had been a bedroom once, but now it had three rows of three chairs with desks attached to them, bookshelves against the wall, and a big chalkboard in front. And there, out the window by which Marya had taken a desk, were the Rosa Mountains. They had only ever existed on a map for her until yesterday; now, in the morning sun, they seemed to gleam as they towered over the landscape, majestic rock palaces embraced by the clouds. It was all Marya could do not to get up and poke her head out the window and just stare. No wonder the giants had been drawn to them.

When Madame Szabo took her place at the chalkboard, Marya snapped to attention. Despite the teacher's diminutive height and her turnip hair, there was something quite commanding about her. And something terrifying.

When Marya was little, there was a woman who used

to come to the market in Torak to sell cheese, and she had this way of looking at you, as if she could see into your soul and she found it lacking. Luka had told Marya that she was a secret witch who kidnapped little girls, and Marya was scared of going to the market for a year.

Madame Szabo looked at the girls the way the cheese witch had. Now Marya remembered Simona's words: *Madame Szabo makes Madame Rosetti look like Auntie Sunshine.*

Once the girls were all seated, Madame Szabo clapped her hands together three times. "Now that the headmaster is done inspiring you," she said—perhaps, Marya noticed, a little sarcastically?—"it is time to begin the work of your education. We know you are all coming in with different levels of knowledge. Some of you may have been to schools before; some of you may have had governesses or been schooled by your families. Others might not know how to read yet, and if so you will have tutoring with Mademoiselle Gris in the library. As the headmaster explained to you, we are doing the work of giving you a good education as well as teaching you how to comport yourself like ladies. Obviously, given your histories, that will be quite a task."

A small, indignant cough came from the back of the room. Marya turned around. Ana-Maria, who was sitting right behind Marya, was looking at Madame Szabo as if she truly were the cheese witch reborn.

Madame Szabo clapped her hands together again so loudly Marya started. Ana-Maria flinched. The teacher turned on her heel and strode out of the room.

Now the girls all looked at each other.

"I don't think she liked that," Elisabet whispered, pulling on one of her black braids.

"Really," said Daria flatly.

"I was just saying," said Elisabet.

As for Ana-Maria, she was blinking rapidly, almost as if she was trying not to cry.

A few more moments passed. "Should I go get her?" Elisabet said.

"No!" hissed Daria.

Next to Marya, Katya slumped in her seat. It seemed the other Rose Hall roommates were getting along about as well as Ana-Maria and Elana were in Marya's room.

Madame Szabo strode back into the room then, took her spot in front of the chalkboard, and clapped three times again.

"As the headmaster explained to you," she said, as if nothing had happened, "we are doing the work of giving you a good education as well as teaching you how to comport yourself like ladies. Given your histories, that will be quite a task." One eyebrow went up. No one made a sound. "Therefore, every moment will be an opportunity for you to practice your comportment. Remember, punctuality, participation, propriety, positivity. These are the rules. When you sit at your desks, you will demonstrate good posture and grace. When you speak, you will enunciate and use proper grammar. You will demonstrate a pleasant disposition at all times. And you will show respect for authority." She surveyed the room meaningfully. "Remember, whoever you were before this"—her eyes fell on Ana-Maria—"it does not matter. You are all here for the same reason. And you have an opportunity that you would be foolish to throw away. Now, would you please stand up and introduce yourselves? Mademoiselle?" She motioned elegantly to Elana. "Introduce yourself and tell me one thing you would like to learn while you are at Dragomir."

If Elana had spent the previous night exploring all the hallways of Dragomir Academy instead of sleeping, there was no sign of it on her face. She gave the teacher a perfectly controlled nod, slid out of her chair gracefully, and stood up. "Good morning, Madame," she said, voice clear and crisp. "My name is Elana."

Madame's eyebrow went up, waiting. Elana started to sit back down, and she proclaimed, "Your full name, Mademoiselle?"

Marya glanced at her roommate. Did she hesitate a moment? "Elana Teitler," she pronounced.

"And something you would like to improve on?"

"I like playing the piano, Madame. I would like to work more on it."

"Hmph. We study music in the second year. Now . . ." She motioned to Katya, who sprang out of her chair as if she'd been bitten.

"My name is—" she started, words tumbling out.

"Eye contact, Mademoiselle," cautioned the teacher.

Katya inhaled sharply and cast her eyes directly on Madame Szabo's. She opened her mouth again, but before she could talk, the teacher interrupted again. "What are you doing with your hands?"

Marya could not help but look. What *was* she doing with her hands? They were clenched in front of her chest, and she seemed to be violently twisting her left hand with her right.

Katya quickly dropped her hands to her sides. "My name is Katya Novak and I'd like to learn to read," she said in a rush, and then practically dove back into her seat.

Madame Szabo cleared her throat, and then it was Marya's turn.

Her stomach twisted. Her mother had trained her to introduce herself properly for the council's visit—to greet them, say her name clearly, and drop in a graceful curtsy.

*We have no other children.*

"Good morning, Madame," she said. "I am Marya Lupu."

"Pardon me?"

Marya glanced around. Katya was no help; she was sitting in her seat, eyes fixed on her desk, chin tucked into her neck. But Elana was giving her a meaningful glance.

What it meant, though, she could not tell.

"I am Marya Lupu!" she said, more loudly this time.

Madame Szabo shook her head slightly, as if in defeat. "There is no need to shout," she said, and then turned to address all the girls. "It is important, in society, to speak precisely, to be clear and understood. Our words are crisp and careful. Ladies do not mumble; they do not drop syllables or swallow words or trip over their sentences. We are not clumsy on our feet, and we shall not be clumsy with our words."

*Speak for yourself,* Marya thought. Words coming out of Madame Szabo's mouth had dimension, depth, music.

Ordinary words became tiny little poems: *mumble*, *syllable*, *swallow*, *clumsy*. So she could probably make *Marya Lupu* sound like a song, but Marya could not.

"And what skill would you like to improve, Marya Lupu?"

Marya's mind grasped for something, anything. "Needlework?" she said.

Madame raised her eyebrow, slightly. "Very good, I'll see that you do."

So went the introductions. No one seemed to do it perfectly, even Ana-Maria, who could not project to Madame's satisfaction. The process involved more lectures on enunciation, as well as posture, bearing, and grace. When she did not like Daria's tone, she clapped again, then made them all sit in silence for five minutes, heads bowed. Marya squeezed her fist under her desk and thought about pretty words and all the things that might be underneath them.

After lunch—in which the girls did, indeed, focus on forks—they had Domestic Arts, where they practiced embroidery, doing row after row of running stitches, backstitches, and split stitches under the guidance of two sixth-year girls. Marya had no trouble demonstrating that her needlework did indeed need to improve.

Then Madame Szabo took them for a "brisk and invigorating" stroll around the grounds. There was more to the Dragomir estate than the mammoth house itself: a series of small cottages for staff was positioned immediately in back of the main building, along with a big carriage house and stables, and just below that a vast pasture where a reddish-brown horse gazed over the fence at the girls as they briskly and invigoratingly strolled by.

It was all Marya could do not to stop and scratch its ears and tell it what a good horse it was.

"I can't believe someone lived here," Elisabet breathed as they walked. "And they just gave this up to make it into a school?"

"Maybe they only had daughters," said Ana-Maria knowingly. "So there was no one to inherit the estate."

"They had one daughter," Elana interjected. "There are portraits of the family on the second floor. But I think something happened to her. She's not in any of the portraits when she's older."

"Really?" Marya asked.

"Maybe she died," breathed Elisabet. "In some tragic accident. And her parents decided to devote their lives to making sure that less-fortunate girls could have help."

"*Troubled* girls," Daria cut in. "Not less-fortunate girls.

We're *troubled* girls."

"Speak for yourself," said Ana-Maria.

"What does that mean?" asked Elisabet.

"You may be troubled, but I am not. This is all just a misunderstanding. You'll see."

Daria crossed her arms.

"My parents summer in the Karakos, but as soon as they return, they'll come."

"Yeah, it sounds like they really care a lot about you," muttered Daria.

Ana-Maria turned on her. "Well, I can see why *you're* here," she snapped.

"Girls!" Up ahead, Madame Szabo had stopped and was staring at them. "You will walk in a straight line and use this time for quiet contemplation. Now follow me and I'll show you the east gardens."

Daria and Ana-Maria glared at each other; then Ana-Maria stalked forward, following the teacher.

"Oh, the *east* gardens," Daria muttered under her breath, and then followed behind them.

"I want to know what happened to their daughter," Marya said, voice low.

"Are you sure she's not in the portraits?" Elisabet added. "That seems so weird."

"Go look," Elana said. "They're all near the library."

"Girls!" snapped their teacher. She gazed at them sternly. Her gaze cut into Marya. "Since you can't seem to follow directions, there will be consequences. No supper tonight for Rose Hall."

Marya's fist clenched.

Elana drew herself up. "Madame," she said, voice full of honey, "I was the one who kept talking. There's no need to punish everyone."

Marya's head snapped to Elana. Marya was the one who'd kept talking, not Elana.

"That's very noble of you," Madame Szabo said, looking distinctly unimpressed, "but as you saw this morning, we do not have individual punishments here at Dragomir. Dragomir girls must think of themselves as a community—you rise, and you fall, as one. Now shall we walk?"

Marya kicked the ground, and the girls all followed.

Thus instead of dinner, the girls went back to their hall, where a rather grumpy-looking Simona met them in the parlor and explained that, yes, if one of them broke a rule, they could all expect to be punished for it, and more, as their hall adviser *she* would have to miss meals along with them, and she did not enjoy missing meals, so perhaps they might consider behaving in the future.

The girls were required to be in the Rose Hall parlor until eight o'clock every night. There, they could read, play approved card games, do needlework, sketch, or practice the "conversational arts." Marya distantly remembered something in the handbook about positive use of leisure time, but it had been too boring to really pay attention to.

Their parlor was a big room, decorated, appropriately enough, with rose-lined wallpaper. Two green velvet sofas sat on either side of a massive fireplace, with two richly embroidered throw pillows on each. There was a table and chairs set up for card games, a small desk, and a few big chairs stationed around the room. A tapestry of a pastoral scene hung on one wall above bookshelves that were packed with books. A large bell hung on the wall, useless, presumably from when this had been a working estate and they'd needed to call to servants.

Tonight Marya and the rest of the girls collapsed onto the sofas while Simona perched on a chair, smoothed out her apron, and leaned forward expectantly.

"So, other than losing your supper," she said, with a little too much emphasis on the supper part, "how was your first day?"

Marya grabbed a pillow and held it close. How was it? She

still didn't know. The headmaster had told them that they'd be educated, that they'd go to work on estates. She was going to transform, to forget all about the girl she was now.

As for the girl she was now, she did not eat, talk, or stand correctly. It was the same thing Mama was always telling her: *Marya, you are not right.* Only here it was: *Marya, you are not right, you are so not right that two centuries ago you would have been put in an asylum, but maybe, if you do everything we tell you, you will have a chance in this world.*

Across from her, Elisabet was asking Simona, "Is it true what the headmaster said? That we will all go work on sorcerers' estates? And we'll live there and everything?"

A wide grin spread across Simona's face. "That's right," she said. "Every one of you. As long as you are able to graduate from here, the Guild will place you on an estate."

Marya leaned forward. "What kind of jobs are there?" she asked quietly.

"All sorts," Simona said. "There's so much to manage for sorcerers! There are the sorts of things that all estates need—maids, staff managers, cooks, governesses. But sorcerers need people to perform more specialized tasks as well. Every estate has an archivist who records details of Dread attacks and the like; and if a sorcerer discovers something, or develops a new spell, someone has to write it down and organize it into volumes. And they need people to transcribe these books for the other sorcerers, and librarians to manage all of them . . ."

Now, this—this was interesting. These were jobs that maybe she could do, that maybe she'd even like. These were opportunities, something else to do besides wait around to be married off.

What would Mama and Papa think, if she had a job at an estate?

"I know it's a lot," Simona said to them. "There are so many rules! And it's hard to take it all in. You can feel . . ." She shook her head and did not finish the thought. "But you can prove yourself here, and you can have a future. It's hard work. But try, and keep trying, even when it's hard. All right?" She looked from one girl to another. Her eyes met Marya's, waiting.

"All right," Marya said.

# More Letters

As the days went on, Madame Szabo did start to teach them real things, things that might be taught to a boy in a household library. And when she was learning about the ways numbers worked together or how invaders had crossed continents to try to conquer Illyria, Marya felt herself forgetting about the troubled girl everyone said she was.

It was everything else that was the problem: she just could not seem to master all the things Dragomir Academy wanted her to so she could show she belonged on a sorcerer's estate. She didn't say the right things, or if she did manage to say the right things, she said them in the wrong way, or she wasn't holding herself well, or her gestures weren't ladylike, or her expression looked sour.

Which was likely because at the time she was thinking sour thoughts.

That was the thing: there was such a gap between the girl she was and the girl she needed to be to have the life they were offering her. They wanted her to be Simona, and it wasn't just that Simona knew how to do everything right; Simona didn't seem to ever think sour thoughts. Really, it was impossible to look at her and see that she had been considered a troubled girl once.

Though, really, it wasn't that clear about the girls of Rose Hall, either.

Sure, they all seemed to have *troubles*: Daria was sullen and quick to anger. Ana-Maria (who still insisted her parents would come to get her) could be haughty. Elisabet and Katya both drove Madame Szabo to despair, Elisabet because she talked a lot and asked too many questions, Katya because she was always fidgeting and had to be reminded to look her teacher in the eye.

As for Elana—well, during the day she was a model Dragomir girl: she walked with an unhurried grace; she sat straight as a rod; she spoke clearly but softly; she displayed an agreeable countenance at all times. She knew exactly how to make herself into the right shape.

But at night she snuck out. Two hours after lights out, nearly every night, Marya heard Elana's feet hit the floor softly, heard the door open, heard her disappear. Then a couple of hours later she would come back and climb into bed.

"I found the music room," she proclaimed one morning. "You wouldn't believe how much sheet music there is in there."

"You can't play the piano in the middle of the night!" Ana-Maria exclaimed. "What's wrong with you?"

"I can play it without *playing* it," Elana said. "I don't have to make noise."

"You're going to get us all in trouble."

"Only if I get caught," Elana said back. "What do you care, anyway? Won't you be leaving us soon?"

"That doesn't mean I want to go without meals or have to clean the bathrooms while I'm here," Ana-Maria said.

Yes, Elana had troubles. But having troubles didn't make someone *troubled*, someone who needed the king to order her to a special school for the good of Illyria. What wasn't Marya seeing? What had these girls all done?

Meanwhile, she had not heard anything from home. There was a boy who came in during meals to deliver letters on occasion; so far none of the girls of Rose Hall had had any.

She knew she shouldn't hope. It could only be her mother who would write. And to write her a letter, Mama would need to decide that *I don't know what to do with you, Marya, but maybe they will* wasn't, perhaps, the last thing she'd want to say to her daughter for six years.

It didn't seem likely. Not anytime soon.

Then, three weeks into the school year, a letter arrived for Marya.

It was breakfast in the dining hall, or, in Dragomir terms, another opportunity for the girls to better themselves. After spending the first weeks working extensively on the proper handling of utensils, now Simona was ready to move on to the next level.

"The ability to make conversation at the table is important in society," she proclaimed. "No one wants to sit next to the girl with nothing to say. A lady might, for instance, inquire about how her compatriots have gotten on since last they dined together, or compliment the food, or bring up a topic that interests the party. So," Simona said, looking around at the group, "does anyone want to try? Daria?"

Daria's eyes widened. "No," she said quickly, and then looked back down.

"No, *thank you*," corrected Simona. "Another time, then. Katya, would you like to start? Perhaps something simple? A comment on the weather."

Katya looked panicked. "I'm sorry," she said, shaking her head. "It's—it's really loud in here."

"That's not really what I meant, but all right. Elisabet?"

Elisabet blinked. "We just woke up and haven't been outside. How are we supposed to talk about the weather?"

It was not going well. They'd spent three weeks barely talking at all, so thinking of conversation as an art was a lot to ask.

Marya was keeping her head down to try to avoid being asked by Simona to bring up a topic that interested the group—because what in the world would that be? This is why she didn't notice the messenger boy until he was right next to Simona, handing her a letter. Ana-Maria turned to her eagerly.

But Simona handed the envelope to Marya.

She nearly gasped. Breath caught, she tore open the letter in a most unladylike way.

*My dear Marya,*

*It took me some time to figure out what happened to you. Your parents suggested you were sent off to some kind of special school for girls, but finally Luka told me the whole story. I had never heard of Dragomir Academy, but Count Andrei was able to give me information after I offered to add some gold detailing to his cloak in the tapestry.*

*I do not really understand what happened to put you in this school—you are certainly not troubled. It seems to me that if the debacle of the sorcerer's visit means anyone needs a special school, it is Anton! I will look into educational opportunities for troubled goats.*

*I do not know if you're able to get much word of the outside world way up there in the mountains. There have been a few unusual Dread sightings of late. The sorcerers were able to push back the clouds before anyone was hurt, and of course they are nowhere near Torak. Still, I'm not sure how much they're sharing with you there, and I thought you should know.*

*The Guild will handle the Dread. And you are safe way up there. While I am dubious about your need to be there, I do believe that this school will be a blessing for you, and it sounds like it will give you options*

*you would not have had otherwise—a great gift. Read*
*everything you can there, for me; learn everything you*
*can. That is the best way to keep the monsters away.*
   *We miss you here, very much.*
   *With love,*
   *Lucille Bandu*

At the bottom, she'd drawn symbols: Dreadbane, fire, diamonds.

*Protection, light in the darkness, courage.*

And there was a postscript:

   *PS. I am not the only one who wanted to say hi.*

And sure enough, there was another letter in the envelope.

   *Hi, Marya,*
   *Madame Bandu said I could write you a letter.*
   *Sometimes I come over here and help with chores.*
   *The boys talk about you all the time. Apparently I play*
   *hide-and-seek wrong. I'm learning, though.*
   *Everything is all right at home. Papa's taken on*

*some more pupils and has been pretty busy. I've been*
*assisting Dr. Bandu here and there. He thinks I might*
*make a good doctor someday.*

*Anton misses you. He's actually pretty nice, once you*
*get to know him.*

*Write back if you can. You can send them to me here*
*at the Bandus'. That's probably better than home.*

*From,*

*Luka*

Marya read both letters over and over again, lost completely in their words. If this was considered bad manners at the table and Simona was chiding her, she did not hear.

Eventually, Madame Rosetti rang the bell and Elana nudged her to stand up. She did so, clutching the letters tightly in her hand. She had nowhere to put them—no pockets, no bag. What if the girls weren't allowed to keep their letters? What if Madame Szabo took them?

She could not lose them, too.

Clutching the letters even tighter, she glanced around. "I'll be right back," she whispered to Elana. And then she turned and ran up to their room as fast as she could. After a quick scan of her area she tucked the letters under her pillow—there!—and then ran back down two flights to

Madame Szabo's classroom.

Of course she was late. The other girls were all sitting at their desks, hands folded, eyes ahead, as the rules relating to punctuality required. Running in breathless, apron amok, one hair ribbon trailing behind her was surely a violation of those rules.

Madame Szabo adjusted the turnip bun on the top of her head and stared at Marya. Marya could not help shrinking a little. "Mademoiselle Lupu, you're late."

Marya ducked into her chair and folded her hands on top of her desk. "I'm so sorry, Madame. I needed to use the bathroom."

Madame's left eyebrow went up. Marya had come to call it the Eyebrow of Disapproval. Could she see the lie on Marya's face? Was she using her cheese-witch powers to read Marya's mind?

"Did I not explain the procedure to you if you have an urgent issue? That you come to class and inform me first? That this was the rule? Katya, tell me, did I or did I not explain this to the class?"

"Um," Katya squeaked. "You did, Madame."

"Therefore, Mademoiselle, you have knowingly broken a very simple rule. No lunch for Rose Hall today."

The other girls groaned. Marya could not help herself;

she burst up from her desk and snapped, "You're punishing everyone because I had to go to the bathroom?"

"Marya, your anger is unseemly, and it is inappropriate to talk back to a teacher. One more outburst from you and Rose Hall will go without dinner, too."

"Sit down, Marya!" hissed Ana-Maria.

"Remember, at Dragomir, if one of you falls, you all fall, just as it will be out in the world. Now, if I may continue . . ."

Face burning, Marya slid back into her chair and fixed her gaze on her desk. Tears stung behind her eyes, but she would not let them fall. It was so unfair. She wouldn't have been late if they hadn't taken her things and hadn't made her fear for the letters. And for all Madame Szabo knew, she really *had* had an emergency. So all the other girls were going to be missing a meal because of her hypothetical emergency?

*Get control of yourself, Marya.*

She clenched her hands tight and tried to concentrate.

They'd been studying Illyrian history leading up to the formation of the Sorcerers' Guild, from the invasions to the natural disasters to the monster incursions to the wars the kingdoms of Dovia had fought against one another for centuries. She had drawn a map of Dovia on the chalkboard, which, three weeks into the school year, was already a monument to the messiness of the continent's past: the kingdoms to the north and east of Illyria had been destroyed in the Wars of the Wolves, and now there were just chalk-dust ghosts where their names had once been.

They were up to the beginnings of the Witching Wars, the decades-long series of conflicts with Kel that had ended two centuries ago with the formation of the Sorcerers' Guild. Madame Szabo began as she did every history lesson: by asking the girls to tell her what they knew about the subject. And then she would spend the next hour telling them all the things they didn't know.

Around her, the other girls were raising their hands, spouting off facts about witches. It was better, they had all discovered, to try to take up as much time as possible with what they *did* know, as it irritated Madame Szabo less. Why she seemed to dislike them so strongly, Marya did not understand. They hadn't even done anything yet.

Madame Szabo had flipped around the board and was writing down what the girls said—the Kellian queen discovered witchcraft in the sixth century; witchcraft was based in chaotic magic; witches called the giants into Illyria at the beginning of the Witching Wars.

Marya tried to concentrate, but her mind kept returning to her letters. Plus there was a fly in the room, and the buzzing was making Marya feel like she had flies crawling all over her skin.

What did Luka mean, it was better to write him at the Bandus' than at home?

Hearing from Madame Bandu and Luka had opened something up in her chest, but that line was like a finger poking right in a tender spot and wiggling around.

It seemed Mama was still angry. And maybe she always would be.

"Marya," Madame Szabo said, interrupting her reverie. "Are you paying attention?"

Marya pressed her foot into the ground, hard. "Yes, Madame."

"You haven't contributed anything. Tell us something about witches."

"Um," Marya said, and then winced inwardly. Madame Szabo hated it when they said "um." She scanned the board quickly for what had already been said. "They started infiltrating Illyria in the seventh century, posing as ordinary people?"

"Yes," Madame Szabo said, "that they did. Then what did they do?"

"Well"—*come on Marya, you know this*—"they cast spells. Like, everyone in the area would lose their vision at once, or sleep through harvesting season, or plant catnip instead of turnips." Marya swallowed, momentarily panicked that Madame Szabo would be offended by the turnip reference. "Or," she went on, "they would all get fevers that lasted for months and months."

"Anything else?"

"Um"—she winced again—"during the war, all the men in one of Illyria's border towns crossed into Kel and surrendered."

Madame Szabo nodded, as if deciding that today Marya was not going to disappoint her. "Yes. Witches started moving into Illyria well before the queen's armies invaded, and they integrated themselves into Illyrian life. How could you tell who was a witch and who wasn't? Anyone?"

Marya exhaled as her eyes went to the other girls, who all shook their heads.

"You couldn't!" Madame Szabo said, arms out. "Any woman could have been a witch; any woman could have been casting spells on your village and you'd have no idea. Now"—she turned to the board—"what are we missing? Anyone?"

She hit the chalk against her list, point after point.

Elisabet raised her hand. She had proven to be the talker of the group, providing a nice counterpoint to Katya, who seemed to do everything she could *not* to talk. "They laid curses all over Illyria. There's one in Lacsat—um, in my village—and every few years the well water turns to manure. It's really foul. I don't understand why the Sorcerers' Guild doesn't send someone to undo it."

Marya grimaced. Yes, the Kellian witches had laid curses like traps all over Illyria during the Witching Wars. These still popped up in Illyria now and again: a few years ago a farmer near Torak had cut down the wrong tree, and as soon as it was felled, it turned into one hundred writhing snakes. He sold his farm and moved to the other side of the kingdom.

"Does anyone know why they don't?" Madame Szabo asked the class. "This is important."

Elana raised her hand. "It's all but impossible for sorcerers to undo a curse when they don't know its origins. And sometimes when they do another curse shows up somewhere else and it's worse."

"That is right," Madame Szabo said. "What else?" She surveyed the group, Eyebrow of Disapproval arched. "Come now. What is the thing everyone knows about witches?"

"They're bad?" Elisabet whispered.

Madame Szabo looked at Elisabet and sighed as if witnessing a tragedy.

Marya straightened. The thing everyone knew about witches was that they had made the Dread.

She raised her hand to answer the question Madame Szabo had asked. But somehow her mind leaped ahead and the words that came out of her mouth were quite different.

"The Dread attacks have been getting worse, right? Could that mean . . . there still might be witches in Illyria?"

At this, most of the girls turned to look at her, wide-eyed. Katya's hand was at her mouth. Elisabet gasped.

A moment of silence. Madame Szabo's eyes narrowed. "Marya Lupu, I will thank you not spread rumors in my class!"

"But, my father, he said that—"

"Are you talking back again? No dinner for the Rose Hall girls either."

At this, an audible groan from the other girls.

"Madame, that's not fair!" Marya said, hands clenched.

"Marya," Ana-Maria hissed warningly.

Their teacher took a step forward. "Fair? You girls are the last to speak on what's fair. Is it fair that you have opportunities so many other girls do not? And then you squander them?"

All the girls stared.

"You are so fortunate, and you don't even know it," Madame Szabo continued. "If it weren't for the Drago-mirs, what would become of you?"

Marya stood up, nearly knocking her chair over. "Madame? I am having an emergency and I need to go to the bathroom."

Madame Szabo's eyes narrowed, considering. "All right, Marya. Since you followed proper procedure."

Marya properly walked out of the room, down the hall, and into the bathroom, and then improperly threw the soap dish on the floor.

# The High Count Arev

The next morning, after the Rose Hall girls ate an enthusiastic breakfast, the entire student body filed into the assembly hall, as Headmaster Iagar had called an all-school meeting. While they were waiting, Marya studied the tapestries in the room. Even after just three weeks of history lessons at Dragomir, she could recognize things in them that she couldn't before. The one on the wall behind the stage was a series of images that depicted the slow fall of the Bolgar queen into madness as her forces moved on Illyria, and here, the one right next to where she was sitting dramatized the Battle of Kovac, in which a band of Ilvanian soldiers crossed into an Illyrian border village and were pushed back by the villagers, led by a local magic wielder—the event that would eventually inspire the formation of the Sorcerers' Guild.

There were so many tapestries all over Dragomir Academy—in the dining hall, in the classrooms, in the hallways—and Marya always wondered about the women who'd woven them. If they were kind, if they had sons, if they had neighbor girls they taught to read.

The Dragomir collection was centuries old; the tapestries had, apparently, all belonged to the count and countess, who had bequeathed them to the school. Marya checked the signature of each one for the little crescent-moon shape that indicated the weaver didn't believe the story. She found none, but she always felt a twinge of excitement every time she looked. It was a secret; more, it was a gift. And it was something that belonged to her, when she had so few things that belonged just to her. Other than that, she was a paper doll in a set.

As Marya gazed at the tapestries in the assembly hall, Madame Rosetti walked in and took her usual place in a chair onstage. Several of the teachers who didn't usually come to the headmaster's addresses gathered in the back, all looking expectant. A moment later, Marya saw why.

The headmaster was striding into the assembly hall, but he was not alone. There was a sorcerer with him.

Just as Marya had had no doubt she was in the presence of a sorcerer when the High Count Georgescu walked through her front door, all the girls of Dragomir Academy seemed to know exactly what the man with the headmaster was. Everyone stood up, good Dragomir girls that they were.

The sorcerer was much younger than the one who had come to Marya's house. While High Count Georgescu looked like you might imagine a sorcerer to look—he had a face that looked carved out of a tree and was about as tall as one—this man did not at all. He was too boyish, his face too open, his smile too wide. He had thick curly reddish-brown hair, pale skin, and greenish brown eyes that greeted the room eagerly.

But still, he was a sorcerer. He had the bearing, some way about him that drew every eye in the room toward him. Maybe that was magic, or maybe that just was what came with being one of the most important people in Illyria.

And of course he had the outfit: a royal blue robe with silver embroidery on the cuffs and those vast sleeves.

Headmaster Iagar took the podium, beaming, jaw

looking even squarer than usual, with the sorcerer right behind him smiling winningly at the room. After her experience with the High Count Georgescu, Marya was surprised to see a sorcerer smile.

"Young ladies of Dragomir Academy," proclaimed the headmaster, motioning for them all to sit. "I have a very special treat for you today. High Count Arev is a sorcerer serving the Melki region, just south of here. As most of you know, a typical apprenticeship involves extensive study over ten years, but the high count proved unusually talented, and after making an exciting discovery—which he will talk to you about—he finished his apprentice work in a mere eight. I invited him here today to inspire you for the work ahead."

After the headmaster was done, the high count took the podium as the girls all applauded. Marya could feel the excitement in the air.

"Young ladies," the high count said, smiling at the group. "It is my great pleasure to be here today to speak to you about the work of a sorcerer."

Marya was sitting between Elana and Katya, the only girls who were willing to associate with her after yesterday's disaster with Madame Szabo. Katya was leaning forward, cat-ear buns pointing directly at the high count as if she really could hear with them. Elana, though, had her arms crossed, and her face was completely blank.

"Sorcery is a difficult and exacting science. The practice only exists because of study, persistence, and vision. If we had been content with what magic could do when we discovered it, Illyria would have been overrun two centuries ago." He turned to the headmaster and deputy headmistress. "Do they know how the sorcerers came to be?"

At the exact same time, Madame Rosetti nodded—*Yes, they know that*—while the headmaster gestured in a way that said *Please, go ahead.*

"Three centuries ago," he proclaimed, "in a small northwest village, a young man suddenly found himself able to work with water in a way not explained by the laws of nature as we knew them. He could sense its location, make it move, even create more water from just a drop, and when a drought hit his village, he was able to save it. At the same time, other young men found themselves with the ability to work fire, to harness wind, to make light and heat, to communicate with animals.

"No one knows exactly why boys found themselves able to wield magic, but all over Illyria, some of them were suddenly masters of nature, not just its subjects, and they turned their talents to helping their villages prosper. Every year another magic wielder or two emerged, and after a generation they began to work together, to share their powers and knowledge, and to see how far they could push their abilities."

Marya found herself holding her breath. The whole room seemed to be. It was one thing to know this history, another altogether to hear a sorcerer tell it.

"Slowly, these first magicians became sorcerers. And their efforts were just in time, as the Witching Wars brought all of Dovia's monsters to Illyrian soil. Drago-mir Academy sits on land once menaced by giants—two centuries ago, you girls would have been afraid of being snatched in your beds. I bet this very estate has tunnels running underneath so its residents could escape if giants attacked."

With a grin, the headmaster nodded. Marya could not help it; she shuddered.

"Meanwhile, the queen of Kel was sending her witches to undermine us from the inside. And we all know the curse the witches left with us. Ever since the men of my order were able to extinguish witchcraft, keeping Illyria safe from the Dread has been our mission, and our obsession. The Dread consumes us so it does not consume Illyria."

Marya was working hard to listen to the high count, though she was still stuck on the idea that the school had secret tunnels specifically for giant attacks.

As the high count was talking, Marya slowly became aware that Elana's posture was growing stiffer and stiffer, as if she were turning into a tree. Her arms were tight around her body, her jaw was set, and her eyes looked cold.

"The headmaster has asked me here to talk about our war against the Dread, since those of you who succeed here will give us important support so we can concentrate on the work of defending Illyria. There are three Dragomir girls working on my estate now, and I do not believe I could do my job without them."

Now it was Marya's turn to stiffen. Pretty words again.

"So, the Dread. Every Illyrian has heard stories, but it is important to separate out truth from myth. This is what we know: the Dread emerges from forests as a sort of fog, or cloud. We do not know yet what causes a Dread cloud to form. We do know that the Dread is attracted to population centers, like villages or estates. It has no interest in animals. Once a cloud reaches a village, it will break off into dreadlings, vaporous creatures who move through the town at night. We don't know precisely how it is the dreadlings do what they do, but in a single night, they can kill an entire town, leaving its citizens bloodless corpses."

Now the whole room was completely still. Even Madame Rosetti was wide-eyed. While everyone knew what the Dread took and what it left behind, hearing an actual sorcerer say it was rather terrifying.

No one knew precisely how the dreadlings killed, because no one had ever survived their attacks, but in Marya's head the foggy creatures wrapped their wispy, cold arms around their prey and absorbed the life from them, bit by bit.

The high count looked solemnly around the room. "This, then, is the sorcerers' charge. The Dread is made of a material no more substantive than smoke, and so no conventional weapon can hurt it. It is a curse, made of magic, and only magic can fight it."

Marya's mind went to the tapestry Madame Bandu was working on, the one that showed Count Andrei shooting arrows at dreadlings in the forest. Of course it was a lie; it was ridiculous to think that an ordinary man could kill dreadlings, especially with a bow and arrow. But she'd never thought to question it until Madame Bandu had told her she could.

"It has been nine years since the Dread has taken a

village. Though its power only grows, so has our ability to predict, track, and contain the monster. Our most important project is to find a way to undo the curse, but until we do, we will keep working on ways to respond to the threat. This is our constant occupation."

Marya was leaning in, waiting for him to tell them what Papa and Madame Bandu had both said—that the Dread attacks were increasing and the sorcerers were barely able to keep up. Though High Count Arev did not strike her as the kind of person who would say he was having trouble keeping up with anything.

And indeed, he did not.

He went on to tell them about the Guild's system: they had guard towers poised near every forest to sight any new Dread clouds; soldiers ready to evacuate any villages in its path; teams of sorcerers prepared to converge on the cloud and dispel it.

"And we are constantly making new discoveries," he continued, eyes sparkling. "Just this year, we figured out how to make a small indoor space completely secure from the Dread—in the palace, the king now has a dreadproof room he can use in an emergency. By the end of the year, we will have a safe space in every estate so a sorcerer could survive an attack."

Marya glanced to either side of her. Katya was wide-eyed and wringing her hands together in her lap. Elana had one eyebrow up, Madame Szabo style.

And that's when she really heard what he'd said. A safe space in every estate for a *sorcerer* to survive an attack.

But what about everyone else?

"Meanwhile," the high count continued, seemingly blissfully unaware of any issues with what he'd said, "the headmaster mentioned my personal invention, and it is my honor to share it with you. For two hundred years, we've had to rely on our eyes to know the Dread is near. But this"—he held up a small glass tube, and though it looked empty, he presented it as if it contained miracles—"is a device that can detect the Dread from several miles away. As each one takes months to make, there are only five in existence right now, but my hope is that someday every sorcerer will be armed with one."

He beamed at the room.

Marya's eyes fixed on the tube, still completely clear. Which was good; if there were Dread nearby surely it would not be, surely the high count would not be standing there, face shining, as if he had invented sunlight.

And still, he did not say anything about the increase in Dread attacks.

Behind her eyes, Marya saw a vision of them all running through tunnels beneath the school, escaping grasping dreadlings.

And suddenly, her hand was in the air. "High Count? Is it true that there's been an unusual amount of Dread activity lately?"

Now every eye in the room was on her. The headmaster popped up, eyebrows knit, but before he could say anything, the high count had drawn himself up. "There are always rumors," he said. "And the threat is always great. But I assure you, never so great that we cannot handle it, with the support of Illyrians like you." He surveyed the room, and one side of his mouth curled up. "Perhaps a demonstration is in order."

The sorcerer reached underneath the lectern and pulled out a glass jar which he held up for the whole room to see.

Inside it was a purple wisp of smoke, writhing in some invisible angry breeze.

Gasps came from the room. Marya found herself stretching upward so she could see, one in a sea of girls now focused entirely on the thing in the jar, as if they were bespelled.

Was that . . . ?

It couldn't be.

"High Count Arev," said Madame Rosetti, standing up, "I do not think it's wise—"

Next to her, the headmaster held up his hand.

The rest of the assembly hall was completely still. The high count grinned. "Yes," he said, "your eyes do not deceive you. This is a small tendril of Dread!"

Nobody moved. Marya could not take her eyes off the thing. It was thrashing violently in the jar now, an angry reddish tone pulsating underneath its purple surface. Marya's stomach turned. Another girl groaned audibly.

It was just a wisp, no bigger than a goose feather and far less substantial. But menace poured off it and filled the room.

"We have been able to capture bits of Dread—too small to form a dreadling, but retaining all its properties—in order to experiment," High Count Arev proclaimed. "That has allowed for great advancements in our fight against this accursed monster. Our inventions aid with detection and protection, but in the end, when the Dread is making its way toward a village"—his eyes swept over the room— "only a sorcerer can face it."

With that, he opened the jar.

The Dread shot out of the glass enclosure up to the ceiling, where it floated above the room, still writhing, still pulsating with something that felt like fury, or maybe it was just hunger.

A couple of girls shrieked. Marya cowered. Was it growing? She couldn't tell. It looked like it was spreading, or else it was just desperately reaching out for more of its kind so it could form a dreadling and do the job it hungered to do: consume everyone in the room.

"High Count!" Madame Rosetti exclaimed. Next to her, the headmaster watched the piece of Dread wide-eyed, like a child at a bonfire.

Eventually, the Dread's writhing slowed. Now it just hovered over their heads.

Like it was waiting for something.

Like it was watching them.

The sorcerer cleared his throat, drawing their attention, and held his hands out, as if gathering air. The energy in the room shifted, and Marya's stomach lurched. Something started shimmering between his hands, as if the texture of the air had changed slightly. High Count Arev thrust the shimmering thing upward, toward the piece of Dread. The Dread sprang toward him like a snake, but the shimmering air hit it, and it reeled backward. Dread and spell hit the ceiling at the same time, and in the next moment the room was filled with wisps of purple smoke and shimmering air.

And then both vanished.

The Dread was gone.

No one moved.

Marya could not breathe.

"Now, of course," High Count Arev proclaimed, "that is just a small bit of Dread. We'd need a team of sorcerers to dissipate a normal-size cloud of Dread, and even more once it collects into dreadlings. But this is our work. This is our calling, young ladies. We are here to protect you."

He glowed at them all. Were they supposed to clap? Marya did not feel like clapping. She felt like hiding under her bed and never coming out. On one side of her, Katya sat completely still, mouth open. On the other, Elana had her arms folded and mouth shut tight.

The headmaster was shaking the hand of the high count, thanking him profusely for the demonstration, while all the girls just watched, still frozen.

That was one wisp of Dread and it was terrifying. What would it be like to see a cloud as big as a village? The kind that her father had told her not even a month ago had appeared far from the nearest forest, without warning?

"They're lying to us," Marya muttered.

Next to her, Elana leaned in. "I know."

"Why would they lie? My father told my family that the Dread threat is growing at dinner. It's a not a secret."

Elana looked around. "Honestly," she whispered, "I don't think they care enough to tell us the truth."

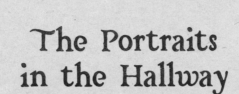

14

# The Portraits
# in the Hallway

More pretty words.

*The Dread is nothing to worry about. The sorcerers will handle it.*

It wasn't too far off, really, from *being ordered to a school for troubled girls is an opportunity.*

She could do nothing about the Dread, but maybe she could find out more about the school. There had to be something they weren't saying.

This week the girls were given the first of their occasional Sunday afternoon free periods, with a list of approved activities—including visiting the library. Elana had said on the first day that that was where the portraits of the Dragomir family were, so that's where Marya was going to go.

The library was on the second floor of the manor, on the other side of the building from the main classrooms. Marya had had no chance to visit before: they were always being led to one place or another in their little duckling line by Simona or Madame Szabo, so that even now walking alone felt strange and dangerous and somehow even shameful.

The entire hallway outside the library was dedicated to portraits of generations of Dragomirs, one after another, culminating in the school's founders: first, a wedding portrait from 715; then one of the count standing with his hand on the shoulder of the countess, who was gazing at a little girl with ringlets, in a red coat, holding a small, green-eyed black cat. It was labeled *Count Ionut and Countess Maria Dragomir and daughter, year 724.* There were two more portraits with the nameless girl in them—in the last she looked maybe a little younger than Marya, still holding the cat. Then time moved forward again three years, and then again to 739. In both of these it was just the count and countess and cat, no daughter.

So they'd lost a daughter, somehow, and founded a school for troubled girls.

There were no more answers on the wall, so Marya headed into the Dragomir Academy library.

She'd pictured something like the library in her house in Torak—bigger, of course, but still in the same family. But the Dragomir library looked like something from an entirely different world. There were dozens of rows of shelves, all reaching way up to the ceiling, so high you'd need to scale a ladder to get to them. It was an entire kingdom's worth of books.

Marya took a deep breath and crossed the threshold, her arms wrapped around her chest. The smell of paper and dust and leather hung thick in the air. She walked slowly, looking from one shelf to another, like a girl in an enchanted forest staring up at the trees.

"First time?"

Marya started. There was a large desk in the center of the room, and a sixth-year girl was sitting at it, smiling helpfully at her.

"Yes."

"It's something, isn't it? The Dragomirs themselves had a famously large library, and the school trustees have only expanded it. A great resource for girls who go to work in libraries on estates."

Marya could only nod.

"I'm Irina. I assist here. Do you know what you're looking for?"

She did not. "Um . . . can I just look around?"

Irina laughed prettily. "Of course. It's the library!"

"Thanks." Suddenly the shelves looked towering and innumerable; she was lost in the forest, with no idea which direction to try to go.

"Are you all right?" Irina asked.

"Yes!" Marya said. In an effort to look like she had purpose, she wandered over to the nearest shelves, which were full of books on needlework, some instruction guides and some academic works with bizarrely dense titles. When her eyes fell on *A Stitch in Time: Reading Illyrian's Past Through Textiles*, something clicked in Marya's head. She flipped through the book and saw what she was hoping she'd find.

A diagram of embroidery symbols. *Dreadbane for protection; diamonds for courage; fire for light in the darkness.*

She ran her hands over the symbols; then, book in hand, headed for one of the tables.

"Marya," a voice whispered.

She looked around. There were tables and desks scattered through the library. Three third-year girls sat at one—one a redhead, one with brown hair, one with black, like another set of paper dolls—all reading silently, separately.

Whenever Marya saw the girls from other classes, they were either making polite conversation at meals, or like this—silent and separate.

And there, at a small table behind them, with a pile of reading primers at her side, was Katya.

Marya went up to her and smiled in greeting; then they stared blankly at each other, Marya fiddling with her braid. The girls were almost always together, so she'd never had an opportunity to run into just one of them somewhere. And so she had no idea what to say now that she had. What had Simona said a lady might talk about? She could not inquire about Katya's day, as Katya's day was exactly the same as hers. The weather? The food?

Should she just stand there, silent and separate?

"You're here," Marya said.

Oh, that was brilliant.

"Yes," Katya said, tapping her hands rapidly against the table. "Mademoiselle Gris is giving me extra tutoring on reading." After the words were out of her mouth, she flushed and looked away.

Katya and Daria hadn't known how to read or write when they came to Dragomir, so the librarian, Mademoiselle Gris, was tutoring them both. Since Madame Szabo seemed to expect them to learn overnight, Marya imagined it was very stressful for everyone involved.

"Lots of girls don't learn to read where I'm from," Marya said quickly. "I had a neighbor—a master weaver, I watched her boys while she worked—she taught me."

"Oh. So that you could teach her boys?"

"Well, I thought so at first, but . . . I think it was just for me. Since my parents hadn't taught me." Marya glanced around, as if they might be behind her still. "I was supposed to keep it secret from them. She thought they might not like it."

Katya scrunched up her forehead. "Why not?"

Marya hesitated. "I don't think they wanted me to . . . know things," she said finally. "I think they thought it would be bad for me for some reason."

She stopped, feeling the click inside her. She hadn't realized it until just then. But in his opening speech the headmaster had said that some people thought it was dangerous for girls to get an education. Maybe her parents were those people.

"My mother tried to teach me, but . . . ," Katya began, "I don't know, the words on the page were so . . . noisy. I think that's why I'm here."

Marya blinked. "You think you're here because you had trouble learning to read?"

Katya looked at the table. "I mean"—she shifted—"there's got to be some reason they wanted me to go here, right?"

"They?"

"My parents."

"You think your parents asked that you come here?"

"Well, yes. How else would the school have known about me?"

Before Marya could answer, Mademoiselle Gris appeared, ready for Katya's tutoring session. Marya had barely seen the librarian; she'd come into Madame Szabo's class once to talk about keeping archives, but that was about it. She was young, maybe a decade older than the sixth-year girls, had a soft, round face, and actually smiled, which made Marya think she was probably the nicest teacher in the school.

And then it occurred to Marya:

She'd come to their class to talk about keeping archives. This library probably had an archive.

Marya excused herself and went back to the main desk.

"Are there, like, archives here?" she asked Irina.

"Of course!"

"I mean, old records of the Dragomir family?"

"Oh, naturally. Noble families always keep everything

because they assume people will care about everything they do years later. They make copies of their own letters, create meticulous family trees. In the case of the Dragomirs, though, we actually do care."

A few minutes later Irina was putting a large box on Marya's table. "There's a lot more," she said, "from earlier generations, but this is all the correspondence we have from the last Count and Countess Dragomir. It's divided by year. I only ask that you keep it that way. Let me know if I can get you anything else."

Marya gazed around at all the shelves. "It must be fun to work here."

"It is," Irina answered. "I'm hoping I can find work in a library on an estate. Of course, Simona gets first choice, assuming the headmaster approves."

"She does?"

"Yeah. Top girl in the class gets first choice. They rank us, so I'm second to her right now. If she messes up, I could move into first."

"Oh," Marya said. They were going to be ranked?

"She probably won't mess up, though. Simona is Little Miss Perfect, right?"

"I . . ." Marya shifted. "She's really nice."

"Well, maybe you all will make a lot of trouble for her,

and then I can move up." She winked. "Anyway. Enjoy your reading. Let me know if I can help you with anything else."

It was the first time since she'd arrived that she'd been able to make a choice about anything, and Marya found her fist clenching, as if to hold on to the feeling. Inhaling, she opened the box and began to go through the files. Judging by the portraits, the girl would have had to have been born in 722 or 723, so Marya flipped to those files first.

And there she was, in a birth record dated 723.

*Nadia Maria Dragomir*

With a glance at the clock, Marya flipped forward to 735 and scanned the letters in that file. Nadia was still with the family; in April the cat, Dracul, disappeared and Nadia was distraught, but Dracul reemerged several days later, looking very pleased with himself, thank goodness!

Marya paged forward. And forward still. And forward still.

The letter about the cat was the last mention of her.

Marya looked through the file again, but there was nothing. And after 735 the correspondence got very thin, as if the Dragomirs had stopped talking to anyone outside the estate.

A shriek came from the middle of the library. Marya jumped up and whirled around. At the table of third-years the redheaded girl was standing straight up, staring at the table in horror, while the two other girls at the table were gaping at her.

One of them breathed, "Tereza, what's wrong?"

"Don't you see that?" the redheaded girl—Tereza—exclaimed, pointing at the book in front of her.

"What?" said the second girl.

"Look at the picture!" Tereza yelled.

Marya stood on her tiptoes, trying to get a look at the book. There was an illustration of some kind of creature—she couldn't tell what. The other girls at the table were looking from it to each other in a way that suggested they saw a lot more wrong with their classmate than with the illustration.

"I don't—" said the brunette.

"Look at it!" she yelled again. "Don't you see?" And then she stumbled violently to the left. Everyone was gaping now—Katya, Marya, the other third-years. Irina popped up from the desk and ran forward.

But before the rest of them could move, Mademoiselle Gris was striding over to the table and grabbed the red-headed girl by the shoulders. "It's all right, Tereza," she said, helping her up. "It will be all right. Come with me."

"What's happening?" asked the brown-haired girl.

Mademoiselle Gris stood up, still holding on to Tereza. "I will be taking her to the infirmary," she said firmly. "She has fallen ill. But she will be fine. Nurse Rieza will look after her."

"Can't anyone else see that?" asked Tereza, desperation in her voice.

"It's all right," Mademoiselle Gris soothed, not very soothingly.

"What's wrong with her?" the brunette demanded.

"Nothing we can't handle. Now, girls, get back to your studies."

With that, Mademoiselle Gris led a crying Tereza out of the library, while the other girls all stared at each other. Irina watched them go and then rushed over to the remaining third-year girls. Marya and Katya exchanged a glance and followed.

"Haven't you seen it happen before?" Irina whispered.

All the girls shook their heads. Marya had definitely never seen anything like that before.

Irina looked around the library again, and then leaned in. "They don't like to talk about it with the younger girls. But it happens sometimes here. They call it mountain madness."

Marya and the others just stared.

"It might be something particular to the Rosa mountains," she continued. "An old curse or something? No one really knows why. Every year a couple of girls get it, usually in their third or fourth year."

"If it's an old curse, why doesn't a sorcerer undo it?" Marya asked.

"It's almost impossible for sorcerers to undo a curse without knowing its origin," one of the third years said. Marya blinked. She'd forgotten. Elana had said that in class, but it was easy to forget classroom material when you were learning about curses that plagued your school.

"Will she get better?" asked Katya, eyes like moons.

The girl nodded. "They have to spend a few weeks in the infirmary with Nurse Rieza, but they're okay when they come out. It happened to a couple of girls in my class my third year, and another in my fourth. They just started . . . seeing things. One said she kept feeling like bugs were crawling under her skin."

"That's awful!" Katya squeaked. Marya shuddered.

"Yeah, it was really bad. She started screaming and thrashing around one night when we were all in bed. Woke the whole hall up. We thought it was the Dread! It took three servants to get her to the infirmary. But she came out two months later and was okay."

"Two months," Marya breathed. "What did they do to her?"

"She said she doesn't remember anything," Irina said.

"But—" Marya started, unsure which of the thousand questions in her head to ask. It felt like that girl should have remembered *something* from two months in the infirmary. "If the mountains are cursed, why do they keep the school here?"

Irina shrugged. "Do you know of another incredibly wealthy count who wants to give his estate to us? Anyway, they can cure it."

"I don't understand why we haven't heard of this," the black-haired girl said.

"You know now. Everyone finds out when it starts happening to someone in their class."

"But what about before?"

Irina threw up her arms. "What are they going to say? 'Hello, welcome to Dragomir, some of you might start hallucinating in a couple of years, but don't worry about it, it'll be fine'?"

"But at least we'd know!" Marya said. "Then we wouldn't be so scared if it happens to one of us." *Like we are right now*, she thought.

Irina shook her head. "I don't think they want anyone to

know. What if it got out? It would only make things harder for us after we graduate, right? If people thought we might be mad? They'd never let us work on sorcerer estates, and then what would we do?"

There was a crack in Irina's voice, then, some desperation that lurked beneath what she was saying.

Marya bit down on her lip. *Some girls might be so ill they have to stay the infirmary for a month, but it will be fine, nothing to worry about.*

More pretty words.

# In the
# Rose Hall Parlor

Rose Hall's nightly parlor time continued to be a fairly awkward affair. A parlor was supposed to be for relaxing and visiting, but the girls did not really know how to do either, at least at Dragomir. Elana and Ana-Maria seemed to always be annoyed with each other, and the girls in the other room seemed just as fractured.

Neither Marya nor Katya had told the others about mountain madness, nor had they talked about it again since Tereza's breakdown. Not talking about mountain madness seemed to be a rule—maybe an unspoken one, but a rule nonetheless, and if you broke rules at Dragomir, everyone paid for it.

So tonight Marya sat and tried to write her brother and Madame Bandu. She had not done it yet, only because there was so much to say, and because her writing was slow and labored. She did not have all the words to say the things she wanted to. She felt seas and eternities away from them, and it would only get worse.

*Dear Madame Bandu and Luka,*

A good start.

*I was really happy to get your letters.*

Maybe if they knew how much she loved getting their letters, they would write more. She considered, fiddling with the feather on the quill as she did so.

*The estate is very nice, but it is hard, too.*

This was all true, and yet it seemed to say nothing.

*We have uniforms. There's a wave pattern on the aprons.*

She chewed on the pen some more. Her heart cracked a little. She couldn't tell Madame Bandu that they'd taken her apron; Marya had promised her that she'd treasure it. Instead she wrote:

*They had bedding for us, so they took Baby Pieter's quilt away. Luka, you will have to remember him.*

She pulled on her braid. She had not so much as said Pieter's name since he died. She and Luka had never talked about him. Even writing it down felt like she was betraying a secret, though she had no idea what that secret was. A rush of panic went through her, and suddenly all she wanted to do was rip up the letter.

But no. She had to say it. She had to tell Luka so he would do this one thing for her.

She closed her eyes. Opened them again, focusing on the empty part of the page.

*We are learning a lot here. We are talking a lot about witches right now. A sorcerer visited and showed us*

*something he invented to detect the Dread from miles*
*away.*

    *How is Anton? How are the boys?*

    *I promise I will read everything I can.*

    *Please write soon.*

    *Love,*

    *Marya*

And then, after considering, she added:

    *PS. Madame, did you learn anything from Count*
*Andrei about the Dragomirs' daughter?*

It had taken her so long to write this, and she'd said so little. She wanted to tell them about the other girls, and how hard it was to talk to them. She wanted to tell them that she always felt like she was doing everything wrong, but she didn't know why. She wanted to tell them that everyone kept saying pretty words to her, but terrible things seemed to lie underneath. She wanted to ask Luka whether their parents ever mentioned her, if he thought maybe Mama might write.

Instead she got out the book on embroidery that she'd borrowed from the school library and studied the symbol chart, and then drew a star at the bottom of the paper.

*Thinking of you from afar.*

She folded up the letter, wrote out the address from Madame Bandu's letters on the envelope, and dropped it in the parlor's outgoing-post box, already counting the days until she might receive a reply.

The parlor was nearly silent. Ana-Maria was writing to her parents, Daria was embroidering, Elana was reading a book from the parlor bookshelf, and Katya and Elisabet were playing some card game Simona had taught them. Simona herself was off at a meeting with the deputy head-mistress, so there was no one to try to get them to have meaningless conversations with each other. But since they didn't know how to have *meaningful* conversations, there was nothing to say.

Marya was itching to get back to the library, to look for some more information about Nadia Dragomir—or gaps where that information should be. And now there was mountain madness. Did the Dragomirs know about it? Could Nadia have gotten it, in the years after the Witching Wars? Maybe before they knew how to treat it?

It had been Elana who had first noticed Nadia Drag-omir in the paintings, so Marya went over to the table where Elana was reading.

"I found some information on the Dragomir's daughter," she whispered, sitting down across from her.

Elana looked up. Marya's chest tightened suddenly; just because Elana had mentioned the pictures didn't mean she cared. She could have gone looking in the archives herself if she'd wanted to. And sitting with other girls was not actually a thing that happened in the Rose Hall parlor.

But Elana's eyes sparkled. "Where?"

"In the library. They have the count's correspondence there. Her name was Nadia. The cat was Dracul."

"That," Elana proclaimed, "is a good name for a cat."

Marya grinned. It was.

"Wait," Elana said. "You said her name was Nadia?"

"Yeah. Why?"

Elana's eyebrows knitted together. "I've seen that name here before. I can't remember where. I'll find it, though. What else?"

"She just disappears after 735. There's no mention of her after that."

"Okay, now, that's weird."

"There aren't many letters either. Like—"

"Like maybe there were more letters once, but they're not there anymore?"

Marya nodded. She wanted to explain everything to

Elana. About mountain madness. About how no one seemed to be telling them the truth, at least not all of it. About how maybe, just maybe, there was something very wrong that no one was talking about. And she couldn't shake the feeling that figuring out why the Dragomirs founded the school could maybe lead to some answers.

But somehow the words got stuck.

"There must be something else," Elana said. "We should go look."

"When the librarian is there," Marya said quickly. "Because we'll need help to find more records." She was not going to start wandering at night with Elana. She would absolutely get them caught.

"If you say so," Elana said, with a knowing grin. "Anyway, look at this." She pushed over her book, called *The Witch's Legacy: The Curse of Kel*, and pointed to the chapter she was reading, which was entitled "On the Origins of Witches."

Marya scanned the first page. It said that scholars were divided over how the women of Kel became witches. They all agreed that there was something about the nature of these women that allowed witchcraft to flourish there, but what was it? Some believed that women pursued witchcraft because they naturally had a defect in their morality;

others, that witchcraft could easily corrupt women because they were naturally weak in character.

Marya looked at Elana. "I . . . don't know why it really matters? Witches are witches, right?"

Elana rolled her eyes. "Right. And women are either evil or weak."

Marya fiddled with a braid.

"If it makes you feel better, the author thinks maybe it's something specific to women in Kel," Elana added, pointing to a paragraph on the next page. "Kel's 'lack of proper social structure, overly permissive society, and history of greedy queens created an environment for witchcraft to take root and flourish.'" She looked up, eyebrows raised. "So you know, maybe Kellian women are more weak or evil than we are here."

"Well, that's a relief," Marya said flatly. How would she feel about these words if she'd just read them in a book, without Elana to tell her it was okay to find them ridiculous?

"Though he gets to Illyrian girls too," Elana said, flipping a few pages ahead. "See?"

Marya looked. The author said that there'd been a concern during the Witching Wars that witches were corrupting Illyrian girls, and that they, too, were turning to witchcraft.

She'd never heard this before. "So Illyria had witches too?" she asked.

She must have spoken louder than she meant to, for Ana-Maria looked up from her letter. "Well, Madame Szabo is clearly a witch," she said.

Marya blinked. And then, before she knew what was happening, she cracked up.

The rest of the girls did too, the laughter filling the air of a parlor that didn't know how to contain such a sound. Ana-Maria had told the first joke in the monthlong history of Rose Hall.

"She can't be a witch," Elisabet said, "otherwise we'd all be turned into spiders by now."

"Or good students," added Elana.

"Even a witch of her powers couldn't do that," Marya said.

"Turning us into spiders would be too obvious," Katya said brightly. "She's just slowly sucking out our spirits."

The only girl who didn't seem to be amused was Daria, who was staring at Marya curiously. "Why are you asking about witches in Illyria?"

"It's this book Elana is reading. I think it's saying that Illyrian girls might have been turned to witchcraft during the Witching Wars. Or people were afraid they would."

"It's true," Daria said. "There was a girl in my family who was a witch."

Now all the girls put down what they were doing and stared.

She shrugged. "A great-great-great-aunt or something. Maybe there's supposed to be another *great*; I don't know. They say there was a Kellian witch in her village and she . . . you know."

"She *what*?" Marya asked. The rest of the girls just gaped.

"I don't know—I just know she was practicing witchcraft. Like, some boy had been pestering her while she was walking and suddenly his hair lit on fire."

Daria was saying this so matter-of-factly, like everyone had a great-something aunt who'd made a boy's hair combust. Marya certainly did not, and, judging by the reactions of the girls in the parlor, none of the rest of them did, either.

"What happened to her?" Elisabet breathed.

"She was sent to an asylum, I guess. They called it a witch asylum; I don't really know what that means, except that I guess you can't just put witches in an ordinary asylum. This was during the Witching Wars. She must have been young, like sixteen or something."

"I've never heard of this," Ana-Maria exclaimed.

Daria lifted her eyebrows. "Probably most families don't like to talk about it. It's not like you'd want it getting out that there was a witch in your family."

"Oh, dear," Ana-Maria said in agreement.

"Mine, you know, every generation there was someone they were afraid would end up like Aunt Magdeline. 'Better behave yourself, or . . .'"

She didn't need to finish the sentence.

"So, that was you, then?" Elisabet asked.

Daria shrugged again. "I guess I should have listened every time my mother told me I needed to act better."

"Mine too," Katya said. "I mean, not directly. But it was all 'what are we going to do with you, we can't handle you.'"

Marya straightened. "Did they tell you they had you sent here?" she said, looking from Katya to Daria, voice strained.

"Not exactly," Katya said.

"If you spend your whole life hearing that maybe you'll end up in an asylum," Daria said, "and suddenly one day you get a letter ordering you to a school for troubled girls. . . ."

"That's awful," Elana said. "People can be so awful."

Marya fiddled with her hair ribbons. Had Katya's and Daria's parents really had them sent here? But how would they even have known about it? They were village girls too, Marya could tell, and even Madame Bandu hadn't heard of the school.

Her stomach was churning as if she might legitimately vomit, and she didn't even know why.

"This isn't an asylum, though," Elisabet said. "It's a school. We're actually learning things—"

"That may be true," Daria said, "but we can't leave. We can't go home."

"Speak for yourself," said Ana-Maria.

Daria turned on her. "You really think you're going to be able to go home."

"I made a mistake," she said. "As soon as my parents feel I've learned my lesson, yes, they will come and get me."

"You're here by order of the king!"

"So we're told," she said. "I'm sure that however they got me in here, they will be able to get me out. They intended to punish me, not send me away."

"Punish you for what?" Elisabet asked.

She hesitated, but only for a moment, then exhaled. "My parents don't have any sons; therefore the estate will go to some second cousin of my father's, who is twenty-five years older than I. They have informed me that when I am of age, I will have to marry him. I told them I would rather eat snails, and locked myself in my rooms for a week. The day I came out, the letter from Dragomir arrived."

All the girls leaned in. But before she could continue, a voice cut through the room like an icy breeze.

"May I ask what you ladies are doing?"

Everyone whirled around. Madame Rosetti was in the doorway, Simona behind her, looking stricken. Madame Rosetti's expression was angry-stern now, a variation on stern Marya had not seen. All the girls froze. Marya's hand clenched around her braid.

But Elana stood up. "We were just talking, Madame."

"You know that talking about your pasts is against the rules here."

"Yes, Madame," the girls repeated.

Or most of the girls. Not Elana, who was still standing up, hands on her hips.

"Why?" Elana asked. "It doesn't make sense."

"I believe the headmaster addressed that in his opening lecture. We want every girl to be on equal footing. More importantly, your job isn't to question the rules; it is to follow them. Is that clear, Mademoiselle?"

Elana did not respond.

"Is that clear?" Madame Rosetti repeated, voice low.

"Yes, Madame," she said, jaw clenched.

Marya dared a glance at Elana, who looked like she might set Madame Rosetti's hair on fire.

"Now," Madame Rosetti gazed around the room, "I am disappointed to see you girls breaking the parlor rules the first time your hall adviser has somewhere else to be. That does not demonstrate good character." Her voice was quiet, measured. "If you break the rules at Dragomir, there are consequences. For one week, after dinner you will go straight to your rooms. No parlor time. Do you understand?"

"Yes, Madame," they all muttered.

"Mademoiselle Teitler?"

"Yes, Madame," Elana said.

"Your job here is to do one thing: To learn to follow the rules. I assure you, this directive is not an arbitrary one, nor are we being needlessly authoritarian. If you think that life beyond the gates of Dragomir will be any different for you girls, I would urge you to disabuse yourself of that notion immediately. You must learn to *follow the rules*. Do not forget again."

With that, she turned and left. Simona stood in the doorway, looking as if she'd walked in to find the girls planning a murder. Maybe hers. And then she turned and followed Madame Rosetti.

Silence in the room. Marya put her head in her hands.

Madame Rosetti was right: they did know the rules. They'd just forgotten; they'd started talking and forgotten. And, yes, it seemed like a silly rule, but half the rules seemed silly; they were still supposed to follow them.

Really, Marya was the one who had started talking. It was her fault.

As Marya was losing herself in these thoughts, Elana stood up, drew herself upward, and stalked toward the door.

"Where are you going?" said Ana-Maria.

Elana turned. "Exploring."

"Now?"

She threw up her arms. "Yes. Now."

"We'll all get in trouble!" Katya said.

"I won't get caught," Elana said.

"How do you know that?" Ana-Maria said.

"I haven't yet, have I?"

"They probably just let you do it," Daria said.

Elana whirled around. "What?"

"You're like her"—she pointed at Ana-Maria—"you just don't talk about it. Your parents are nobility too. It's obvious. I bet you're super rich. I bet you live in a house like this." She gestured toward the lavish parlor.

Elana's eyes narrowed. "You don't know anything," she said.

"I know you can break the rules over and over again and not get in trouble for it." Daria crossed her arms.

"Because they haven't caught me!"

Marya closed her eyes. She did not understand. Something was happening here and she could not figure it out.

"Fine," Daria said, straightening. "Maybe you just don't care who you get in trouble."

At that, Elana turned on her heel and charged out the door. Daria blew air out of her mouth and flopped on the sofa.

Before Marya knew what she was doing, she sprung up and went after Elana.

"What is going on?" she hissed, catching Elana's arm a few steps down the hall.

"I have to get out of here," Elana said.

"Why don't you just go back to our bedroom? I can make sure Ana-Maria doesn't come in for a while."

She shook her head. "I'm going to go look for those tunnels High Count Arev mentioned."

"Now?"

"Yes. Right now."

Marya looked around, then lowered her voice. "Why do

you do this? Why do you sneak around?"

Elana straightened, and in that moment, she looked to Marya every bit the daughter of a noble. "Because," she said, "if I do what they say, that means I am everything they say about me. And I'm not. Do you understand? I'm not."

And then she turned and slipped down the hallway and out of sight.

The girls were quiet the next day. At breakfast, Simona didn't seem to have any interest in guiding them in conversation, and none of them had any interest in having one. Elana looked as if she hadn't slept, and maybe she had not. As for Marya, the pieces of the evening kept flying around in her head, but she couldn't put them together in a way that explained how it had gone so badly so quickly. Except that everyone was hurt and upset, and it had started with her.

It was a relief then when the messenger boy came to their table that night at dinner. Marya's heart leaped— maybe her mother had finally written?—but it was not Marya he had a letter for.

Ana-Maria's letter from her family had come.

As if understanding the solemnity of the occasion, the

boy handed Ana-Maria her letter with the dignity of a royal servant.

"Finally!" Ana-Maria said.

The girls all stared. Every day she'd been writing her parents; every day she'd been confident that a letter was coming soon, that their coach would pull through the gates and a footman would fling open the doors and Ana-Maria would saunter out, climb into the carriage, and leave the school forever.

Now Ana-Maria acted the lady she had been telling them she was all along. Her posture was perfect, her countenance eager, her words to the messenger boy crisp and clear. She opened the letter delicately—ladies do not rip envelopes—and unfolded it.

"'Dear Ana-Maria,'" she read.

And stopped.

Her eyes popped. Her face twisted, then fell.

She put her hands over her face and began to cry.

"What is it?" Elana, who was sitting next to her, asked. "What's wrong?"

Ana-Maria only cried harder.

Elana grabbed the letter and scanned it.

"Elana!" Simona said. "I don't think that's—"

But then Ana-Maria sprang out of her seat and ran out

of the dining hall, and Simona jumped up to follow her.

The girls all stared at each other, except for Elana, whose eyes were stuck to the letter.

"What is it?" Elisabet whispered. "Is everyone all right?"

Elana's lips pursed. Her eyebrows twitched. "Her parents," she said, voice tight, "say that as she was ordered to a school for troubled girls, she has disgraced the family. They say they do not wish for her to write them anymore." Elana's words caught for a moment. She swallowed. "They no longer consider her their daughter."

# Missing Pieces

The girls of Rose Hall became an even quieter group after that. While they'd had little to say to each other before, now the silence had body and weight. It plodded behind them everywhere they went, lurked in the back of their classroom, tucked itself into bed in their rooms at night.

Even though Ana-Maria's insistence that her parents were coming to get her had seemed less and less likely, her confidence more and more absurd, no one could blame Ana-Maria for wanting to believe she didn't really belong there.

They were troubled girls, cast off by their families, isolated in this academy way up in the mountains; they had to be taught how to sit, how to walk, how to eat soup, how to speak. They needed rules about how they could dress, how they could spend their time, what they could talk about. And as the weeks went on, it seemed that Dragomir Academy was the only home the girls had. None of the girls got letters from their families.

Including Marya.

Maybe her parents no longer considered her their daughter, just like Ana-Maria's. Maybe now, while they were all girls, none of them were daughters anymore.

Madame Bandu, though, wrote every week. Marya still hadn't gotten any reply from her or Luka to her first letter; it would be at least a month from the time she wrote a letter for a response to arrive (unless Madame felt compelled to pay for a messenger, which there was no good reason for her to do, as much as Marya might very much want it). There was part of her that was afraid that they wouldn't write back ever again once they'd gotten her letter, that somehow her mention of Baby Pieter was a huge mistake. That sentence sat with her always, a burning ember in her chest.

It was autumn in Illyria, and it was getting cold in the

mountains. There were fires going in the rooms now, their colors matching the tree canopy outside the window. The school supplied the girls with coats for their outdoor walks now, and when they came back, their cheeks were chapped and their noses red.

Dragomir continued to promise them opportunity in one moment and in the next show them how little they deserved it. Marya couldn't stop thinking about Nadia Dragomir, about what had happened to her. If she could fill in the blanks about why the Dragomirs had started this school, maybe she could figure out what the teachers weren't telling them.

So, on the first Sunday free period they had after the disastrous evening in the parlor, Marya headed back to the library to see if she could find out anything else. Today the library was empty of students, save Marya, thanks to some vomiting-based illness that was sweeping through the school and had nearly half the girls in their rooms or in the infirmary.

Today Mademoiselle Gris was working at the library desk by herself, with no sign of of Irina. "What can I help you with, Marya?" she asked.

Marya still had not talked to the librarian much, but she greeted Marya cheerfully and didn't treat her like she was doing something wrong in that cheese witch-ish way Madame Szabo had.

"Is Irina here?"

"She's come down with the pesky stomach illness so many of you girls have, I'm afraid to say. But I'd be happy to help you find something."

Marya paused. She hadn't told Irina exactly what she was looking for in the Dragomir archives and Irina hadn't asked. But there was no reason not to tell, was there?

When she explained to Mademoiselle Gris that she was looking for more information about Nadia Dragomir, the librarian just looked puzzled. "You mean, there's nothing that mentions what happened to her in the Dragomir's personal papers and correspondence?"

Marya shook her head. "There's not much at all after 735," she said.

The librarian frowned. "That's very peculiar. I haven't worked on those archives myself, but I can't imagine why they'd be so incomplete." She chewed on her lip. Marya almost giggled; you'd never see Madame Rosetti do that. "We have a box of some of the countess's personal effects—books, needlework. No letters, though, I'm afraid; those would have been in with the files you'd looked at if they were saved at all. And there should be a trove related to the founding of the school." She considered a moment. "Let me try something else." Her eyes caught Marya's and she grinned. "Archives are such treasures, aren't they? I don't always see a first-year girl taking an interest. Maybe you'll be a librarian someday!"

Marya looked up at her. "Maybe," she said quietly.

"Well, work hard. The headmaster chooses the girls who get such important positions personally. You'll want to impress him." With a wink, she headed off to look for her something else.

She returned a few minutes later with another box for Marya to examine, this time a collection of documents related to the founding of Dragomir Academy. There were blueprints for the building of cottages for faculty and staff—including, Marya noticed, a connection to the estate's tunnels in case of giant attack. A several-page document estimating what kind of staff they'd need for the school. A few different drawings suggesting how to convert the existing estate to a school. And pages upon pages of contracts that made no sense to Marya.

"Marya."

Marya looked up from the box to find Elana standing above her.

"I was going to look at the music books," she said,

motioning over to the shelves. "What are you doing?"

"I—" She flushed. She'd talked with Elana that night in the parlor about going to the library, but after Elana had stormed off, it hadn't seemed like she'd want any part of something Marya was doing. Marya took a breath. "I'm looking for more about Nadia Dragomir. Do you want to look with me?"

"Sure," Elana said, sitting down. She looked a little wary, and Marya could not blame her. And so, as Marya caught Elana up on everything she'd found and hadn't found, she tried to sound as friendly and eager as possible. "Even Mademoiselle Gris thinks it's weird that there are so few letters after 735."

"They're obviously trying to hide something," Elana said. "If she'd gotten sick and died, I feel like there'd be something here. There's no way Count Dragomir would never mention her in a letter again. Whatever it was, they didn't want people to know about it."

Marya's eyes widened. "Maybe she committed a crime or something? And went to prison?"

Elana let out a small laugh. "They don't put the daughters of counts in prison."

"But"—Marya studied the documents in front of her—"she had to have been troubled somehow, right? Something happened to their daughter, and they founded a school for troubled girls? Her parents thought that if she'd had a proper education, things would have been different?"

Elana shrugged. "Maybe. But that still doesn't tell us why her father wanted to act like she just disappeared into thin air."

"Is that what you think happened?"

"Well, he's the one who would have ordered the letters copied, and saved everything, right?"

Marya chewed on her lip. It was certainly possible that Nadia had gotten mountain madness. If she'd gone mad before they had a cure and had to go to an asylum, he'd want to hide it. *Here, have our estate; our daughter went mad in it. It'll probably be fine, though.*

She could not explain mountain madness to Elana here in the library, with Mademoiselle Gris lingering somewhere behind them. She'd have to tell her later.

Still. It was something, being here with another girl, just talking. It was something to have someone to share this with.

"Look," Elana said, passing another letter to Marya.

Marya took it and read it over. This one was from a representative for Count Dragomir announcing the count's intent to transfer the deed for Dragomir Hall and its surrounding lands to the crown for its use in establishing *a reformatory school for Illyria's most disturbed young ladies.*

Marya's eyes could not help but linger on that phrase.

"Who knew that *troubled girls* would be an improvement?" Elana muttered.

But it was a sentence near the end of the letter that really caught Marya's attention:

*The count and countess would appreciate the immediate completion of the service the crown has agreed to provide, in which case all will transpire smoothly.*

She read the line several times.

"What service?" she asked.

"My question exactly," Elana said.

"Does this mean that they made an agreement with the king? Like, they give up their estate and the king . . . does something for them?"

"It sounds like it."

Marya sat back in her chair. Elana was studying the letter again, face etched in concentration. With a glance around for Mademoiselle Gris, Marya leaned in. "Don't you think it's weird?" she whispered. "That they're training us to work on sorcerers' estates even though we're . . . you know . . ."

"Troubled?" Elana raised her eyebrows. "No. I don't. What better place to keep an eye on someone?"

Marya blinked.

"Seriously. If you think someone is a threat somehow, where would you put them?"

*Illyria's most disturbed young ladies.*

"But . . . are we really . . . ?" She couldn't finish the sentence.

Again, Elana knew what she could not say. "Someone must think each of us is a serious problem, right? I know why I'm here. Do you know why you're here?"

Flushing, Marya nodded slightly. There was the reason she knew about, and the possible reason that she did not want to think about. The ember in her chest burned.

"It's almost dinnertime," called a voice behind them. Mademoiselle Gris. Elana and Marya straightened, trying to look very much like girls who were not doing anything the school wouldn't want them to do. "Simona will be here to fetch you in a minute. Did you find what you're looking for?"

"Not really," Marya said quietly. If Simona was fetching them, they would not be able to talk more until later.

"Well, come here next free period, and I'll look for other boxes to pull for you. Always happy to help girls interested in history!"

Later, in the parlor, Marya wrote to Madame Bandu, telling her what she'd discovered. *What could the king do for the Dragomirs, do you think?* She also told her what Mademoiselle Gris had said, about pleasing the headmaster so she could work in a sorcerer's library someday. Finally, she added another embroidery symbol from the book at the bottom—cat whiskers, for uncovering secrets.

Just as she had addressed the letter and put it in the box, a wave of queasiness hit her. She sat back quickly. Simona suddenly stood up and exclaimed, "Marya, are you all right?"

No, she was not all right. It had started to feel like something in her stomach was rapidly turning rancid, and that rancid thing was infecting everything else around it with rancidness, and soon she herself would be a rancid, decaying thing. Marya ran to the bathroom, reminded suddenly that there was a vomiting-based illness going around.

Some time later, Simona walked Marya to the infirmary, where Nurse Rieza immediately ushered her into a bed, which was conveniently the only place in the entire world Marya wanted to be. She felt like a squeezed-out rag, one that had done all it could do in this world and was now ready to be released from its earthly burdens.

\* \* \*

When Marya awoke, it was the next day. She'd been aware of little the night before, other than her own desire to lie in a miserable heap on the floor, but now she was able to take in her surroundings.

The infirmary was about the size of Rose Hall, with eight beds arranged in two rows and a large desk near the front entrance. There were several large armoires arranged around the room, and in the back a small office. The door to the office was open, showing Nurse Rieza sitting at her desk, reading.

There were five other girls in the infirmary—four older girls and, in the bed next to her, Elisabet, looking like a miserable heap.

Something needled Marya's brain, something out of place or missing. Which was strange, as she'd never been here before, barely even heard of the infirmary, except in the library that day that—

Tereza. The mountain madness. *Nurse Rieza keeps them in the infirmary for a few weeks*, Irina had said. Since that day, Marya had been checking the third-years' table for Tereza's return, and unless she'd just happened to get out of the infirmary exactly when Marya went into the infirmary, something was weird.

"Elisabet," she whispered.

Elisabet pushed herself up. "Oh! You're alive now!"

"I seem to be. Hey, how long have you been here?"

Elisabet threw up her hands, as if time had no meaning.

Elisabet hadn't been in class for a day before Marya got sick in the parlor. She had disappeared just as Ana-Maria had reemerged from three days in the infirmary, looking wobbly. "Did you see a third-year girl in here named Tereza? Bright red hair?"

Elisabet looked around the room. "Not that I remember? There was just that one third-year, you know, the one with the sneeze? Why?"

Marya glanced into Nurse Rieza's office, then shook her head. It was too much, again. "It's not important. I have to go talk to Nurse Rieza about something." Marya got up, and then immediately remembered why she was in the infirmary in the first place. Her legs wobbled, and her body felt like someone had thrown a bucket of ice water on it.

"Um, are you going to almost die again?"

"No. No, I'm okay." Marya took a deep breath and then headed over to the small office.

As soon as she got there, Nurse Rieza stood and took a step forward. "What are you doing? Are you all right?"

She was not, not really. The body, it seems, requires

some moisture to function, and Marya no longer had any of that. So she sank into the chair in front of Nurse Rieza's desk.

"There's a bell!" Nurse Rieza proclaimed. "It is for ringing when you need me! So you don't need to stand up and walk all the way across the infirmary to get me when you are sick, thus becoming so weak you need to sink into a chair in my office! Have you had your remedy yet? Drink this, little sips, there you go."

Nurse Rieza pushed a bottle of something toward Marya. It tasted gingery and warm. Her stomach gurgled, though out of protest or gratitude Marya couldn't tell.

"You will have some sips of that every two hours, and that should help avoid any further . . . incidents. Now . . . you came to see me, against orders?"

"Thank you," Marya said unsteadily. Now that she was here, she realized she had no plan. "I was wondering how long might I have to stay in here?"

There. That was a reasonable question, and pretty good for a girl with no moisture in her body.

"That is up to me. I will release you when I feel it is safe to do so, and not a moment before. For instance, I would like to believe you can stand upright effectively, and I do not, as of yet, believe that."

"Right."

"I would also suggest that you might get out of here more quickly if you followed my orders, which include staying in bed."

"I'm sorry. I just wondered what would happen if I had to be here a long time. Like, if I didn't get better."

"Are you concerned you have something different from the other girls?"

"No, I—I just wondered. . . ."

"I assure you, Marya, that I am more than capable of managing stomach upset. And that is all this is. Though I am not a physician, I am highly qualified to take care of the maladies of schoolgirls. But there is a doctor who comes by once a week, and who I can call in, in emergencies. I could certainly arrange a consultation if you're not comfortable with my care."

Marya took two more sips of her drink. Being subtle wasn't working, so she was just going to have to be unsubtle. "I saw a girl in the library, Tereza. She got . . . sick."

At this, Nurse Rieza's eyebrows went up. But when she didn't speak, Marya plowed ahead. She could always blame the vomiting. "A sixth-year girl said she had something called mountain madness."

"I see," Nurse Rieza said, face now expressionless.

"Well. I understand why you are concerned, but there has not been, as of yet, any vomiting associated with mountain madness."

"No, I just—I wanted to make sure she is all right."

"She will be. She is getting the best of care."

"Where?"

"Pardon me?"

"Where is she getting the best of care? Is there another room in the infirmary?"

"Ah. Well, that, I'm afraid, is school business."

"I just . . . wanted to visit her." This was a stroke of inspiration, possibly brought on by the triumph of keeping the ginger drink down. "I saw what happened, and I thought maybe I could bring her a book or something. From the library. After I feel better."

"Hmm. Well, that's very kind of you. But Tereza is quarantined. I'm sure you understand." And with that, Nurse Rieza stood up and motioned toward the door, and Marya could do nothing but stand up—and she could barely do that—and go back to her bed.

She could feel Nurse Rieza's eyes on her, and so she just shook her head slightly toward Elisabet, planning on telling her later, perhaps after the nap that she felt very much like taking at that moment.

She did not awaken again until evening, when the messenger boy's voice woke her. And as he spoke to Nurse Rieza, she pointed him in Marya's direction.

Marya's heart leaped at the thought it could be a response from Madame Bandu, or Luka. She tried to prop herself up. But he was not heading for her. The letter in his hand was for Elisabet, and Marya tried to pretend it was just illness churning in her stomach.

She watched as surprise crossed Elisabet's face, then something like joy.

"I haven't gotten any mail yet," she whispered to Marya as she reached for the letter.

Marya pressed her lips together. Someone else's happiness should not have made her unhappy. There was just so little to go around.

But as Elisabet read, the joy in her face completely disappeared. She went completely gray. She sucked in a breath, and it sounded like a sob.

Marya sat straight up. "What? What it is?"

Elisabet did not respond. She just stared at the letter, as if willing the contents to change.

"What happened?" Marya repeated.

Elisabet turned to her and stared. Her mouth opened, but the words did not come.

"It's from my aunt," she said after a moment.

"Okay," Marya said.

"My parents are all right. My sister, too."

"Okay," Marya said. It was hard to breathe, suddenly.

"They were staying with my aunt when it happened."

Now Marya could not speak.

"But everyone else . . ." She swallowed. Closed her eyes. Opened them. Turned to Marya, eyes like the sea. "The Dread came to Lacsat. The whole village is gone."

# The Many
# Uses of Fire

The next morning the headmaster called a school-wide assembly. Forty students and a dozen teachers filed solemnly into the assembly hall. Nurse Rieza even ushered in all the students from the infirmary, except Elisabet, who had been given a sleeping draft after her shock.

Word of the destruction of Lacsat had already spread to the entire school. The Dread had not taken a village in eight years; the sorcerers' watch protected all the towns near enough to forests to be in danger, and even in cases where they could not repel a Dread cloud, they were always able to evacuate the villages in time.

But Lacsat was nowhere near a forest.

Marya sat rigid in the hard wooden seat as the headmaster walked into the room, accompanied as always by Madame Rosetti.

And behind them was High Count Arev. The sorcerer had not been back since he spoke to the students over a month ago, but here he was again in his majestic blue robes, though this time he was not smiling at all.

"By now," the headmaster began as he took the podium, voice as somber as a grave, "you have heard of the terrible fate of the people of Lacsat."

Marya squeezed her eyes shut. *We don't know precisely how it is the dreadlings do what they do, but in a single night, they can kill an entire town, leaving its citizens bloodless corpses,* the High Count Arev had said.

"As you may be aware," the headmaster continued, "Lacsat is not one of the villages typically under sorcerer watch, as it is not located close enough to a forest to be in danger. The Guild confirms that this Dread cloud did not originate in any forest. Now, I'm sure you're all wondering what this means for us all at Dragomir Academy. We have always considered ourselves quite safe from the Dread up here in the mountains, but in light of these developments,

I have petitioned the Guild to allow High Count Arev to live on the grounds, and they have agreed."

A murmur passed through the room, as High Count Arev nodded solemnly.

"Ladies of Dragomir," the high count proclaimed, taking the podium, "I am sorry to be addressing you under these terrible circumstances. I came here a month ago with assurances that we were making great progress in our continual battle against the Dread. But I am afraid the witches' curse is more devious than even we knew. With that said"—he held up a hand—"the Sorcerers' Guild has taken nothing for granted these past two hundred years. We have been hard at work mastering magic, giving it order and structure, and we will meet this new chaos head on."

Marya swallowed. His words were reassuring, but then what else was he going to tell them? That the Sorcerers' Guild wasn't up to it?

Daria's hand went up. "What would make the Dread change its behavior all of a sudden?" she asked.

Daria clearly suspected the same thing as Marya—that no one was going to simply tell them the whole story. They'd have to ask.

Marya felt the entire room lean in as the high count

cleared his throat. "We are still in the process of investigating. There had been an uptick in Dread activity in the previous year or so, and it's possible the two events are related. Rest assured we are looking into every possibility."

Again, the whole room seemed to react at once. Marya and Elana exchanged a look.

Daria raised her hand again. "But what I was asking was, well, if the Dread is from an old curse, how could it just change like that without—"

"Mademoiselle, as I said, we are looking into every possible cause."

Daria folded her arms and sat back on the bench. Marya's brain grabbed on to the sentence that she had not finished and turned it around until she could see how it was supposed to end.

Whatever was going on, the grown-ups were not telling them the whole truth.

Marya hesitated only for a moment before raising her hand. "If the Dread are suddenly changing behavior after two hundred years, is it possible that . . . well, could it be that the Kellian witches are back?"

Daria caught her eye and gave her a swift nod. Now every girl in the room was leaning forward, waiting wide-eyed for the sorcerer's next words. The witches were an old monster, like the giants and the pricolici; they appeared only in history books, tapestries, and the tales of storytellers—and in the great and terrible shadow of the Dread. They were not supposed to be something to be afraid of now, something that could be living in your village, poisoning your crops, laying down curses, turning your mind against itself without you even suspecting a thing.

"As I said, we are exploring all possibilities. Right now, all you need to know is that the entire Sorcerers' Guild is putting all its resources into discovering what brought this curse to Lacsat so we can prevent future attacks. In the meantime, I am here to protect you. I will be here on the grounds for the foreseeable future."

With that, the headmaster thanked him profusely on behalf of Dragomir and dismissed the girls to their classes. Still, the sorcerer's last assurance to them hung in the air, where Marya could examine it.

Why would they send a sorcerer to protect Dragomir Academy?

As the girls headed to Madame Szabo's room after the assembly, Marya's brain whirled. Everything had changed, and then changed again. She sidled up next to Elana and whispered, "Could the Guild think the Dread would come here?"

"I don't know," Elana whispered back. "But it seems like it. Why else would he be here?"

"I don't understand why they couldn't just say that the witches are back," Daria muttered. "They obviously are. Someone has to be causing it to change, right?"

"They don't want to worry us, I guess," Elana said, rolling her eyes.

"Too late," Katya whispered.

There was no way that Simona didn't know her ducklings were talking behind her, but perhaps she'd decided that, since the destroyed town had been home to one of their own, she wasn't going to make a big deal about rules.

Sometimes Simona was nice like that.

But as soon as they crossed the threshold into Madame Szabo's class, they stopped talking. Madame was never nice like that; in fact she was already giving them her best cheese-witch look, as if nothing had changed.

But Daria either did not see the look, or simply did not care. As soon as they were all settled, she raised her hand and asked, "Is there a reason they think the Dread would attack Dragomir?"

At that question, Madame Szabo's mouth formed a

long, thin, admirably straight line. "What would make you ask such a thing?"

". . . Because they're assigning a sorcerer here?"

Madame Szabo exhaled. "I am sure that is simply a precaution."

"But why do they think we need protecting?" Daria asked. "Does it have something to do with witches? Would they target the school?"

Marya and all the rest of the girls watched Madame Szabo carefully.

"Such a thought is fanciful, Daria," she said, Eyebrow of Disapproval fully active as she surveyed them all. "Fancy does not show good character. Fancy shows an idle, uneducated mind. Ladies at Dragomir are to keep their minds on—"

"Pardon me, may I interrupt?"

Madame Szabo's head swerved toward the door, where High Count Arev stood. The expression on her face said that no, no, he most certainly could not interrupt, now or ever. But the words out of her mouth were "Certainly, High Count."

He strode in, gliding into the room as if the wind bore him. "I couldn't help overhearing what you were saying. Madame Sabel—"

"Szabo," she corrected.

"Yes," he agreed. "I commend you on urging these girls to remember to be practical. Practicality is a fine quality in a lady."

"Well, thank you, High Count—"

"However, times such as these require expanding our idea of what is practical. Limited thinking will not help us defend our kingdom!"

Madame Szabo's mouth fell open in a decidedly unladylike way.

"This is Illyria, and we are constantly under attack. It is wise to be wary. And these times especially call for suspicion." He looked at them all meaningfully. "Trust your instincts."

Madame Szabo's head twitched slightly. "Of course, High Count. It is simply that these girls are here because their instincts are not necessarily—"

"Their instincts seem fine to me!" he proclaimed. "They are asking the questions they should be asking. Do not discourage suspicion among these girls, because that suspicion could save Illyria someday." He was beaming at them now, the solemn sorcerer of the morning gone, as if he could only hold that persona for so long.

"High Count," Marya said, "may we ask you questions?"

"Certainly! Certainly!" He stepped in front of the class, right next to Madame Szabo. "I hope you do not mind, Madame?"

"Oh," Madame Szabo said, slightly adjusting the bun on the top of her head. "No. No, not at all."

He grinned, and then turned his attention back to Marya. "What would you like to know?"

Everything. Marya wanted to know everything. She glanced around the room, and the other girls nodded slightly at her. The High Count Arev liked to talk. So they needed to get him talking. Maybe then he would actually tell them something.

"So, let's say there are witches again, and they're here in Illyria," she said finally. "Could they be controlling the Dread?"

"Well, that is certainly a possibility, yes."

"So maybe there would be a reason Lacsat was attacked?"

He nodded. "Again, we are open to all possibilities. That is the only way we will uncover the truth."

Marya frowned. There were no answers in his answers.

"So . . ." Elana raised her hand. "Do you have any theories on why witches might have sent the Dread to Lacsat?"

He blinked. "Well, as I said, witches sending the Dread is just one possibility. Another is that there is something particular about Lacsat that attracted the Dread. Or perhaps that this particular Dread cloud originated somewhere outside a forest, and Lacsat had the terrible luck of being the nearest village."

Now, they were getting somewhere.

Ana-Maria raised her hand then, but did not wait for the high count to call on her to speak. "But this is all a change. So something had to have caused that change, right?"

The high count looked around the room and grinned. "This is what I mean," he added, turning to Madame Szabo. "Good Illyrians ask questions. Now, you must understand: part of a sorcerer's job is to keep Illyria's people calm. But, between us"—he leaned forward, his voice inviting them all into his world and all its wonderful secrets —"it is not unreasonable to suspect witch involvement. After all, who does chaos in Illyria serve? Who does it serve if Illyria's most powerful protectors are occupied by unpredictable Dread attacks? Kel."

*Who does it serve?* It was the same question Madame Bandu had told her to ask about the stories Illyria told about itself.

And yes, if the sorcerers were occupied trying to predict an unpredictable Dread, it would serve Kel.

But how would it serve Kel if the Dread attacked Dragomir?

"So there could be witches in Illyria right now." Ana-Maria said. "They could have been here for a long time. Waiting. Just like before."

High Count Arev straightened then. But he did not deny it. "If there are," he said, "we will find them."

"Then what happens?" asked Daria. "When you find them?"

"Ah, well. That is a question. During the early days of the Witching Wars, we simply put them to death. But of course, that ultimately added to our troubles, for reasons we understand now."

"What reasons?" Daria asked.

"Ah, well, it's simple. If you understand the principal of magical permanence . . . you do know about magical permanence, yes?"

Madame Szabo cleared her throat. "We do not cover magical theory until year three, when our girls are more mature."

He whirled around. "But these discoveries are part of Illyria's legacy. Surely, you are instilling in these young women a sense of pride in the discoveries of the sorcerers?"

"Illyrian pride is one of the principal tenets of our

philosophy. But as I'm sure you know"—she smiled coldly—"there are so many things about Illyria of which to be proud."

He laughed. "Yes! So true. But, it certainly won't hurt the girls to get a little bit of magical theory now, would it?" He turned to the class and pulled back the sleeves of his robe. "It was a great Illyrian magical scholar who uncovered many of the basic principles of magical behavior. And the first principle, that of magical permanence, tells us that magic cannot be destroyed, only changed or transferred. Which means if you try to destroy a magical being, that magic will be released somewhere else in ways we cannot predict or control. Hence, all the magic of the witches we killed back in the beginning of the Witching Wars either transferred to new witches or appeared somewhere else in the kingdom as an uncontrollable magical entity and would wreak havoc. You should have seen what happened when magic emerged in the Satamarian pigs!" He laughed. "Eventually, King Danut and his sorcerers began to imprison witches in cells that interfered with their ability to do magic. It was a drain on resources, of course, to imprison witches for their lifetimes in these asylums, but it was necessary."

Daria sat back, as Marya eyed her. So, that was it,

then. They put Kellian witches in witch asylums, the same places they put Illyrian girls who had become witches, like Daria's distant aunt.

Katya raised her hand. She sucked in a nervous breath, and then the question tumbled out of her mouth. "Why did we get sorcerers when Kel got witches?"

At this, Madame Szabo straightened. "Katya, you should know better—"

"Excellent question, Mademoiselle," the high count interrupted. "And one that no one really has the answer to. Of course"—he rubbed his hands together—"there are theories. Let's say, for instance, two different countries discover fire," he said, now pacing. "In one country, the people study it and learn its secrets, learn how to use it to heat their homes and cook their foods, how to control it, how to use it to make life better for everyone. In the other country, they see fire only as a means of destruction. They learn how to feed the flames to burn longer and hotter, and how to set it upon their enemies, how to use it to destroy what others have built."

Katya glanced around the room, clearly to see if the other girls had understood. "But," Katya asked, "why do we have *sorcerers* and they have *witches*?"

Now he gave Madame Szabo a look that clearly said,

*What is wrong with these girls? I just explained that.*

Madame Szabo said flatly, "I can't imagine why that wasn't clear."

The sorcerer tried again. "Magic is a great power, and a very few of us are blessed to be able to manipulate it. Here in Illyria, a kingdom of learning and values, we use our fire—or our magic, you see; the fire was a metaphor—in a certain way. We have tamed and created order out of it; we have organized the council to find those young Illyrians with the ability to wield magic, and the Guild to train them to respect it, to use it only to fight the Dread and help the kingdom. In Kel, the queen was the first person to learn how to manipulate magic, and she and her disciples saw in it only the potential for chaos—a means to curse, to destroy, to take over the kingdoms of Dovia. That is how magic spread in Kel—whether through coercion or infection, we know not."

And there it was, again. Just as in the book she and Elana had looked it. Defect in morality or defect in character.

Marya shivered. Did they think there was a witch here, biding her time? She raised her hand. "If witches look like everyone else, how do we recognize one?"

He nodded solemnly. "Well," he said, "that is the

question. In the past the witches did everything they could to blend in, to weave themselves into the fabric of Illyria. So, how do you recognize a witch? Ask yourself, what does a witch want? A witch wants to destabilize Illyria. She wants to undermine us in any way she can. Remember what they did before: they destroyed crops and livestock; they sowed fear and suspicion; they spread chaos and madness. So we must be wary. How might someone undermine Illyria? Perhaps through exerting some kind of unnatural influence on people in power. Perhaps through weakening the health or strength of Illyria's people, or keeping them distracted so they don't notice the threats around them. Perhaps it means diminishing their faith in the sorcerers or the king, spreading doubt or dissent. Or perhaps"—and here he seemed to put more weight on his words—"it means spreading witchcraft to susceptible young girls."

The words stopped Marya cold.

*They* were the susceptible young girls. They were troubled girls, sent here by the king to work on their character, because they were a threat to Illyria.

Did the Guild think they were in danger of becoming witches?

# 18

# The Fire Salamander

It was possible she was wrong.

It was possible she'd put together the pieces badly, that maybe there was another reason the Guild had put a sorcerer in Dragomir.

But she couldn't shake the feeling that they believed either the girls were in danger, or the girls were themselves a danger.

*Is it that you're naturally evil or naturally weak?*

She remembered, then, playing sorcerer with her brother when they were little, waving their hands in the air and pretending to enchant the chickens, and how upset her mother had been. Marya had thought she was upset that they were playing together, but no. She was upset because it looked like Marya was playing at being a witch.

She would never become a witch. She would never hurt animals or ruin crops or make people sick. She would never try to harm Illyria, or anyone in it. Whatever they felt was in her nature or her character, *that* was not.

There was no time to talk this through, and no time for Marya and Elana to look for more information about Nadia Dragomir. Meanwhile, the threat of the Dread was still there, and the question of why the Dragomirs had founded the school—or why the king had asked them to—seemed even more pressing. Twice, Marya sat down and tried to write Madame Bandu about it, but she could not begin to find the words. More, the thought of telling her—the one person who seemed to think there was nothing wrong with her—that the school suspected Marya might be susceptible to witchcraft made her heart feel like it was being boiled.

So she told her in her head. *Madame, I think they believe we could become witches. I wouldn't ever—you know that, right? If I do well here, I could have a good job, but I don't know how to do well here, when I seem to do everything so badly.*

*Madame, I know I've made mistakes. I know I've done really bad things. But I would never do that.*

The High Count Arev seemed to be keeping a close eye on them. He was always around—in the hallways, in the dining hall, on the grounds, even occasionally popping up in class with Madame Szabo, where he freely offered his commentary and additional insights.

One thing was for sure: Madame Szabo was not a witch; otherwise she would have turned him into an Albian newt.

It was a welcome distraction when, one morning at breakfast, Marya spied Tereza at the third-year table. It felt like it had been an eon since Tereza had broken down in the library, and Marya had never figured out where she'd gone.

"May I be excused a moment?" Marya asked Simona quickly.

Tereza looked thinner than Marya remembered, paler, and really drained, as if a dreadling had started to feast on her and then got bored and floated away. When Marya tapped her on the shoulder, she jumped.

"Yes?" Tereza said. Her expression was cold, but her eyes danced around the room.

"Hi," Marya said. "I just wondered—I saw what happened . . . in the library."

With a violent blink, Tereza shifted away from Marya.

It would be nice, Marya thought, if once in a while she went into a situation with some kind of plan, as opposed to simply opening her mouth and seeing whatever came out.

"I didn't mean to . . . ," she started. "I just wanted to see if you were okay."

"Oh." Tereza looked around the dining hall, as if wondering how many other girls had seen her overcome with mountain madness, and if they all might try to talk to her too. "I am well."

Marya inhaled. "If you don't mind my asking, where were you?"

Tereza cocked her head. "Uh, the infirmary?" She laughed slightly. "It is where one goes when one is sick."

"But I was there!" Marya said. "I was sick. I was there for a couple of days, and I looked for you, and you weren't there."

"Oh, not the regular infirmary. I had my own room."

"Where?"

She looked at Marya as if Marya might be the one suffering a bout of madness. "Why do you care?" she asked, eyes narrowing.

It was a good question. There was a perfectly logical explanation for why she wasn't in the infirmary; she was in a private room, as made sense for someone with something called mountain madness. And here she was, back and completely fine, just as she was supposed to be.

But Marya couldn't help herself. "I just wondered."

Tereza shrugged. "Listen, I don't know what everyone's saying, but what happened to me was completely normal. It happens to plenty of girls here. They said so."

Her voice was perfectly controlled, but her eyes flickered everywhere. And Marya realized: she was scared.

When she sat back at her table, she felt queasy. She should not have asked. Still, all the questions about the school were rattling around in her brain at once.

These thoughts were interrupted by the delivery boy, who slid a letter next to her, with Madame Bandu's handwriting gleaming up from the page.

Tucking the letter under her apron, Marya asked Simona if she might be excused to go to the bathroom before class. She rolled her eyes in a *you know how Madame Szabo is* way.

"Yes, just be back here before the bell."

"All right."

Gathering herself, Marya walked out of the room as gracefully as she could, and then broke into a run. The only thing she wanted more than to read her letter was to know that it would be safe. So, as she had done every time a letter arrived since the first one, she ran all the way up to her room, tucked it under her pillow, and then ran all the way back down again, until she reached the dining hall, where she walked back in as gracefully as she could.

It was an interminable day. Madame Szabo decided that they were slacking in their enunciation, so she had them recite the same four lines from "The Ballad of Bezna Forest" again and again, correcting what felt like every syllable. Apparently she did not breathe right either.

Finally, after dinner, Marya could not stand it anymore. She slipped back into her room while the other girls headed for the parlor, lay on her bed, and tore open the letter.

> My dear Marya,
>
> It did my heart so much good to hear from you. I am glad you are all right up there, and that you are learning.
>
> It's funny that you ask about the Dragomir daughter. I have been researching the family since I found out where you were. The Dragomirs were renowned tapestry collectors, and had the biggest private collection in Illyria once upon a time. I hope the tapestries are still at the estate.

*Interestingly enough, the Countess Dragomir was not from nobility; she was from a village not far from Torak—the younger daughter of a seamstress, and quite the accomplished needleworker herself. I'm sure the count marrying a village girl was a great society scandal in their time!*

*They donated the estate to the crown in 740, and then they seem to have disappeared. I cannot find much information on their daughter, but I will keep looking, and let you know if I can find anything else.*

*On another note, I am so sorry they took Baby Pieter's quilt. I know it must hurt tremendously. Remember, Pieter is in your mind, in your heart, in your memories, not in a quilt, and losing the quilt doesn't mean anything about how much you care about him.*

*It's not your fault. None of it is.*

*With love,*

*Lucille Bandu*

*PS. In case they took the apron I made for you as well, I am starting on another one. I will put some protection against thievery in the stitching this time.*

And, at the bottom, two symbols—a fire salamander and what looked like a bird's wing.

The next letter was Luka's. It read, simply:

> *Dear Marya,*
> *Don't worry, I never forgot Pieter.*
> *Mama and Papa like to pretend bad things don't*
> *happen.*
> *But you can talk about them with me.*
> *Anton is good. He misses you.*
> *From,*
> *Luka*

Marya gasped. Her heart pressed against her chest; it felt like it might burst through.

*I never forgot Pieter.*

Even writing Pieter's name down, she'd felt like she was breaking open the sky.

*It's not your fault.*

Simona came into the room then, and Marya's hand flew to her chest.

"Marya, are you all right?"

"Yes."

"You're supposed to be in the parlor now."

"I'm coming," Marya said. As soon as Simona turned her back, she stuffed the letters under her pillow again, and wiped quickly at her eyes, making sure they were dry.

It was hard to walk into the parlor when you felt like your heart was going to fall out. Marya kept her hand pressed there.

The rest of the girls were in their usual places, including Elisabet, who had finally come back from the infirmary. She looked like a ghost. She didn't seem to want to talk about the destruction of her village, and none of them knew what to say to her after *I'm sorry*. Dragomir had not trained them in this kind of conversation.

The fire in the fireplace burned bright and hot. Someone had opened a window slightly, and the autumn night wind was creeping in and toying with the old servants' bell on the wall, which occasionally let out a desultory ping in response.

With a glare at the bell, she sat at the little table by the bookshelf with her embroidery book from the library and looked up the symbols Madame had added to the letter.

The fire salamander meant *wisdom*.

And the bird wing: *protection against giants*.

Marya let out a little laugh and sat back. Madame Bandu had a sense of humor. No, she did not need protection against giants now, though if she'd been here when the Dragomirs had been, she might have needed it.

In fact—

In fact, Marya realized, sitting straight up, the Dragomirs did think they needed it. She'd seen the pattern before—right here, on one of the throw pillows on the couch.

Marya's heart quickened. In front of her, Ana-Maria was curled up on one of the sofas reading, the pillows cradled in her arms.

"Ana-Maria? Could I see that pillow for a minute?" Marya smiled benignly, like it was a completely normal thing to ask.

"Uh, okay."

It hadn't even occurred to Marya that there might be symbols in the embroidery here; everything was so fancy, and Madame Bandu had said the symbols were the language of village women.

But the Countess Dragomir was a village woman.

And yes, there was the same bird-wing shape running in strips across the pillow, framing sections of intricate swirls—the snake, protection against pricolici—and of bells, protection against capcaun. A border of dreadbane—witchbane, it was called then—bordered the pillow.

Marya ran her fingers over the pillow. It was all here, protection against all of Dovia's monsters, at least the ones that existed when the Dragomirs were alive.

"What are you doing?" Ana-Maria asked, eyebrows knotted.

"I'm reading the pillow," Marya said.

With a heavy sigh, Ana-Maria went back to her book.

Next, the other pillow. It was just as richly embroidered, but the pattern was completely different.

The spiderweb: *omen*.

The beetle: *menace*.

The tulip: *daughter*.

Marya put the book down. The wind whistled. The bell sputtered. The fire flickered.

*Think, Marya.*

The story was here, in the house. Maybe not in letters, but in clues the countess had left behind. The count had left no record; his letters were gone, leaving just silence and empty spaces where Nadia had been.

*We have a box of some of the countess's personal effects: books, needlework.*

Marya's breath caught. She slid next to Elana, who was playing a tile game by herself.

"Elana," she whispered, "do you know where the library archives are?"

With a glance over at Simona, who was occupied with

her own needlework, Elana nodded. "There's a big storage room behind the library. Why?"

"We should visit them. I found something."

"You want to go when we get free time again?"

"No," Marya whispered. "Tonight."

"Really?"

"Yes."

She should wait. She knew she should wait. But she had no idea when they'd be given any free time again. It could be next week; it could be two months. She had to know now.

The embroidery language was from the villages, and it was dying out; it was possible that no one had ever seen the meaning in the countess's needlework before.

It was possible that she might discover something important about the school, something that might help them figure out what had happened. Maybe even what was happening right now.

Marya was no witch.

# 19

# The Tulip

Elana said the halls were generally clear by two hours after lights out, so Marya got in her nightgown and robe and lay in bed, waiting, until she felt a tapping on her shoulder. Marya put on her slippers and followed Elana to the door.

Of course, as soon as the door opened, Ana-Maria sat up.

"Not you, too," she said.

Marya wanted to explain that she had a plan, that she was going to do something that would help. But part of moving silently is you don't talk, so Marya just shrugged and followed Elana out the door.

They took a side stairway down to the second floor, then moved past the classrooms. Marya's heart tightened when they passed Madame Szabo's; if any teacher had no human need for sleep it would be her. But the classroom was empty. Everything, in fact, was empty, and everything was open, as if they wanted the girls to snoop around. Or else never believed they actually would.

They passed the Dragomir portraits, and Marya felt Nadia and Dracul looking on.

The moonlight through the windows was bright enough to illuminate their way as they moved through the library, so they did not have to risk lighting any of the lamps. They still had not spoken; even whispering felt like too much of a risk. They punished everyone when one girl broke the rules; what would they do when two did?

No, no, Marya told herself; they would not get caught. Elana never got caught.

Elana led her to the other side of the library and through another door. There were no windows here, no moonlight, so Elana lit the lamp and closed the door behind them. "I present you the archive room," she said, throwing her arms out as the smell of must rushed to greet them.

"How did you find this?" Marya asked. It was a treasure trove, hidden behind an ordinary door in the back of the library. The archive room was less than half the size of the library proper but seemed to have the same number of shelves, all filled with stacks of books and boxes of various sizes.

Elana shrugged. "I like to know where everything is."

Marya explained to Elana about the embroidery language, and about the pillows she'd found and the librarian's offhand mention of a box of the countess's personal effects.

"So," Elana said, nodding, "Count Dragomir hid whatever happened to their daughter, but maybe the countess wanted to leave a record somehow, in a way he'd never find."

Marya studied her companion. Elana's lips were tight. It was clear to Marya by this time that her parents must be nobility, even though she never talked about it. You could dress the girls the same and tell them their pasts don't matter, but in Illyria people would always be able to tell where you come from.

And Countess Dragomir had come from a village, Madame Bandu had said; she was a seamstress's daughter. Her mother had probably passed on the embroidery language to her, and she had left her story in Dragomir

Academy, in the pillows, and maybe elsewhere.

With that, they began to move around the room, scanning the shelves.

"Elisabet looks so broken," Elana said, as she walked down one of the aisles.

"I know."

"I can't imagine almost everyone I know just being . . . gone."

"No," Marya said, the word catching in her throat. "Do you know anything about Lacsat?"

Elana shook her head. "I didn't even know that was where she was from until this happened."

"She mentioned it once," Marya said. "Almost by accident, in class. That there was an old curse there. Her well water turned to manure, I think?"

With that, Elana stopped. Something passed over her face. "Marya. I think . . . I think I remember where I saw Nadia's name. Stay here, I'll be right back."

And before Marya could ask any questions, she was out the door again.

Marya went back to the shelves. She found a whole section of archives of student records. Those stopped at 948, meaning that current student files were somewhere else. Meaning that, somewhere, there was a file on Marya. But that wasn't Marya's concern right now, and neither were the old student files—they would probably be fascinating reading, but Marya was on a mission.

But next to these files sat three boxes labeled *Countess Maria Dragomir, Personal Effects*, and they were right next to the box of papers Irina had brought her.

Taking a breath, Marya put the boxes on the floor. Two were the same size as the other boxes Marya had looked through; one was flat and the size of a window.

The first box Marya went through was full of the countess's embroidery-practice fabrics, each one carefully wrapped in white muslin, with little strips of muslin tucked into the fabric's folds.

An archivist must have done that, Marya thought. She thought these practice fabrics were important to keep, and she knew how to keep them well.

The Rose Hall girls worked on practice fabrics at least twice a week in needlework lessons. Marya's were covered in awkward stitches and tiny pinpricks of blood. The countess, though, her work was intricate, masterful, and gorgeous.

The first fabric had row after row of patterns: ornate interlocking diamonds and circles and flower shapes in different configurations, all with perfect tiny stitches, creating what looked like a completely different fabric. It would have taken Marya approximately one hundred and fifty years to make just one row of what the countess had done here.

The next piece of fabric was a match for the pillow in their parlor: row after row of bird wings, snakes, bells, and witchbane. You could see the countess experimenting with different sizes and shapes and ways of connecting them until she settled on something that felt right.

The practice for the other pillow in their parlor was in there too—spiderweb, beetle, tulip; spiderweb, beetle, tulip. *Omen, menace, daughter.*

Marya shivered.

There were other pieces, scattered rows of different symbols, some of which Marya knew, some of which she did not; maybe they were for pillows that now sat in other parlors. If she didn't come up with anything else, she'd investigate these.

As she unfolded the next piece, Marya sucked in a breath.

It was row after row of witchbane, all on its own this time, all in the same tight, perfect pattern—no experimentation or variation, just the exact same stitches again and again. It didn't feel like practice, not like the others. It felt like a prayer.

The next piece was exactly the same.

As was the last piece.

She looked at all three pieces laid out next to each other, and suddenly she no longer saw prayer. She saw desperation.

Marya pressed her lips together. It was not an answer, but it was something.

"I found it!" Elana was standing in the doorway, looking triumphant, holding a large book in her hands. "Look." She crouched down next to Marya. "It's a book of folk songs from the area—someone went all around Illyria collecting them so they don't disappear. This volume is from the north. There's lots of stuff about giants and the Bolgars, but here, look."

She laid the book down on the floor. It was full of piano music; Mama had a stack of books just like this at home, and when Marya was little, she used to pretend the notes were actually some strange written language.

And in a way, they were.

The song Elana was pointing to was called "Nadia's Curse," and below that was written *second half of the eighth century*.

"The time's right," Elana said, running her hands along the notes. And she read:

*The wind blows ill in the mountains*
*The moon does not shine there*
*The girls, they do not know themselves*
*Daughters of the mountains, beware*

"Nadia's curse," Marya repeated.

The girls, they do not know themselves.

"It might not be the same, but . . . the daughter of the count would be well known to the people in these parts. If something happened to her . . . I don't know what 'curse' this could be referring to, though."

"I do," Marya said. "Or, I might."

It was then that Marya told Elana what she knew of mountain madness, as quickly as she could. Elana listened, eyes wide.

"Okay," Elana said, shaking her head rapidly. "Well, we need to talk about that more thoroughly later. But it sounds like maybe Nadia went mad? And they had to send her away?"

"Look at these," Marya said, showing Elana the fabrics in front of her. If mountain madness was a curse, and the countess feared her daughter getting it, feared that she had gotten it, these fabrics fit that story.

"So, if Lacsat has a lingering curse, and Dragomir has one too . . . ," Elana began.

"Maybe the sorcerers think the Dread is attracted to curses," Marya whispered.

"Maybe," Elana said. "Let's see what's in these." She started going through the box of books, and Marya opened the flat one. The contents were wrapped in a piece of muslin as big as a blanket. Breath caught, Marya unfolded the wrapping to discover . . .

Something incredible.

It was an apron made of the smoothest silk, and every inch of it was covered in the countess's intricate embroidery. There were four panels covered in rows of different patterns, and behind those panels were hundreds of tulips.

*My daughter, my daughter, my daughter.*

"I found something," Marya said, voice hushed.

"Can you read it?" Elana whispered.

Marya shook her head. There were too many symbols, and the tulip was the only one she knew. "I'll have to take it up to our room," she said, though she cringed a little as she said it.

"Okay," Elana said.

"Okay," Marya said.

After the two girls went through the last box, they

cleaned up after themselves as carefully as they possibly could, trying to leave no trace that they'd been there. Mademoiselle Gris was kinder than any other teacher at school, but maybe that kindness ended when girls snuck into her archives at night and took things.

*Details, Marya.*

The two-hundred-year-old apron had been carefully packaged, and all Marya could do was make a silent vow that she would put it back just the way she found it, before folding it up and tucking it under her arm.

"Let's go," she said.

Elana reached for her hand and squeezed it; then the two girls crept silently back to Rose Hall.

# The Maze

There would be no decoding the apron that night. Marya could not light a lamp in the parlor, nor in their room; if Simona saw the light under the door, it would be all over. And, as Marya lay awake in bed she realized that what she needed—time and space to sit with the book and the apron, where no one could disturb her—was nearly impossible to find.

So she would have to steal it.

She spent the rest of the night planning. Her best chance was to figure out a way to get some time alone from Simona, who actually possessed human empathy, and the time to do it was dinner time, when there was nothing else planned for the day but parlor time, which Simona was also in charge of.

So at the end of the school day, when Simona came to walk them to dinner, Marya slumped over to her. "Simona," she said, sagging, "I don't feel well. I don't want dinner. Can I just go back to the room and lie down?"

Her head cocked. "Do you need to go to the infirmary?"

"No," Marya said. "I think I just have to go to bed."

She could feel Elana, in the line with the other girls, watching her carefully. But Marya dared not meet her eye.

Simona's lips mushed together. She considered Marya, a searching look that said, *Can I trust you not to break any rules?*

Yes, Marya thought, you can trust me. I'm lying in order to go break some rules, but you can trust me.

"All right, Marya," Simona said finally. "Straight to the room, though. And I'll come check on you after dinner. And if you get any worse, go to the infirmary, promise?"

"I promise," Marya said, forcing her face to remain completely blank.

Simona dismissed her then, and a sagging, dragging

Marya headed up to Rose Hall.

As soon as she crossed the threshold into their wing, she started to run. She had exactly one hour to herself, one hour before Simona and the other girls would come upstairs and she'd need to be resting in bed. After fetching the apron from her dresser, where she'd unceremoniously stuffed it the night before, she spread it out on the big table in the parlor.

The fire in the fireplace was freshly fed, and the room was even stuffier than usual, so Marya cracked the window a bit, and the autumn wind welcomed the chance to invade the room. Immediately, the servants' bell started its familiar arrhythmic grousing. Marya glared at it. It clinked at her in response.

"Nobody uses you anymore," she said.

*Clink. Clink. Clink.*

"Fine. Be that way." She leaped up and in two steps was at the wall, where she unhooked the bell's clapper and hid it under the sofa cushion.

Now she was ready.

She beheld the apron, the hundreds of tulips staring back up at her like a challenge. The four panels across the midsection had four different sets of symbols, and there was an identical border around all three. Of course, it was not Nadia doing the telling; it was her mother, who'd clearly spent a couple of years on this and then left it at Dragomir Hall, maybe for—what had the count's letter said? *Illyria's most disturbed young ladies?*—to find.

"Okay, countess," Marya whispered to herself. "Tell me what happened to your daughter."

Chewing on her lip, Marya took a piece of paper and drew the apron, with the border and three panels. She wrote down:

*Background: tulips—daughter.*

Then, book in hand, she recorded the symbols.

*Border: waves—eternity*

*Panel #1:*
*Spiderweb—omen*
*Spider—treachery, corruption*

*Panel #2:*
*Butterfly—transformation*
*River—border between good and evil*

*Panel #3:*
*Maze—confusion, journey, trap*
*Empty hands—sorrow*

*Panel #4:*
*Tentacles—peril*
*Mountains—barriers*

There was more to read, though. The spiders seemed to be dangling off one spiderweb and also weaving another. The butterflies changed colors over the course of the panel. The maze grew more and more complicated over each row. She made notes about it all, and then she stood back and looked from the paper to the apron.

It was like a story, to be read one panel after the other, and in the background, always, *my daughter, my daughter, my daughter.*

She'd thought that perhaps Nadia Dragomir had gotten mountain madness, but there was nothing here that really suggested madness or illness. The embroidery book had symbols for both, but neither was on the apron. It looked like Nadia had been sent away, far away. And something bad had happened. There was evil woven into this story.

*Omen, treachery, corruption; transformation, bor-
der between good and evil; confusion, journey, trap,
sorrow, barriers, peril*

And the practice panels, the desperation. *Protection from
witchcraft, protection from witchcraft, protection from witchcraft.*

The wind wove its way through the room. The embroidery started to dance in front of Marya's eyes. The tulips
blurred into the panels. The butterfly slowly transformed,
row by row, until at the very last row the colors were the
complete opposite of what they'd been, crossing the border from good to evil. The tentacles wrapped around the
mountains, lurking.

And then she realized:

Nadia Dragomir was a witch.

Marya's eyes went to the bookshelf, to the history book
Elana had showed her. During the Witching Wars, Illyrian girls had been corrupted by Kellian witches. Nadia
Dragmoir could have been one of those girls. It all fit:
*treachery, corruption, transformation, evil.*

*Journey. Trap. Sorrow.*

Nadia had been sent away. Not just to an asylum, but to
a *witch* asylum.

And that was why she disappeared from the archives.

Why Count Dragomir left no trace of what happened to her.

Why they wanted to leave their estate behind.

Why her mother put the story in a secret language, one her husband did not speak.

It wasn't everything. That letter in the school archives implied that the king had performed some kind of service after the count donated his estate. And it didn't explain how the school came to be.

But maybe it explained something else.

Marya sat back. There was something else here she wasn't seeing. She'd been so convinced that Nadia Dragomir had been *victim* to mountain madness, same as that handful of Dragomir girls each year; it made sense.

*Nadia's curse.*

Peril. Tentacles around mountains.

*The girls, they do not know themselves.*

What if Nadia's curse wasn't about what happened *to* her, but something she did? What if *she'd* cursed the estate, left behind this madness to afflict anyone who was here, at a time when not even sorcerers knew how to cure it?

If that was the case, maybe the sorcerers could fix it now. If they knew the origins of the curse that caused mountain madness, High Count Arev could lift it, permanently.

And if that's what was attracting the Dread, like the curse on the well in Lacsat . . .

The clock on the mantel ticked forward. Marya glanced at it. The girls would be back soon; she wanted to talk to Elana about all this, but it would be late that night, at the earliest, before she and Elana were in their room, and even then Ana-Maria might yell at them for whispering to each other and breaking the rules.

But this was bigger than them now. Someone needed to know what she'd discovered.

The headmaster had told them to come see him in his office with any concerns, any time. So that's what Marya was going to do.

She was no witch.

She gathered the library book and—since she couldn't exactly bring the antique apron she'd purloined from the archives to the headmaster's office—her notes, and headed to the stairs.

The headmaster's office was in the east wing on the first floor at the end of the hallway. Marya ran down one flight of the grand staircase—even though the girls were at dinner, it didn't seem smart to go traipsing through the other halls, and she didn't have Elana to guide her—then across to the back stairs next to the infirmary and all the way down. Everyone was still in the dining hall, so the hallway was completely quiet.

Except for the sounds of Marya's increasingly rapid heartbeat filling her ears.

The hallway was filled with wall-size tapestries, all Illyrian landscapes, which Marya now knew were from the 600s, when the nobility suddenly wanted to gaze upon Illyria's natural wonders instead of its historical terrors. One showed the Rosa Mountains, another the Donau River, another a scene from the Fantoma Forest, where the trees were the size of giants. Marya instinctively checked the signatures for the telltale moon, but *this forest has lots of big trees* was probably not something someone would lie about.

Then she was outside the headmaster's door. It was ajar, with light spilling out in a way that said, *Come see me with concerns at any time.*

Still, now that she was there, she hesitated. It seemed suddenly quite likely that she might vomit, and she should probably immediately go—

"Is someone there?" the headmaster called. "Please, come in."

With a deep breath, Marya entered.

Headmaster Iagar's office was actually two connected rooms—the first, an elegant parlor with a divan and three chairs and walls covered entirely in bookshelves; then, connected to it, a study, with a desk, a tall armchair, a file cabinet much like the one in her father's study, and walls covered entirely in bookshelves.

The headmaster was standing in back, behind his desk, flipping through papers from the file cabinet.

"Marya Lupu." He sat at his desk and put down the file he was reading. "Please, pull up a seat," he said, motioning to a small chair in the corner.

"Um . . ." Marya found herself unable to stop looking around her. Besides books, there were so many strange objects lining the shelves: little figurines and glass orbs and silver trinkets, the sort of things that noblemen collected. Her father had a gold statue of a horse that had been given to him by Count Masteri, and he valued it like a crown; he would envy a man who had so many treasures.

"I always tell girls to come see me anytime, but they rarely take me up on it." The headmaster smiled pleasantly at her. He really was so polished; even his words seemed to shine.

Marya's eyes fell on his desk. There was a stack of seven

folders there, each with a name on it. She recognized Irina's name on top.

*Focus, Marya.*

She still clutched the library book and her notes in her hand. The headmaster's eyes fell on them, and back to her.

"So," she began, "I was wondering about why the high count was here, and why the Sorcerers' Guild might think the Dread could attack here."

He held up a hand. "It is only a precaution."

"Right," Marya said. It was going to be hard to have this conversation when he insisted on speaking in empty words that she had to pretend to believe meant something. "I heard about mountain madness?"

"Ah." He folded his hands together. "Yes. I can imagine that would be a bit frightening. Believe me, any afflicted girls make a full recovery. We are well-practiced in techniques to combat its effects; do not worry."

"Uh-huh. So, it might be a curse, right?"

"That is a theory, yes."

"I think I might have found the origin," she said.

Now his eyes sharpened. He sat back in his chair, considering her. "Tell me more," he said.

"So, there used to be this language of embroidery

symbols, among village women. They passed it on, mother to daughter."

"Marya"—he held up a hand—"you seem very nervous. Take a deep breath. Take your time."

She flushed. If she seemed very nervous, it was probably because she was very nervous. "It's all in this book I got from the library, if you want to see," she said, handing it to him. "There's a whole chapter on the history and everything, and a code, see? The Countess Dragomir was from a village near mine. Her mother was a seamstress. So she would have known this language." She glanced up at him and he nodded, like he was following. "And she used it on the things she made. The pillows in our parlor, she embroidered them. One has codes for protection against witches, capcaun, pricolici, giants, and this was during the Witching Wars, right, so it makes sense. And, um, she left an apron here too, and I think it tells the story of what happened to her daughter."

His eyebrows popped up, as if he was having difficulty following. Which Marya couldn't blame him for.

"Anyway," she continued, "I was wondering what happened to Nadia—that's her daughter's name—because she disappears from the portraits, you know, next to the library? So I started looking in the library."

He steepled his hands. "And that's where you found this apron," he said slowly.

"Yes," she said, as if there was no more to the story. "So, I think maybe Nadia Dragomir was a witch."

Now, now he looked surprised.

"The apron says"—she showed him her paper—"here, see? This is *omen*, *treachery*, the line between good and evil. At first I thought maybe she had mountain madness, but there's nothing about any kind of ailment here. But you can see she transformed into something bad." She was rambling now. Her face and ears were flaming hot; they themselves might start warming the entire room. "And there's more. There's a reference to eternity, peril, and the mountains. And I thought that might mean, if Nadia was a witch, that she'd left a curse here in the mountains."

"Marya—" he started.

"If you know the origin of the curse, you can undo it, right? I mean, not you, but a sorcerer. The High Count Arev could. We learned that in class."

*Of course he knows about undoing curses, Marya.*

"I don't know for sure," she went on, "but it's a theory. I thought High Count Arev could try. And then maybe there wouldn't be a curse here anymore. In case, you know, the Dread is attracted to places with lingering witch magic

283

or something. Like in Lacsat."

"Marya—" he said again.

"There's an old curse in Lacsat. In a well. Elisabet told us in class—not like she was talking about her home but we were talking about curses. So I thought what if that's what's attracting the witches?"

"Marya"—he clapped his hands together—"I truly appreciate your concern for the school. And I'm sure this embroidery language is fascinating business. But I must tell you that Nadia Dragomir had the river pox and died in 735."

Marya sat back, stunned.

"Her parents were heartbroken. Her mother went a bit mad with grief, I'm afraid. Believed it had been a witch's doing. Eventually the count gave the estate to the king; he thought it was best for the countess to move away."

"Oh."

"It's all right, Marya," he said. "You found the embroidery language and got excited. I don't blame you."

Marya stared at the floor, feeling her face burn up.

"But!" He held up a hand. "I'm glad you're here. There's something I wanted to give to you." Standing up, he went to his cabinet and returned with a small bundle. The moment Marya saw it, she gasped.

He had Baby Pieter's quilt.

"I believe this is yours?"

Marya nodded, fighting back the tears that were blossoming in her eyes.

"I apologize," he said. "I meant to ask you about this some time ago, but I've been distracted. Our staff was going through the first-year girls' things and pulled this aside."

She could not speak. There was part of her that wanted to reach for the blanket, hold it close. But she could not move.

"It was apparent to me that this wasn't a mundane bit of bedding, and I wondered if it had personal value," he continued, bowing his head slightly. "I can see by your face that it does."

Marya still did not say anything.

"My dear girl," he said, voice suddenly hushed, "are you all right? Did this belong to your little brother who passed away?" His eyes pried into her. "It did, didn't it? I'm so sorry we ever took it. The staff can be overenthusiastic in their job sometimes, and I suppose they did not know. But it's yours now."

With that, Pieter's quilt was in her arms. Headmaster Iagar dismissed her, and in a few moments she found herself huddled in the stairwell opposite his office.

"I'm so sorry," she whispered to the quilt. "I'm so sorry."

She had fallen asleep. Pieter had had a fever and she'd spent the day bringing him broth and wiping his forehead, promising him she'd take care of him, and then she'd fallen asleep and when she woke up he was gone.

She cradled the quilt, feeling as if she'd been run over by a carriage. She should go back to Rose Hall, but she could not move, could not do anything but hold the blanket and think about how very, very sorry she was, what a sorry, sorry girl.

It was some time before she thought to wonder:

How did the headmaster know about Baby Pieter?

# 21

# The Butterfly

Eventually Marya made her way back up to Rose Hall, still clutching the quilt to her. She didn't know how long she'd been gone, but the hallways were dark now; she'd missed parlor time altogether.

She wanted more than anything to head right for her bed, but as she passed the parlor, she saw Simona there, alone, sitting in a chair crying.

"Simona?" Marya asked, stopping.

The older girl looked up as Marya stepped into the room. "Oh, Marya!" she exclaimed. "I'm sorry, I forgot to check on you. Are you all right?"

Marya swallowed and nodded, though she was in no way all right. "What's wrong?" she asked tentatively.

Simona made a shrugging gesture and wiped her eyes. "Listen, if you're feeling well enough, you better go down to the kitchen. That's where the rest of the girls are, serving out their punishment."

"Punishment?"

"Yes. Madame Rosetti came to tell us that Elana was seen in the library shelves last night after hours."

Marya froze.

"I'm sure you understand how serious this is. The Rose Hall girls are to do all the dishes from dinner, no matter how long it takes. It would be better for everyone if you were down there with them, in case Madame Rosetti checks in."

"Yes, of course," Marya whispered.

Simona looked away. "I'll be down to check on you later. I just need . . ."

"Okay."

"You should put that away first," she said, gesturing to the quilt that Marya was clutching. Then, Simona turned away, a dismissal.

Marya could not breathe now. As she went to her room

to put Pieter's quilt away, Simona's words hung above her. They had fangs. *Your fault, your fault. Elana got in trouble because of you. They're all in trouble because of you. Simona was upset because she might lose her rank, because of you.*

*Your fault, your fault.*

And it was all for nothing. She'd been wrong about Nadia, and the headmaster probably thought she was more foolish than ever before.

She put the quilt away in her trunk, because she'd told the headmaster she would, and then she took off for the kitchens, as though she could fix this all if she got there fast enough.

The kitchens were in the west part of the basement, directly underneath the dining hall. They were massive, as you'd expect for a place that made food for forty girls and dozens of faculty and staff every day. And, as you'd also expect, making that quantity of food for one meal generated a lot of dishes.

When Marya arrived, the Rose Hall girls were all down by the sinks, wearing big white kitchen aprons, their hair tied back with kerchiefs. Marya didn't know how long they'd been working, but the pile of dirty dishes seemed to be about one thousand times the size of the pile of clean dishes.

Her blood coursed through her body, hot and stinging.

They were all there—Daria, Katya, Elana, Ana-Maria, and Elisabet, all working slightly apart from each other, all looking somewhere between upset and absolutely furious.

Marya kept her eyes on the floor as she picked an apron and kerchief off the counter and took a space near a pile of dishes. She glanced at Elana, whose gaze was fixed entirely on the pot she was scrubbing, as if she might be able to clean it with her eyes if she glared hard enough.

"Where were you, Marya?" asked Ana-Maria flatly. "I thought you were feeling sick, but you weren't in our room."

Now, all the girls turned to look at her, except Elana, who kept on with her scouring.

"I'm here now," Marya said quietly.

"Say, Elana," Ana-Maria called, still looking at Marya, "what happened last night anyway? I thought you never get caught." She looked pointedly at Marya.

Elana shook her head and did not reply.

"It was my fault," Marya said, voice quiet. "Elana was helping me. If we got caught, that's why. Be mad at me, not her."

Elisabet whirled around. "We can be mad at both of you! Did either of you think about what would happen if you got caught? Did you think what would happen to the rest of us?"

Marya wiped her eyes quickly. Just when she thought she couldn't feel any worse, the girl whose town had been consumed by the Dread was yelling at her. "I'm sorry," she said, and turned on the kitchen faucet.

"You were lucky to have missed Madame Rosetti," Elisabet continued. "She was furious. At all of us. She said we wouldn't last here unless we started monitoring each other."

"You should tell Madame Rosetti it was you," Katya said, voice strained. "She gave Elana an earful."

"I will," Marya whispered. It was like the ceiling was pressing down on her, physically crushing her.

"Not now, though," Elisabet snapped. "We need you now to help with the dishes so we can finish before we graduate."

"At least Marya knows how to wash dishes," Daria grumbled. "Those two have no idea." She motioned over at Elana and Ana-Maria.

"I'm doing the best I can!" Ana-Maria called.

Marya gulped. The girls had never been like this before. *Your fault, your fault.*

She put her head down and started to scrub a particularly

dirty pot. It seemed to have mashed potatoes indelibly glued to the bottom.

"Do you really think they'd kick us all out?" Katya asked, voice a whisper.

"I hope not," Daria said. "I don't have anywhere to go if I get expelled. A neighbor was visiting my parents when the messenger arrived with my letter, and she told the entire village. My sister had been engaged to a doctor, and before I'd even left to come here, the engagement was called off. I don't have any brothers; the only chance my family has is for her to marry well, so they basically had to disown me for that to happen."

"We have to stop getting in trouble," Katya said.

"It's not 'we,'" Elisabet grumbled.

"I'm sorry," Marya said again. "I'm sorry!"

"It's not just you," Ana-Maria said, waving over to Elana. "You asked her to help you for a reason. And she's the one that got caught."

Someone probably saw Elana when she went to get the sheet music collection while Marya was holed up in the archive room.

"It is my fault," was all she could say.

"Elana's been flouting the rules since she got here. I know what kind of girl she is. Just because her father's a count she thinks she can get away with anything. Maybe your parents will welcome you back, Elana, but some of us aren't so lucky."

At this, Elana dropped the pot she was washing and regarded the room. "They will not welcome me back," she spat, eyes red. "I assure you. And my father will make sure no one else does either."

The tone in her voice made Marya wince.

"So why do you do it then?" Elisabet asked, arms out. "Why do you keep breaking the rules?"

"I don't know!" Elana exclaimed, tears running down her cheeks. "I don't know! I didn't mean to get everyone in trouble. I'm sorry!"

No one was cleaning anymore. All the girls were staring at each other.

Ana-Maria was looking at Elana suspiciously. "Who is your father?"

Elana threw up her hands. "He's a sorcerer. My father is a sorcerer, all right? High Count Teitler. He's the one who had me sent here; he had to be. And so obviously he never wants to see me again. I am a disgrace to him and my mother. They told me that."

Absolute silence then. Elana turned back around to her sink and buried her head in her work. When she spoke again, it was so soft it was hard to hear her. "So I don't have anywhere to go either."

Simona walked into the room then. There was no sign that she'd been crying; her face was smooth, her eyes dry, her posture perfect, as always. Whatever she was feeling, she had stuffed it down.

"I came to help," she said briskly. "I bet you need all that you can get." She donned an apron, stood next to Katya, and began to dry the plates she was washing.

Marya gulped. No one else knew about the ranking system, not yet. Simona had never told them that she had something to lose.

They all had something to lose.

What would happen if they didn't make it here? Would they be sent to asylums? What if they got mountain madness there, and no one knew what it was or cared, because everyone already thought they were mad?

Marya turned back to her work, trying to push every other thought out of her head.

It was silent in the room then for several minutes. With Simona there, they would not fight, and if they were not fighting they had nothing to say to each other.

After Marya moved from one mashed potato–encrusted pot to the next, she thought she heard some kind of whimper come from Elana. She glanced over to find her friend's gaze focused on the sink, her face in some horrible mask.

Marya's stomach flipped over. "Elana?"

Elana dropped the pot she was washing. A sharp intake of breath came from her, then some kind of yelp. Backing away from the sink, she whirled around, staring at the kitchen as if dreadlings were coming from every corner.

"Elana!" Simona exclaimed. "Are you all right?"

She was definitely not all right. Elana looked like she didn't know where she was. She held her hands out in front of her, gaping at them as if they were on fire. "Do you see this?" she yelled. "Do you see?" She held out her hands to the room. "What's happening?"

Everyone froze.

"What's happening to me?" Elana yelled again. Marya's whole body turned to ice. Elana stumbled toward her, and she recoiled.

"Elana." It was Simona, suddenly sounding very much in control. She strode forward. "It's all right. Girls, stay back. I know what to do."

Marya could not react; she could not think. From the looks on the other girls' faces, they couldn't either.

Carefully, Simona put her arm around Elana's shoulder

and led her out of the kitchen. "It's going to be all right, Elana. I promise," she murmured. "You're seeing things, but they can help you. It's going to be all right."

All the girls of Rose Hall watched, completely still, as Simona led Elana out. It had happened so fast that Marya could not process what she was seeing, but when the pair were gone, Katya shot her a look that was full of meaning and she understood.

"What was that?" Daria asked, voice trembling.

Marya swallowed. "It's called mountain madness," she said, throat thick. Eyes fixed on the floor, she told everyone about that day in the library with Tereza, and what Irina the sixth-year had told them.

"Irina said it usually happens to girls after they've been here a couple of years," Katya added.

"Usually," Daria said pointedly.

A silence fell over the room like a spell. The echo of Elana's cries still hung in the air. The horror that had contorted her face lingered in the kitchen, a creeping miasma that made it hard to breathe. It took everything Marya had not to give herself to it entirely. She felt like she was choking.

"I don't understand," Elisabet said, voice cracking. "Why does this happen?"

"They think it's a curse," Katya said. Marya winced.

"No one will want us if they think we're mad," Ana-Maria exclaimed. "How will we ever get placed on estates?"

Marya could not talk. There was no room for her theories now. None of it mattered.

"They say everyone will get better," Katya said weakly.

"What if we don't?" Daria asked.

There was no answer.

The girls worked in the kitchen for another two hours, not talking, all caught in the worlds of their heads— leaving Marya with nothing to do but scrub pots and marinate in her shame.

When the girls got back up to their rooms, Simona, looking extraordinarily exhausted, was just getting ready to head down to the kitchens to find them. She sat them all down and explained mountain madness, assuring them again and again that this was completely treatable and Elana would be just fine.

No one said anything. Maybe they believed her, or maybe they were too tired to talk.

As the other girls headed off to bed, Marya lingered. "Simona?"

Simona looked at her, ready to assuage all her concerns,

because that's just who Simona was.

"Will Elana really be all right?" Marya asked, voice cracking.

Simona motioned for Marya to sit down. "Yes, she will. It just takes a while."

"How do you know for sure?" Marya asked. She was clutching one of the countess's pillows as if it could physically protect her from giants.

Simona gazed at her. "Because. It happened to me. I had mountain madness."

Marya's eyes went wide.

"Yes, well." Simona flashed her a tight smile. "As you can see, I am perfectly fine now. But it is not something I talk about. The school does not wish to create a panic. Or cause girls to suspect each other of madness. People can be very judgmental here, you know." She glanced away. "I did tell them that I thought we should prepare girls. But the headmaster knows best, of course." She said that like she did not really believe it was true. "Still, I would have liked to have known."

"What happened?" Marya asked. "Was it like with Elana?"

"Not really? I was just sitting in class one day and suddenly I thought spiders were crawling all over me, first one, then two, then a dozen, then a hundred. And then I realized the class was just going on as normal, and if spiders were appearing out of nowhere, crawling all over me, it probably wouldn't." She laughed slightly, though there was no humor in her laugh. "So I just sat there with the spiders."

Marya stared at her. Simona was telling the story so blithely, as if talking about some tale she heard at dinner.

"So, what happened?" she asked

"Nothing. Class ended, and I stood up. Nothing was there. But then it kept happening. Or it would feel like the spiders were underneath my skin, scuttling in my veins. Madame Rosetti was our teacher that year, and I did not want to be caught fidgeting, you can imagine! So I said nothing. I thought I was going mad. If people knew, what would they think?"

Marya shook her head slightly. If she'd felt like spiders were running around inside her body she would have had a really hard time pretending like nothing was happening. But she was not Simona.

"I tried to hide it, pretended everything was fine. And then one night when I was sleeping, I dreamed a giant spider was sitting on my chest, tying me up. But it felt so real. So I started screaming and fighting, trying to get it off me. Next thing I knew, I was in a bed in the infirmary, days later."

And now Marya remembered Irina's words: *A girl in my class had it. . . . She started screaming and thrashing around one night when we were all in bed. Woke the whole hall up. We thought it was the Dread! It took three servants to get her to the infirmary.*

That was Simona. ". . . What did they do?" Marya asked quietly. "How did they make you better?"

Simona looked away. "I don't remember much. I had a private room somewhere, until the end when I woke up to find that they'd moved me to the regular infirmary. And I had no idea how much time was passing. You know when you think you haven't been able to fall asleep, but then you realize that it's almost morning, all this time has passed, and you must have slept? That's what it was like. It was six weeks, but I didn't know. I remember lying in the little room. I remember having horrible dreams, where I couldn't move at all. I remember . . ." She pressed her lips together and shook her head.

"What?"

"Well, I'm not sure it actually happened. It seems strange."

"You can tell me," Marya said. Simona never talked

about herself, never said anything personal, but it was late, the fire was dying, they were both exhausted, and she seemed to want to talk.

". . . I thought I remembered a sorcerer in my room. An old one with a scarlet cloak. But it was probably a dream," Simona said. "Or . . . something."

"But you were fine? Afterward?"

Her mouth twitched. "I had nightmares. For a long time. I still do, on occasion." She shrugged, as if what she was saying didn't matter to her at all. "I don't know, maybe it was just me. My mind plays tricks on me sometimes." Then she shook her head rapidly. "I don't mean it that way."

"Okay."

"Please don't tell anyone I said that."

"I won't!"

"Not even any of the other girls. Not Elana. If they knew—"

"I won't!"

"People don't understand. They're so ignorant. They'll think you're dangerous. . . . Anyway, I didn't mean it like *that*. I just meant that, sometimes, the dreams come back." She started rubbing her arm. "That's all. I'm not used to talking about this. After I got back, no one wanted to talk about it. No one asked me anything. They just pretended like it didn't happen."

Marya flushed. What would she have done? She didn't know.

"This school does not encourage us to care for one another," Simona said. Then she immediately straightened. "Not that I'm not grateful. I want to get a good job where I can make a difference. So please don't tell anyone."

"I won't," Marya said again.

"I had cousins. They were twins, my age. We were best friends. And when I was eight, the Dread came to their town. Everyone was gone." She looked at the fire for a moment. "So I'm glad for the school, really. I can be in a position to help. Do you understand?"

Marya nodded, because it seemed like the thing to do.

But it was hard to believe she herself could ever be in a position to help anyone.

All she did, it seemed, was hurt people.

# 22

# The Spiderweb

Marya spent the next few days going to her meals, to her classes, and everything else she was supposed to do, and that was all she had the will for. She felt like her mind had detached somehow from her body—not completely, just enough to feel like she was always half there, half observing herself.

She kept the quilt tucked away in her trunk. She never looked at it, but she was always aware of it, folded up and tucked into a corner in her mind.

She'd left the book on embroidery in the headmaster's

office, and her notes, too. There would be no more symbols in her letters to Madame Bandu, and if Madame sent them, she would not be able to read them.

*Dear Madame Bandu, I lost the book. I made a mistake. Someone who helped me got hurt. She's sick and it's my fault.*

She didn't even know where Elana was now. And even if she did, would Elana want to see her?

Marya was sitting in Madame Szabo's room when she realized the teacher was calling her name, in a way that suggested she'd been calling it for some time. Marya looked up to discover Madame Rosetti in the doorway, staring at her and looking impatient.

"Marya," Madame Rosetti said, "please come with me."

Madame Rosetti wordlessly guided her down the long hallway, through the great hall, and to her office. Marya's heart, which had been lying dormant, suddenly sped up. Was this it? Was she getting kicked out?

Madame Rosetti's office was much starker than Headmaster Iagar's, which made sense, since the deputy headmistress herself was much starker than the headmaster. There was no sitting room, just an austere-looking desk, several chairs, and one small knickknack-less bookshelf, neatly arranged. The only evidence that an actual human with interests and tastes used the room was a small, well-trimmed fern on the windowsill. If you saw the office, you would think the inhabitant liked neatness, books, and at least one potted plant. And that's about it.

"Sit, Marya," Madame said, motioning to the chair in front of her desk. She did the same, then folded her hands together and nodded slightly, as if answering a question Marya had not asked. "How are you?"

Marya's mouth opened slightly, like a door that had fallen off its hinge. It is hard to answer questions when your mind is only half in your body, no matter who they come from. But when you are suddenly in Madame Rosetti's austere office, for no clear reason, and she asks you to evaluate your physical and emotional well-being, also for no clear reason, your brain will go as blank as her walls.

"Fine?" Marya said, after too long a beat.

"Good, good," said Madame Rosetti. Though the expression on her face was as stern as ever, Marya felt the discomfort emanating from the deputy headmistress like too-strong perfume. It did not help.

A moment. "The headmaster asked me to speak to you. He is away from the school for the day."

This was it. She was being kicked out. Where could she go? Could Madame Bandu take her in without her parents' permission? Or would they just condemn her to an asylum?

"As you know, this is a difficult time in Illyria. We are discovering that the world is not as we thought it was. This can be a shock. The Sorcerers' Guild is all over Illyria now, trying to identify dangers where they were not looking before. And they found something."

Marya sat straight up. "Did something happen to Torak? Did the Dread come?"

Madame lifted up a hand. "No, no. The Dread is not there. Torak is fine. They caught her in time."

The relief hit Marya first, followed quickly by confusion. "Caught who?"

Madame Rosetti's mouth twitched. "Tell me about this, Marya," she said, reaching into a drawer in her desk. "It was in your belongings."

It was Madame Bandu's apron.

Marya gasped and reached for it without even thinking.

"The headmaster told me that you said that there were spells woven into some embroidery?" she asked, speaking carefully.

"What? No! Not spells. Symbols!"

Madame looked confused. "Symbols for spells?"

"No! Just symbols! That mean normal things." She looked around the room frantically, as if there might be an explanation attached to the wall.

"I see. And the woman who wove this for you, she's been writing to you, correct? Do you still have those letters?"

"I don't understand," Marya said. "How do you know that?"

"The headmaster told me," she said. "The Sorcerers' Guild notified the headmaster." She glanced down at a piece of paper on her desk. "I believe there was some concern raised over this woman's influence on you."

The sentences were swirling around her slowly, hovering just out of her grasp—as if toying with her. And when they finally struck, Marya burst out of her chair. "You think Madame Bandu is a witch?"

Madame Rosetti raised herself up. "Marya, please sit back down. *I* do not think anything. The Sorcerers' Guild contacted the headmaster because Lucille Bandu was arrested two nights ago. In their interview with townspeople they discovered that she and you had a close relationship. And our mail logs show you've been corresponding with her."

Marya was trembling all over. "But—but—it's impossible," she said, once she could speak. "I know her. She's good to me." She was sputtering, she could tell, but it was the best she could do.

"Such is the way of witches, Marya," Madame said,

looking almost kind. "That is what High Count Arev told us—they infiltrate, ingratiate. In the Witching Wars, we discovered witches who had been here for decades."

"It's not true!" Marya exclaimed. "It just isn't!"

"I am sorry, Marya. I'm sure this is a shock to you. And I'm afraid there's something else."

Marya simply gawked. How could there be anything else?

"Yesterday morning, it seems, your brother disappeared. He'd been spending a lot of time with the Bandu family of late, so there is some concern."

"My brother . . . Luka . . . Madame would never hurt Luka! Luka is fine! Maybe he just ran away! Our parents are awful! He loved the Bandus too." Marya's eyes were so thick with tears that Madame Rosetti was just a blur now.

"It's all right, Marya," Madame Rosetti said gently. "I will let you know as soon as we hear that your brother is safe. Meanwhile, if you did keep those letters, the Guild would love to see them. They are investigating all of the arrested witches looking for any connection to Kel. You can imagine how important that is to the kingdom. And if you think of anything that Madame Bandu ever did or said that might help the sorcerers, please let me or High Count Arev know."

At the mention of that name, Marya's brain snapped into focus.

High Count Arev was a sorcerer. He had power with the Guild.

"Where would I find High Count Arev?" Marya asked. "If I did think of something," she added quickly.

"I believe he was planning to spend the day in the library."

Marya clenched her fists, hard. She had to find him, right now, before they did something to Madame Bandu. She inhaled, trying to breathe around the feeling that had taken up residence in her chest. Exhaled. Inhaled again.

"I know this has been a shock. If you'd like, please go to the infirmary and Nurse Rieza can give you something to calm your nerves. I'll send word to Madame Szabo that you won't be back today."

"Please," Marya said, "I would like that."

She would definitely need something to calm her nerves later. But right now, she had somewhere else to be.

As soon as she got into the hallway, she started running for the library.

Madame Bandu was not a witch. Marya knew that. Madame Bandu cared about Illyria. She was good, and kind; she would never hurt anyone. She had not tried to corrupt Marya; she'd taught her to read, offered her a place at her side.

Marya would convince the high count that this was all a mistake, and then Madame Bandu could help her find Luka.

As she ran, questions swarmed in her mind like bats. How could this have happened? Had Marya's parents said something? Had one of her clients gotten upset? Or—

*Do you see this symbol here? This symbol says, I don't believe you. I think you are lying.*

Was that it? Did someone find one of her crescent moons and figure out what it meant? Did they decide it was treason, that she was trying to undermine Illyria?

She wasn't. It was just a mark; that was all.

When Marya got to the library, she found High Count Arev sitting at a table with Mademoiselle Gris, going over something in an enormous book.

As Marya rushed in, Mademoiselle Gris looked up. "What can I do for you, Marya?" she asked, and then her head cocked. "Are you all right?"

"I need to speak with High Count Arev, if that's okay."

"Certainly, young lady," he said, looking up. "Would you like to sit?"

So Marya did, smoothing her skirt under her as she'd

been taught. She was trying so hard to keep herself together, to be the girl they'd been trying to teach her to be. Young ladies did not show excess emotion. They did not get upset. They spoke in even tones, kept their voices clear but not loud. They kept their posture rigid and their gestures restrained and graceful. If they needed to persuade, they avoided specious arguments and irrationality.

"I'm from Torak. There was a woman there, who was arrested under suspicion of being a witch—"

He nodded solemnly. "I am sure that is very frightening. To think, a witch in your own town!"

"I—No. I mean—There's no witch. I mean. She's not a witch. It's a mistake."

"Ah." He nodded solemnly. "I understand."

"You do?"

"No one likes to think there's a witch in their village."

"No, that's not it!"

He blinked, startled.

Marya's eyes filled. Why could she not hold herself together? When it mattered so much?

"What I mean is, I know her. The woman who was arrested. I've been taking care of her boys since—for a few years."

He straightened. "I see. And you feel ashamed that you

did not suspect anything. I assure you, Marya, greater people than you have been taken in—"

"No!"

High Count Arev squinted at her, as if he could not quite understand what she was made of—perhaps bits of machinery or riverbed rocks or goat parts.

Mademoiselle Gris cleared her throat pointedly at Marya.

"I'm not taken in," she breathed. "I know her, and she cannot be a witch."

"Oh," he nodded, as if he now understood what she was made of. He folded his hands together and leaned toward her. "Young lady. The way the Torak witch conducted herself is exactly the way witches have been operating in Illyria before the Witching Wars. The witch is the person you would least expect, the one who seems the most trustworthy, a neighbor, a friend. Why, I heard this one was a master weaver. She interacted with the most important people in Illyria. It was her job to record history! Imagine what a witch could do in that position."

"I don't understand," Marya breathed.

"If you wanted to undermine Illyria, what better way to do it than through altering history? Why, think of the power, Marya! I know it must seem to you that the books you read and the tapestries you admire are objective recordings of fact, but what if someone chose to alter that fact? What if they chose to paint the Battle of Vastya Pass as a failure of planning or King Danut as mad?"

"But Madame Bandu doesn't do that. She just takes commissions from noblemen and—"

"And sets down their stories for the historical record." He sat back, as if his point was made.

"I—" She closed her eyes. She was trying so hard not to cry—everything would be lost if she cried; no one would listen to her—but they were not listening to her now, and despair was swelling up "What if he is lying?" she said. "What if *he's* making up stories to make himself sound like a hero? What does the weaver do then?"

Now the high count straightened. His eyebrows twitched, he steepled his hands together, and he eyed her like she herself might be a tapestry with secrets to unknot. "I don't understand your meaning."

Something was wrong. Marya knew that, and while she did not know precisely what, she knew she should stop talking, feign ignorance; she absolutely should not tell him her meaning. And yet—

"It's just a symbol," she said. "That's all it is. She's not a witch. It's just a symbol for other weavers. She's not trying to undermine anything."

That's when she felt a hand on her shoulder. "Marya," said Mademoiselle Gris, "I believe you should be in class."

The high count stood up, bowing his head at Mademoiselle Gris. "Madame, I believe the young lady was trying to tell me something."

"The young lady is making a spectacle of herself," said Mademoiselle Gris coldly. "If she has something to tell you, she can do it when she has regained her composure." The librarian moved her hand to Marya's arm and pulled her up, hard. "I apologize, High Count, for our student's behavior."

With her hand firmly on Marya's arm, Madame Gris steered Marya to the entrance of the library. A girl working at one of the desks watched them, wide-eyed, the way you might watch a guard marching a prisoner through the town square on his way to the dungeons. And that's just how Marya felt. Like she was being marched to the dungeons, or wherever they sent people who could not follow rules, could not comport themselves, could not manage to say things in a way that would make someone listen, even when everything was on the line. Madame Bandu was in terrible trouble, and Marya had a member of the Sorcerers'

Guild right here, and she could not say the right things, in the right way, to save her.

And maybe she'd made it worse.

Or almost had.

Because—Marya realized—maybe, just maybe, Mademoiselle Gris had stopped her from revealing a secret that would have gotten a lot of people in trouble.

And maybe she'd done that on purpose.

Maybe she knew.

Mademoiselle Gris led her out of the library and into the hall, where she whirled around and stared down at Marya.

"Marya," she whispered, "you must be careful during times like these."

"You know . . . do you know about the weavers' symbols?"

Mademoiselle Gris waved her hand in the air. "I don't know anything about that and I do not want to know. But I do know that you need to watch yourself. People will see witches everywhere, don't you understand? Even here. Even among young girls."

"But—that's what's happening! Madame Bandu isn't a witch."

Mademoiselle Gris looked around the hallway. "That

may well be true," she whispered. "But"—and here she met Marya's gaze—"if they've decided she is, there's nothing you can do about it. There's nothing anyone can do for her. You need to save yourself."

# 23

# The Spider

Marya stared at Mademoiselle Gris's retreating back, her words replaying over and over in Marya's brain.

*If they've decided she is a witch, there's nothing anyone can do about it.*

There was nothing Marya could do. In a lifetime of feeling helpless, she had never felt so much so. All she wanted to do was lie down on the stairs, curl into a ball, and stay there. But a sixth-year passed her and shot her a suspicious look, as if maybe she needed to be imprisoned for the rest of her life. So she headed for the infirmary, which at least was better than class.

Where was Madame Bandu now? And where was Luka? She could not imagine where he had gone, or why.

When she got to the infirmary, Nurse Rieza gave her a robe, a nightgown, and slippers, and then led her to a bed and gave her something to drink that tasted like cloves. And though her thoughts were careening around her head like overenthusiastic goats, drowsiness grabbed her in its bony claws and pulled her down, down, down, and soon she was asleep.

When Marya woke up, it was dark in the infirmary. There was only one other girl there, a lanky fourth-year several beds down who was snoring slightly in her sleep. It took Marya several moments for her mind to settle into her body, and several more moments to figure out where exactly that body was in space, and several more moments to register why she felt so sad and scared.

It felt like she was eight again, and Pieter had just died. Pieter.

She flipped over in the bed and stared at the ceiling.

The headmaster had known about him, and Marya could not think of any reason why that should be so, unless Pieter's death was the reason she was here, the reason she was so troubled that she had to be locked away, watched, transformed, put on a sorcerer's estate to be watched some more.

*Your fault, your fault.*

And now she was completely alone. Her parents did not care about her. Madame Bandu had been arrested. Her brother was missing. And the only person here who had been like a friend to her had mountain madness, because Marya had gotten her in trouble.

And Marya had not even tried to find her, to visit her.

Elana, she thought in the moment, would not have been stopped by private rooms and quarantines, and yet Marya had let herself be stopped.

She squeezed her eyes shut so hard that it hurt.

Fine. She could not do anything for Madame Bandu. She could not find Luka. She could do nothing for Pieter. But she would find Elana, because Elana was, maybe, her friend.

There was a dim light on in the office, and a shadow of someone at the desk, head buried in a book. Not Nurse Rieza; a woman whose shape Marya didn't recognize. So Marya tightened her robe, slid her slippers on, and headed into the office.

The woman at the desk was quite young, maybe a couple of years older than Simona, and she looked rather alarmed to see one of her charges upright and walking around.

"Um," she said, putting her book aside. "Hello. I'm Mademoiselle Karon. What can I do for you? You're Marya Lupu, correct?"

Marya did everything she could to tame the thoughts in her brain, which were somehow both manic and sluggish at the same time, like drunk chickens.

*Think, Marya.*

"I was wondering," she said carefully, "if I could have a private room."

She hadn't really known she was going to say it until she said it, but it seemed like a decent strategy, especially for one conceived by drunk chickens.

"Unfortunately, we don't have private rooms."

"Don't you? My friend Elana, she's in one right now. In quarantine. She has"—and here, Marya leaned in, as if there were anyone to hear her—"mountain madness."

"Oh," said Mademoiselle, blinking in distress, "I'm just the night nurse. I haven't been here for very long. I'm afraid there are no private rooms, as far as I know. All we have is the infirmary here."

"But . . . where do the girls with mountain madness go?"

"I don't, um . . . Nurse Rieza will be back in the morning. As I said, I've only been here a few weeks. I can administer medication, you see. I have another draft for you prepared if you think it would help."

Marya blinked. No. She did not need bony hands pulling her into sleep and holding her there anymore.

"It's all right," she said, after a moment. "I can sleep. I'll sleep."

The young woman seemed visibly relieved. "If you change your mind . . ."

"I will," Marya said. And with that, she headed out of her office and back to her bed, where she closed her eyes and pretended to sleep.

She counted to one hundred. And then two hundred. And then three. When that was done, she propped herself up in bed slightly.

Mademoiselle Karon was back to her book. She did not even glance up. So Marya slipped out of bed and out of the infirmary. Of course, she did not have a plan. Marya did not make plans. She merely followed her impulses, broke rules, created chaos, and got other people in trouble.

It was late, and it seemed like the entire school was asleep—not just the students and whatever staff slept in the main house, but the mansion itself. As if it was satisfied with its work for the day, had dimmed the lamps, put on its nightdress, and tucked itself into bed for the night.

Did it know that not everyone was in bed? That there was a girl creeping down the grand staircase under the cover of darkness? Or did it think that maybe this was just another dream? Did girls tiptoe in and out of Dragomir's dreams all the time?

If she could not find where the quarantine rooms were, what she needed was information.

And the only place she could think to find it was the headmaster's office. Surely if a student contracted a disease particular to the region, a disease that might or might not have been caused by an old curse, that information would be in her file. Wasn't that the sort of thing files were for?

The problem with going to the headmaster's office was that it tended to be where the headmaster was. But it was the middle of the night, and even the headmaster needed to sleep, didn't he?

She crept down one of the back staircases, willing the mansion to stay asleep, and to keep everyone else asleep too.

*I am just a dream*

*just a dream*

*just a dream*

The mansion did not stir.

But when she got downstairs, she discovered that while

the mansion might be asleep, the headmaster was not. Light was spilling out of his office and, in the quiet of the night, she heard the sound of paper ruffling.

Marya froze. Maybe he did not sleep after all.

No, she told herself, that was ridiculous. He was up late because he was busy, but eventually he would have to go to sleep. Eventually his office would be empty.

She was in this now. She was not going to give up.

But where to hide? She could tuck herself behind the stairwell, but she had no idea where the headmaster's quarters were; he might actually use that stairwell. It might be hard to explain to him why she was standing there in the middle of the night. And she needed to be close enough to see when he left.

There was nothing else to do but hide behind one of the tapestries.

So, with a deep breath, Marya dove across the hallway and ducked behind the tapestry of the Fantoma Forest. Two centuries worth of dust hit her immediately, and then swirled up into her nasal passages as if returning to a long-lost home. She sneezed twice.

Footsteps, then. Heart in her throat, Marya pressed herself against the wall, just a shadow in the night. It was dark enough in the hallway that he would not notice, right?

The footsteps reached the doorway of the office. Silence, then. She imagined him looking down the hallway.

*Just a mouse,* she thought at him. *Just a sneezy mouse.*

One moment.

Two.

Then the footsteps receded into his office.

Now Marya could not move even if she wanted to; she was completely frozen with terror. She would be here behind this tapestry until the end of time. They would find her still-frozen body in a hundred years and think, *Wow, what a terrible hiding place this girl chose.*

How long had she been back there? She had no sense of time. The minutes folded in on themselves and unfolded again. Time might possibly have stopped; she did not know.

Then, footsteps again. Out of the office and right past her, down the hallway.

Still, she waited. She counted to five hundred. And then one hundred again.

Silence.

Only then did she duck back into the hallway, which was completely dark now. The headmaster's door was closed, and no light crept out from under the doorway.

Heart racing, Marya snuck inside. She shut the door slowly behind her, quietly enough that she did not startle the tapestries, and then turned on the light. Then, to the file cabinet.

The student files took up two drawers in the cabinet: the sixth- and fifth-year files in one, the rest in another. Each year the files grew progressively thicker, and Marya could barely help herself; she wanted to take them out and read them, one by one.

The bottom drawer was locked. Marya tugged at it, to no avail.

So she flipped back to the smallest section, the first-years. And there:

*Teitler, Elana*

And right behind it:

*Lupu, Marya*

Marya's fingers twitched.

The headmaster was gone. The building was asleep. The tapestries would not tell.

And before she knew it, both files were out and spread on the floor before her.

And she found—

Nothing.

That is, nothing that she could read.

Both files were pages and pages of notes in a language Marya didn't know, hadn't ever even seen before. One page after another, completely illegible to her.

Useless.

Just like she was.

Marya put her head in her hands. She had no other options. Everything she tried failed. She could do nothing for Madame Bandu, she could do nothing for Elana, she could do nothing for the Countess Dragomir, she could do nothing for herself.

"I thought someone was in here."

The voice came from behind her. Marya jumped up and found herself face-to-face with the headmaster.

"I'd just stepped out to the kitchens," he said, taking a step closer. "I do get hungry."

The headmaster strode into the office, where Marya was standing perfectly still in between the two files, like a monument to her own perfidy.

"Did you discover anything interesting in those files?" he asked, nodding to the paper at her feet.

There was nothing to do but tell the truth. ". . . I couldn't read them."

"No. Most girls cannot read ancient Messapic." He took another step forward. "When you run a school for troubled girls, you learn to take certain precautions."

Marya felt like she was burning, like she would soon turn to ash.

"Marya, I have seen hundreds of girls come through this school, and none of them has ever surprised me. Did you really think you were the first girl to come into my office saying she thinks she's discovered the secret to mountain madness? Did you really think you were so special that you could figure out something no one else had in two centuries?"

"No, I—"

"The secret in the embroidery was an interesting twist, though. I've never heard that one before! But still, it's the same story. You follow the rules at first, and then you decide that maybe they don't apply to you. Take Mademoiselle Teitler, here." He gestured toward her file. "From the beginning I expected that she would need to prove something to me, to the school, to herself. And she did. She snuck out nearly every night—oh yes, Marya, we know that. We know everything. Do you really think a girl could act that way and we wouldn't know?"

Yes. She had thought that. And so had Elana.

"Some girls like her get their disobedience out of their system and become model students if we give them the chance. Others . . ." He threw up his hands. "But she will feel better after we help her, I know that."

He was standing in front of Marya now, smiling down at her in the way you might smile at a dissection well done.

"What about you, Marya? You have been in close contact with a witch. Do you think she might have had some influence on you?"

Marya took a step back. "She's not—"

"Not a witch. You really believe that."

"I do!"

"You think you know better than the Guild. The king."

"No, but—"

"Then, what? Tell me, Marya."

"I know her!"

"Isn't it at all possible that you've been deceived?"

"No."

"Or perhaps," he said, "that you've been enchanted?"

"No!"

"Perhaps that you are working for her?"

"No—"

"I don't mean that you'd do it intentionally. But how can you say, with absolute certainty, that you haven't been bespelled by the Torakian witch?"

"Because she's not a witch!"

"So you are saying that you are not bespelled, that you are absolutely in control of your actions?"

"Yes."

"So you are here in my office, not because you are under some spell, but of your own volition?"

Wasn't that what he just asked? "Yes!"

And then everything went black.

# The Sanitarium

**W**hen Marya next regained consciousness, she was in a small, white room with a plain door and a single small window, outfitted with an infirmary bed, a blanket, and a bedside table with a lantern on it. She was completely alone.

She sat up, though her head felt like wool, and her muscles felt like particularly wet mud.

Where was she? She had no idea. She should be panicking—she felt for certain that panicking would be the right reaction now—and yet her body seemed to have

forgotten exactly how one did that. Her heart beat desul-
torily, her blood crept sluggishly through her veins, and her
thoughts felt like they were occurring somewhere near her
body, but still outside it.

And she could not figure out what had happened.

She was Marya; she knew that much. She was made of
wool and mud, and something else. Maybe sticks?

Her conversation with the headmaster floated around
in her head hazily, like a story she'd heard once when she
was half asleep.

She reached out to the memory, trying to find something in it to hang on to. But there was nothing. She was
grasping at air.

She put one leg on the floor, then the other, conscious
that the process was much harder than it should have been.

And no wonder. Her legs were made of sticks and mud.
You needed muscles to move, and she did not have any of
those. She wobbled and braced herself on the bed.

It hurt to be made of sticks and mud.

Marya squeezed her eyes shut.

In that moment she wanted, more than anything, more
than two working legs, even, to know exactly where she
was, because right now it felt like the whole world was this
strange, small white room. There were no sounds coming

from anywhere. And if her feeling was right, if the whole world was this strange white room, then she was completely, truly alone. Then there was nobody left.

Marya inhaled, and then propelled herself toward the door, legs regaining some memory of how to work as she did so. A few steps, and then she was there.

Marya pulled on the doorknob. It did not open.

At first she thought maybe the same fog that had overtaken her legs had taken over her arms, too, that she no longer had the strength or skill to work things like doorknobs. She tried again, and again, nothing.

And then she realized:

She was locked in.

She rattled the doorknob, tugged with both hands. Nothing. She could not get out.

But where was she? She climbed back on her bed to peer out the small window above it, and then she gasped.

She was not at Dragomir at all.

She was on the ground floor of what seemed to be a remote cottage. The mountains shimmered in the distance, and there was no sign of the school at all.

Or of anything else she recognized.

The cottage was surrounded by nothing but trees. No other buildings, no sign of people.

Marya tried to open the window, but that was locked too. She was trapped.

Now the panic was starting. She could feel it rising from her stomach like flames.

She ran back to the door and started pounding on it and yelling, though she had no idea if anyone was around, and if they were, were they the sort of people she would want to hear her?

It didn't matter. Nobody came.

She was all alone.

Marya rested her head against the unforgiving door and tried to get her breath back. After a few moments she sat back on the bed, hugging her knees to her chest. It felt there should be something else to try, but her mind was as blank as the room.

All she could do was reach into her memories again and look for something solid, and she tried, she tried as hard as she could. But there was nothing there but fog.

She sat like that for some time in the quiet, stark white room. So lost was she in her own thoughts that she barely heard the footsteps until they were right outside her room.

The doorknob turned, and the door opened.

Whoever she was expecting to see—Nurse Rieza? Simona? The headmaster? Madame Rosetti?—it was not the tall figure in rich blue robes in the doorway. High Count Arev stood there, clapping his hands together as if she were an old friend he had not seen in years.

"Ah, you're awake," he said with a grin.

Instinctively, she pressed herself against the wall. "Where am I?"

He took a step into the room, holding his hands out as if to calm a frightened animal. "It's all right. There's nothing to worry about."

"Where am I?" she repeated. "What are you doing here?"

"I'm sure this must be very frightening for you," he said, taking another step. "Do you know who you are?"

"I'm . . . Marya!"

"Good, good. I'm High Count Arev, if you don't remember me."

She stared. Had he lost his mind? "Of course I remember you!"

"Good, good," he said again. "That's good. Now, please know you're perfectly safe here."

"Where's here?"

"You're in a sanitarium, away from harm. And you're in good hands, I promise. We will be able to heal you."

"Heal me? Heal me of what?"

He nodded, as if expecting her to say that. "I under-stand that you might not remember. Everything must be so confusing. If you'd just calm down—"

"Please," she said, "tell me what's happening."

"I'm afraid that you're ill, Marya," he said, his voice softening. "There's a malady unique to these mountains that some girls fall victim to, but rest assured—"

"Mountain madness? I don't have mountain madness!"

"Ah, you know about it! Then you must know it's easily curable with some bed rest and treatment."

"Yes, but I don't have it!"

"You do, Marya. Perhaps it doesn't feel like it, but you do."

"According to who?"

"The headmaster."

Marya blinked. The headmaster. Of course—she'd been in his office. He'd asked her if she was bespelled.

And when she told him she wasn't, the alternative in his mind must have been that she was mad.

"I just wanted to find my . . . friend."

Marya stopped. *Elana*. Was she here? This was the place with the rooms that Simona and Tereza thought were just off the infirmary. The sanitarium, High Count Arev had called it. It was definitely not just off the infirmary.

"You seem quite distressed, Marya. I could give you something for your nerves."

"Listen," Marya said, trying to steady her voice. "I don't have mountain madness. Maybe the headmaster thinks you'd have to be mad to sneak into his office, but that's just—I'm not. But Elana—Elana thought her hands were on fire. And Tereza thought pictures were moving and Simona felt like a giant spider was sitting on her chest in the middle of the night." She swallowed. "Please. You have to listen to me."

He smiled at her warmly. "I believe I will take the headmaster's word over yours," he said, a note of laughter in his voice.

"But—" she sputtered. "But . . . what if he's wrong?"

"You need rest, Marya."

The exhaustion slammed into her then. She had no energy to argue. And it didn't matter; even if she had the energy, it wouldn't work. He thought she was mad.

The high count pulled a small chair up next to the bed. "The headmaster told me that the madness came upon you suddenly," he said, voice soothing. "That you were in his office and then you started shrieking. Do you remember?"

"No. No. That's not what happened."

"Girls in your condition do not always remember," he said.

It was true that there was time Marya could not account for: she'd been talking to the headmaster; then everything went dark.

"You must not exhaust yourself, young lady. Your system has had quite a shock."

Yes, she was exhausted. Yes, her system had had a shock. And yes, she remembered nothing. She kept trying to reach and reach into her mind and there was nothing there.

All she wanted to do was sleep now.

"What happened does not matter," he went on. "What matters is what will happen now. Now, you will rest and heal. And when you come out of here, it will all be over and your life can go forward. I will be ministering to you. I have an elixir for you. It will help you rest. You must have sleep."

There was a vial in his hands. The fluid inside was the color of liquefied grass. Maybe she was mad. Even if she wasn't mad, she was so tired.

"How . . . how do you cure me?" she asked. "Does it hurt?"

"No," he said. "Not a bit. The madness is a sickness, so

like with all sicknesses, we need to draw it out of the body. And that is what I will do while you are sleeping. You will not feel a thing."

It seemed so easy. He just drew the madness out, let it hang in the air and float away. Marya's hypothetical madness would sail along in the sky until it found a nice cottage somewhere, where it would tuck itself in by the fire and have a nice long nap.

There was the principle of magical permanence. Was there a principle of madness permanence? Maybe she had Tereza's madness, and Tereza had had Simona's madness, and maybe hers would be passed on to generations of Dragomir girls.

"I think Nadia Dragomir cursed the school," she said. "Maybe you could check for a hidden curse? Since you're a sorcerer."

"Mmm," he said. "Yes, certainly."

Suddenly there was a noise from the hallway behind him. He sprang out of his chair and whirled around to look.

Elana, in a nightgown and bare feet, stumbled into the room, moving as if her legs, too, were made of sticks and mud.

"Young lady!" the high count exclaimed. "What—how

did you get out of your room?"

She held her hands out to him, as if there were proof there. "You know how! I told you how!"

Marya gaped at Elana, her head suddenly feeling quite clear. Elana was too thin, too pale. Her eyes were sunken and rimmed in red. And the expression on her face—she looked like she'd spent the night in the Fantoma Forest and barely survived the ordeal.

"Elana," Marya whispered.

Elana's head whipped to her. "Marya? Is it you? Are you really here?"

"I'm here," Marya said.

Elana held her hands out. "Do you see it too?" Her voice was desperate.

Marya felt her heart crack. Elana's hands were just hands—there was nothing unusual about them. She pressed her lips together.

"Oh," Elana said, dropping her hands. "Oh."

Marya stared.

Yes, Elana looked mad.

"I must have left your door unlocked," High Count Arev said, straightening his robes. "I apologize, Elana. I will be more careful in the future. Now, we should get you back to your room. You should not be out of bed. I—"

He stopped. An expression skated over his face, too quick for Marya to tell what it was. His hand went into his robe and he pulled out a small glass tube with wisps of gray smoke inside. He just stared at it, in much the same way Elana had stared at her hands. And, as he watched, the smoke began to thicken.

"What is that? Marya asked, even though she knew. He'd shown them at the assembly. Besides, there was only one name for the feeling coming over her.

"The Dread," he breathed.

Marya sat straight up. Elana fell against the bed, and Marya instinctively grabbed her hand.

"Where?" Marya asked.

He went to the window and peered out. "I don't . . . I don't see anything." He glanced at the little tube again. The smoke inside it was writhing now. "Stay there," he said, and stalked out of the room.

Elana moved herself onto the bed next to Marya. "Is this really happening?"

Marya nodded and squeezed Elana's hand again. She leaned her head against Marya's shoulder and exhaled softly.

"We're with a sorcerer," Marya whispered. "We'll be safe."

High Count Arev rushed back into the room, carrying two shawls and two pairs of slippers in his hand. "We need to leave, girls. Put these on. I have a carriage out front."

"What—" Marya started.

"The Dread is to the northwest, in the mountains. It will head toward the location with the most people, so we should be safe for now. But we need to leave here, and get as far away as possible. There's no way of knowing how fast it will move—it could be hours before it heads south, or it could be minutes. Come on, quickly now."

Marya shot a desperate look at Elana, who was shooting her a desperate look back. There was nothing to do but move. Marya sprang up and pulled Elana with her, all exhaustion forgotten. There was nothing like the approach of a monstrous bloodsucking cloud to wake you up.

"Can you move?" she whispered.

Elana nodded. "My legs hurt. I'm slow."

"It's okay," Marya said. "We aren't going far. Here." She wrapped the shawl around Elana's shoulders, then threw her own shawl on, picked up the lantern, and headed outside, her friend in tow.

And then she stopped. They were in front of a two-story cottage surrounded by trees, just off the road. Marya's window had overlooked the east side, where nothing hung in the sky but the sun.

The carriage was pulled up in front, its driver struggling with two majestic black horses that looked as if they very much wanted to run as fast as they could away from the spot where they were. High Count Arev was tying a trunk on top. In the distance, the Rosa Mountains spread across the landscape.

And to the west, somewhere between them and the mountains, a roiling patch of fog the color of a bruise inched slowly across the horizon.

"Oh," Marya gasped.

"Oh," Elana echoed.

"Look." Marya pointed into the mountains, where a small estate stood perched in the foothills. Dragomir.

How far was the cloud from the school? How far were they? Would the Dread arrive before they could get there? Did the school even see it coming? The sun would be setting soon. And the sorcerer that was supposed to protect them wasn't there.

"Let's go!" yelled the high count.

Marya grabbed Elana's hand and they ran toward the coach, as the high count shouted instructions at the driver. "Drive southeast," he said, pointing. "As fast as you can."

Marya pulled to a stop just outside the carriage door.

What was he doing? "The school's that way!" She pointed up the road.

"Yes, I know. That's why we're going this way! Hurry now!"

"What—what about the school?"

"What *about* the school?" the high count replied.

"You said the Dread would go where the most people are," Marya said.

He stared at her as if trying to discern some sense in what she was saying. Then, understanding crossed over his face. He straightened. "I am afraid that is true. And that is why we want to head away from there. I'm sure they'll see it coming and evacuate."

"You're . . . sure? Does the headmaster have one of those tube things?"

"Of course he does not. They're only for sorcerers."

"But then we have to warn them!"

"And ride into certain death? I think not!"

"But you're a sorcerer!" Marya said. "This is what you do!"

Next to her, Elana was gaping at the Dread and completely still, as if she herself were bespelled.

The high count scoffed. "I couldn't do anything against a cloud of Dread by myself. And the kingdom certainly does not want to lose a promising young sorcerer in defense of a girls' school. And I must notify the other sorcerers about this Dread appearance. Now, I'm getting in this carriage and we are driving southeast. Are you coming with me?"

Marya's mouth was hanging open. She could barely think as the sorcerer's words kept smashing into her face like waves in a storm.

The road lay in front of them—one way would take them toward safety, the other to Dragomir Academy. There was no way of telling how long it would take to walk to the school, if there was any hope of warning them before the Dread came. And if the Dread did come, no one would survive.

The sorcerer hopped in the carriage and yelled, "Last chance! What are you going to do?"

A noise burst out of Marya's mouth, an incomprehensible syllable that meant something like *How dare you?* and *I hate you* and *I'm scared.*

She did not even look at Elana. She didn't have to; she knew what Elana would do. Elana was the sort of girl who would run headlong into the monsters.

And now, she was, too.

"We're going to the school!" Marya yelled. Elana

squeezed her hand tight.

"Suit yourself," he said, climbing into the carriage. The driver cast them a look, and then shook his head and let loose the reins.

And then they were gone.

# The Road at Night

Neither Marya nor Elana spoke as the carriage sped down the road in the opposite direction from the Dread and the school. It wasn't until it disappeared around a bend that either girl could even move.

Now they were truly alone.

The Dread still hung in the sky. It did not even appear to be moving; it seemed to be in no rush, as if it had all the time in the world.

And somehow that did not make Marya feel any better.

The sky was growing darker. If no one at Dragomir had

sighted the Dread, they certainly would not now. Marya turned to look at Elana, who still appeared as if she'd been haunted. Maybe even more now than she had when she'd first appeared in Marya's room.

"They're so awful," she breathed. "They're all so awful."

Marya could not speak. The sorcerers were supposed to be the heroes of Illyria, given everything the kingdom had as a reward for keeping its people safe from the monsters that lurked in the forest. She pictured High Count Arev alone in the coach now. What was he telling himself about the choice he'd just made? Did he feel like the horrid, self-ish coward in a fancy robe that he was?

"We need to go," Marya said. "We have to walk. . . . Can you walk?"

"Yes," Elana said, voice full of determination. "My legs feel stronger. I just . . . I've been in that bed for days. I think."

Evening was settling into the land, carrying with it the promise of dark. They were in their nightclothes with nothing but robes and shawls to protect them against the cold, the lantern to guide them in the night. All they had was the road ahead, the school on the horizon, and the absolute terror of what might happen if they failed.

The Dread hung in the distance, and Marya tried not

to look, not to even think about the sickening cloud that hovered above them, ever nearer as they walked, though she herself felt like dread was filtering into her body and might soon overtake her. The light from the lantern helped them keep to their path as the distant school fell into the shadow of the night.

How long a walk was it? There was no real way to tell, just like there was no way to tell when the Dread would strike. All the things they'd learned in school so far, all the recitation and enunciation, none of it mattered for now, facing an inevitable Dread attack with no one to stop it and no idea if they'd be able to evacuate in time.

Still they kept walking.

"Are you doing okay?" Marya asked Elana, after a time.

"Yeah," Elana said. "I feel—I feel like my brain is inside my body again. The cold air helps. That probably sounds silly."

"No, I get it."

"I don't remember much," Elana said quietly. "Everything I remember seems like it was probably a dream. Do you know how long I was in there? I can't tell."

"You were in there a few days before me. But I don't know how long I was there."

"Simona brought me to the infirmary, and then Nurse

Rieza called the headmaster. I remember that. And then . . . I'm not sure. I was here." She swallowed. "I do feel . . . mad. I was in the kitchen cleaning up, and then, suddenly . . . I saw the water in the sink start to swell, like it was going to fill the room and drown us all. And then . . ."

"You thought your hands were on fire," Marya said quietly.

A moment. "I know they're not on fire, but . . . it feels that way. And I dream . . . the strangest things." She looked away. "What about you?" she asked, after a moment. "Do you . . . have mountain madness? Is that why you were brought there?"

". . . The high count said I do."

"But you don't remember anything."

"No. The last thing I remember, before I was here, is that I was in the headmaster's office—"

"You were? Why?"

"I was trying to find out where you were."

Elana's voice grew soft. "You were?"

"Well . . . yeah." Marya swallowed. "I wanted to find you. I felt bad; I should have earlier. But—"

"You're telling me that you snuck into the headmaster's office?" Was that a note of laughter in Elana's voice? "And you, what, went through his files?"

"I did," Marya said, a smile twitching on her lips.

"Even I haven't done that, Marya," said Elana. "So what happened?"

"The headmaster caught me. He asked me if I'd been bewitched. And then . . . well, I don't know."

"You really don't remember anything?"

"No," Marya said. "I just woke up there."

"Did they tell you anything?"

"The high count said that I'd started shrieking. But I feel like I'd remember that. It just feels like maybe . . ." She stopped. The words were too dangerous to say out loud. But it felt like, maybe, the headmaster had wanted her to say that Madame Bandu had put her under a spell, that that was why she was acting the way she had. And it felt like, maybe, if she had said it, he would have forgotten she'd ever gone into his office; she could have gone back to her room and gone to sleep and it would have been like none of it ever happened.

But why?

Something was bothering her, a puckered seam in the fabric of the story that was pressing against her side. But no matter how much she searched for it, she couldn't find the source.

"Maybe what?" Elana asked.

She shook her head. It sounded mad.

Instead she told Elana about the apron and what she'd decoded in it, and her ill-fated trip to see the headmaster, because she had not been able to talk to Elana since. Even as she reconstructed it for Elana, she felt the story she'd told him about Nadia take on an absurd shape, as if she was ridiculous for ever having believed it.

But Elana only said, "I don't believe him."

"You don't?"

"No. If Nadia had just died like that, there would have been something in the archives that said so. Letters, funeral arrangements, condolence notes. My father received dozens of them when his father died and saved them all for the estate archives."

"But why would he lie?"

"I don't know. I don't understand any of it. But if we can get through this, we'll find out, okay?"

Marya nodded.

It was good to have a friend.

Because it was dark and quiet and their journey was long, they could forget about what lay at the end of it for a bit. They could see nothing now but the road ahead as lit by the purloined lantern, and that was all they chose to think about.

But then, suddenly, a glow on the horizon: the lights around the school had been lit, as they always were in the evening.

Both girls stopped. If there were activity, if people were evacuating, surely there would be coaches equipped with lanterns making their way from the school to the road. There would be some fluttering of the glow coming from the school as people moved around. There would be some sign of something.

"They don't know," Elana whispered.

"They don't know," Marya agreed.

The girls quickened their pace. It had passed from dusk into twilight, and it seemed like they were no closer to the school. She was tired. Her feet hurt. These slippers were not made for walking outside at night, but they seemed ever so slightly better than her bare feet. She was really cold. Her robe was nothing. Her robe was paper, a prayer, a breath. The shawl helped, but what good was a shawl and a breath?

Worst of all, she couldn't see the Dread anymore. The night sky had gotten cloudy, and the Dread was, perhaps, hiding itself among its innocuous brethren.

Every once in a while she asked Elana if she was okay, and Elana said yes, even though she surely was not. Every once in a while Elana asked her if she was okay, and she said yes, though she definitely was not.

And still they kept walking.

The school shone on the horizon. Marya looked away when she could, in the hopes that when she looked back she would see signs of the coach house and stables lit up, of carriages leaving the school. And in fear that the lights would be encased in cloud, and they'd see that they were too late.

At some point Marya registered that the sound of the wind had changed, that there was in the distance some kind of odd, rhythmic noise that felt out of place in this quiet night.

Elana squeezed her shoulder. She'd heard it, too.

"Maybe we should get off the road," she whispered.

Marya nodded. They were two girls walking an empty road at night, in a land once haunted by giants, in a kingdom on the brink of war, in a place currently menaced by the Dread. Together, the girls ducked off the road and hid behind a tree, Marya covering the lantern with her robe.

Now a light was up on the road behind them, and the rhythmic noise resolved itself into horses and a carriage. Heading in the direction of the school. Fast.

Marya squeezed Elana's hand. Maybe the high count had changed his mind and was coming back. Maybe someone else had sighted the Dread and was coming to warn the school. Maybe they were saved. And yet neither girl could bring herself to come out from behind the tree. Because it was night on a lonely road, and maybe they were safer in the dark.

But it did not appear that they would get to make that choice, for the carriage began to slow as it approached them, and then stopped altogether just where they'd ducked off the road.

They'd been seen. Marya did not dare breathe.

Someone leaped from the carriage and shone the lantern on the side of the road. "Hello?" he called. "Is someone there?"

When the words settled on Marya, she leaped out from behind the tree.

"If you need help," said the voice, "I can—wait, is that . . . Marya?"

"Luka!" With a great gasp, Marya sprang toward her brother. His arms opened wide, and as she fell into them, he took her close and held her.

"I can't believe it's you," he murmured.

No. No, she could not believe this, either.

"We should go," he said. "The Dread's coming!" Luka was driving an open-air carriage that sat four people with a platform for the driver. He helped Elana up into the seating area while Marya perched herself next to the driver's seat.

"I'm sure there's a really good reason why you're on the road at night in your nightgowns?" he said as he climbed in next to her. "Didn't you see the Dread?"

"Yes. That's why we were . . ." The weight of the story suddenly seemed that it might crush her, and they did not have time to be crushed. "Elana and I," she said simply, "we were in a cottage back there. We saw the Dread and . . . we have to warn the school."

She stopped. Luka had already signaled to the horses to turn around, which was the natural thing to do. He thought he'd rescued them, and now they'd go as fast as they possibly could in the opposite direction. He stopped and squinted at her. "You were in a cottage, and you saw the Dread coming and . . . you started walking toward the school, which is miles away, in your nightgowns? To warn them?"

"Yes," Marya said.

With his hands tightening around the reins, he let out a long, slow breath. "Well," he said, "we'd better get moving, then."

"Thank you," Marya breathed.

"Can't have you do something so foolish and not be there to witness it," he muttered, flicking the reins.

The horses started to canter toward the school, where all was still quiet. Now that she was not walking anymore, Marya's body decided to register what exactly she was doing, and suddenly her lungs could not seem to get air. She closed her eyes and breathed, and breathed again.

*It's okay, Marya,* she told herself. *It's okay.*

It was nothing close to okay, but it helped to pretend.

"Marya," Luka muttered, "I have to tell you something."

"Madame Bandu was arrested for being a witch," she said.

"Yes . . . Dr. Bandu came to the house. He told me Madame Bandu had been arrested late in the night, and that she'd instructed him to send me to get you. She said you were in trouble. He gave me the carriage, money for the trip, and directions. I've been driving since yesterday morning."

"In trouble?" Marya repeated.

"Dr. Bandu didn't know why. She told him when they came to get her. She thinks that's why they arrested her."

". . . Because of me?"

"Because she found something out about the school. But she couldn't say anything else."

Marya could not process it all. That was why they'd arrested her? Madame Bandu thought that they arrested her not because they thought she was a witch, but because they thought she knew something? But wasn't she arrested for witchcraft?

"They told me you were missing," Marya said, after a moment.

"When Dr. Bandu came over, I just left. I dropped him at his house and came straight here. I didn't tell Mama and Papa. I was afraid . . ." He stopped.

"That they wouldn't let you go."

Luka did not respond.

"Luka, have Mama and Papa said anything about why I'm here?"

"They . . . haven't said anything."

No. They likely hadn't mentioned her since she left.

"I just wonder if it's. . . because of Pieter."

"Marya! What does that even mean?"

"Because I fell asleep."

Luka let out a long exhale. "It wasn't your fault, Marya," he said quietly. "He was sick and he died, that's all."

"But they told the headmaster about Pieter. He knew."

"Marya," Luka said, "Mama and Papa have not talked to anyone at that school. And even if they had, there's no way they would mention Pieter to anyone. You know that."

She clamped her mouth shut. She could not manage to hold all of this in her brain at once. She was practically vibrating with it all.

"It wasn't your fault, Marya," he went on, voice almost a whisper. "There's nothing you could have done. I've been assisting Dr. Bandu, and sometimes when kids have fevers there's just . . . nothing anyone can do. Even a doctor. I don't know. I just wish . . . I wish we'd talked about it." His hands clutched the reins, "I wish we'd realized we could have stuck together."

The road had started to climb up the foothills, and as they turned around a bend, the lamps from the school illuminated enough of the sky that they could see the sickly smear of Dread in the sky. Though they had not seen any signs of it moving, it was now somehow close, too close, impossibly close.

"Hurry," she whispered.

Luka nodded and loosened the reins. Anxious, the horses were only too happy to run. Marya scanned the landscape, looking to see if the cloud was changing, if it was quickening, if it looked like dreadlings were beginning to form.

How would they even evacuate the school? Did they

have enough horses and carriages for everyone? Even if they did, was there time to get them all ready? What if they were asleep? It must have been late by then, so late, and the girls of Rose Hall were surely in bed. But maybe the older girls were still up; maybe Madame Rosetti had seen the Dread and gotten everyone ready; maybe maybe maybe it would be okay.

As soon as the carriage arrived in front of the school, Luka jumped down, Marya and Elana right behind him. Luka threw open the doors to the school and the girls ran in and found—

No one. It was silent. The whole school was asleep.

So Marya took a deep breath and yelled, "The Dread is coming!"

# The Dread

A moment later, Marya heard the sound of a door opening, and footsteps running down the hallway toward them. Madame Rosetti appeared around the corner, still in her dress and boots.

"Marya! Elana! What are you—"

"Madame Rosetti," Marya said, straightening. "It's the Dread. It's nearby."

Her eyebrows knitted together. "That's preposterous!" she exclaimed. "You girls are in quarantine. You need to come with me right now."

The deputy headmistress looked back and forth between the girls, both breathing hard, their slippers covered with dirt, the hems of their nightgowns filthy, their hair messy. She didn't believe them, Marya realized. She thought this was mountain madness. And no wonder—they both looked like they'd crawled here.

As Elana and Marya exchanged a frantic glance, Luka stepped forward, back straight, chin high. He bowed—not a deep, respectful bow, but the sort of bow you give someone to tell them they are supposed to be respectful to you, the bow of a boy everyone thinks will be a sorcerer one day. "Madame," he said, voice low and rich, "I am Luka Lupu. My sister is telling the truth. There is a cloud of Dread within striking distance of here. I saw it with my own eyes. The school needs to evacuate immediately."

Madame Rosetti blinked. "Well," she said. "Well." And then she strode outside.

Luka shrugged at Marya, as if in apology, but she did not care. It was not news that people wouldn't take her seriously, and right now it was life or death that they take someone seriously. Luka knew how to act like an ostentatious brat, and an ostentatious brat was exactly what Marya needed.

Madame Rosetti rushed back in, all her composure

gone. This, somehow, was the scariest thing Marya had seen today. "We need to find High Count Arev," she breathed. "Wasn't he at the sanitarium with you?"

Elana raised her eyebrows at Marya. "He saw the Dread and ran away," Marya said.

Madame Rosetti's eye twitched. "I see. Well. Will you excuse me? I must go to my office and sound the alarm."

She disappeared down the hallway again, as fast and efficient as a curse.

There was an alarm? Marya glanced at Elana, who shrugged. Maybe they'd mentioned it in the handbook.

Sure enough, the distant sound of ringing bells came from the corridor and from somewhere above; then Madame Rosetti returned, brushing invisible dirt off her skirt quite intensely.

"Well," she said, words clipped, "I cannot seem to rouse the headmaster. I know he was in his office working late this evening. But now it is locked, and he's not answering."

"Maybe his office is dreadproofed," Elana muttered.

Madame Rosetti stared at her a moment. Marya did too. High Count Arev had said that there was a procedure— a small space, the sort that could fit one person, could be dreadproofed.

Maybe *that* was what High Count Arev had been doing

at the school this whole time.

"I see," Madame Rosetti said again. She looked from Elana to Marya to Luka. "I guess it's up to us, then." Her chest rose and fell. "Would one of you run down to the kitchens, please? One of the boys will be there still. Make sure they heard the bells in the staff quarters. He'll know what to do. Elana, I believe you know the fastest route to the kitchens?"

There was not even a hint of reprobation in her voice. Elana took off running.

"Should I go get the carriages?" Marya asked, voice squeaky. "Is there time?"

Madame Rosetti turned to her. "No. It's too dangerous on the roads. We'll use the tunnels the Dragomirs built for the giants. This is our procedure in case of Dread attack. The tunnels lead to houses far away, and if the messengers do their jobs, there will be coaches waiting. The faculty will lead the students in groups through them."

"But won't the Dread . . . ?"

"It's our best chance. The tunnels run deep and should provide some protection. I will be accompanying the Rose Hall girls. It was supposed to be the headmaster and I, but . . ." Her voice was flat, controlled, but suddenly Marya felt the anger coming off her like heat from a fire.

Then, trampling down the stairs, came the sixth-year girls, wearing robes and boots, faces set in masks of shock and fear, with Mademoiselle Gris and another teacher accompanying them. As Madame Rosetti spoke to Mademoiselle Gris quietly, Marya caught the eyes of Irina, the library aide. The sixth year looked at her, full of panic, as if Marya had any reassurance to give her.

Then more footsteps. The fourth-year girls, with two more faculty members. Then the second-years. Then the third-years: Marya saw Tereza in the middle of the group.

Marya frowned. Where were the Rose Hall girls?

Then came Nurse Rieza, with Mademoiselle Karon and the girl who'd been in the infirmary when Marya was there.

Then the fifth-years, with Madame Szabo. They were down the stairs and out the hallway.

And then quiet. The stairs settled, as if they'd done their job for the night.

Where were the Rose Hall girls?

That's when Marya remembered:

The bell.

"The Rose Hall alarm . . . is that the bell in the parlor?"

"Yes. Simona will hear it and know what to do."

She shook her head frantically. "It's broken. I—I broke

it. I took the clapper off. They don't know. I have to go get them."

Whatever Madame Rosetti's reaction was, Marya did not see. She'd already started running.

*Marya.*

*Marya, Marya, Marya.*

*What did you do, Marya?*

Of all the mistakes she'd ever made, it was this one small action of breaking that infuriating bell that would do them all in. Somewhere, her mother was thinking, *I told you so, Marya*, without even knowing why.

She ran up the four flights of stairs, even though her legs were screaming at her, were threatening to stop working at any moment if she did not treat them with more care, but she did not have time for such things. If they all survived this, somehow, she would apologize to her legs later.

All was quiet in Rose Hall. The parlor was empty, and there on the wall hung the broken bell, swinging back and forth silently, a monument to Marya's terminal dysfunction.

First she pounded on Simona's door. One breath. Two. Three. Then Simona burst out into the hallway.

"What is it? . . . Marya? What are you doing here? You're supposed to be in the infirmary. Now"—she took a step out into the hallway and began to speak in deliberately soothing tones—"come with me. I'll just—"

Marya took a step back. "No! Simona, listen. The Dread is outside. We need to evacuate—"

"Oh, Marya—"

"The bell is broken! Listen to me!"

Her voice cracked. They'd said she had mountain madness, and now no one would ever believe her, about anything, ever again.

The commotion must have awakened the other girls, who were emerging from their rooms now and were watching Marya, agape.

Marya inhaled. "Listen, Simona," she said carefully. "You told me that you were afraid people wouldn't take you seriously after you had mountain madness. I need you to take me seriously now. The Dread is outside"—at this, a yelp from one of the other girls—"and everyone else has evacuated. Madame Rosetti is waiting for us downstairs. Elana is too. We need to go, now. Please. Listen to me!"

The other girls did not move, just stared at Marya, as if her words themselves had frozen them. Simona blinked once. Then again. Then she turned. "Girls, get your robes, then go to the great hall, now. Marya will lead the way."

Marya gasped in relief. As the other girls grabbed their

robes, she bounced on her feet, then propelled herself forward as soon as Simona waved them ahead. She went first, followed by Ana-Maria, then Elisabet, Daria, and Katya, then Simona right behind.

With the Rose Hall girls following her, Marya led the way to the grand staircase. They were not safe yet. They were so far away from being safe—they had to get through the building, to the tunnels, and then make the miles-long trek through them, to some house somewhere, where there were, supposedly, carriages waiting. If it all worked.

But they were on their way to being safe. And that, at least, was something. It was something that could keep Marya going forward, despite that whispering voice that told her she should just give up, that there was no hope, that everyone was doomed and it was her fault. As long as she could move forward, as long as she could hear the footsteps of the other girls behind her, there was hope. There was hope as they went down the first flight, then the second, then the third; there was hope as they hit the last one, as they rounded the landing to get to the great hall. And then—

Marya screamed.

The front hall was filled with fog, deep purple, throbbing with veins of red and malice. Marya felt the warmth drain from her body as four pieces of the fog resolved themselves into vaguely human shapes that filled the hall from floor to ceiling.

The cloud had transformed. Now it was ready to kill.

The only thing more terrifying than the Dread proved to be the Dread in creature form: the roiling, angry cloud had become giants of purple fog, as tall as the great hall itself. The four dreadlings were shaped like elongated human shadows, with loping legs and arms that hung too low and oddly limply. Their heads were too thin, too long, with depressions for eyes and a giant, ravenous maw.

The terrible creatures were hovering a few yards away from Madame Rosetti, Luka, and Elana, who were huddled against a wall, Madame Rosetti holding the other two close to her. For a moment, nobody moved. The dreadlings floated above the floor and seemed to have no interest in attacking when they could just float there and observe their prey shrinking in mortal terror.

"Girls, run!" Madame Rosetti shouted. "Now!"

And then another scream sounded behind Marya, and bodies pressed into her. She whirled around to find that another dreadling had appeared on the landing, filling the space available to it. It reached its arms out as if to grab for them, to envelop them in shadow. Marya and the other girls ran down the stairs, and as they did so, the other dreadling twisted through the air behind them.

Madame Rosetti pushed Elana and Luka toward the rest of them.

"Simona!" she shouted. "Get everyone to the tunnels! Go!"

While this was happening, the dreadlings simply hung in the air, watching them—or what looked like watching them. It was hard to say, as they only had hollows for eyes. They did not seem in any hurry to attack at all, despite the scurrying around.

Perhaps because they knew there was no escape.

The girls of Rose Hall, plus Luka, slowly inched from the great hall to the hallway, with Simona motioning them to the staircase at the hall's end. She walked backward slowly, slowly, the rest of them following her lead.

The dreadlings still floated in the air, watching, watching.

And then Marya realized—

"Madame Rosetti!" Marya cried then.

The deputy headmistress was still on the other side of the great hall, holding her arms out in the air, hands up, as if to compel the dreadlings' attention.

"Go," she hissed, not moving.

"Are you coming?"

"I'll be right behind you."

She was lying. Marya knew she was lying, knew she thought that the only chance the girls had was for her to remain, to keep the Dread focused on her.

"Go now. All of you. That is an order."

Rage flared in Marya, even amid all the fear. She wanted to run to the other end of the school, pound on the headmaster's door, yell at him that he was a traitor and a coward and a liar, let those words linger in his head for the rest of his life. But a man who would hide in a dread-proofed room while his students and colleagues were killed probably did not let words like that linger.

Luka tugged on her robe, pulling her forward. "Marya, we have to go," he said. Marya started backing up, one step at a time, while the five dreadlings watched. She peeked behind her. Simona was nearly at the back staircase now, and still the Dread had not moved. She stopped. Daria and Katya were right in front of her.

Then, in a blink of an eye, everything shifted. Another dreadling appeared in the hallway, right behind Simona.

"Simona!" Elana yelled. But Simona did not need a warning—she whirled around and yelped, and then Daria grabbed her dress and pulled her backward.

The new dreadling floated toward them, pushing the girls back to the great hall, where the other dreadlings were waiting.

Only then did they start to close in, and Madame Rosetti stumbled into the center of the room.

They were being herded.

Soon they were all gathered, with the six dreadlings surrounding them all. There was no way out.

Some of the girls were sobbing, but Marya did not cry until Luka grabbed her hand. Then the tears came flowing, hot against her cheeks. Luka was crying too, and she squeezed his hand back. After their whole lives, after so many years of letting their parents pit them against one another, they'd found each other. And it was too late.

The dreadlings continued to close, moving as one unit. Marya and her friends huddled into each other, because that was all they had left. Elana was on the other side of her, breathing like she was trying to suck in her last gasps of air.

"I'm sorry, girls," Madame Rosetti said, voice breaking. "I failed you. I am so sorry."

Now the dreadlings were elongating, their arms stretching toward the cowering group, and fog began to pour down from their hands.

"No!" Elana shouted. "No! Stop!"

Elana stepped forward in front of Marya, staring at her hands as if they were once again on fire.

"It wasn't a dream!" she yelled. "They lied! It wasn't a dream!"

And then she stuck her hands straight above their heads, the room tilted, and Marya felt her breath leave her lungs, as if sucked out.

Elana let out a howl of rage, and in that moment, the dreadlings suddenly jerked back, as if punched. They tried to close in again, but as the fog began to pour from them, it was pushed back, once again.

All around them, the air shimmered.

Elana's eyes were fixed on the dreadlings, and her knees started buckling, as if something was trying to crush her. But the dreadlings did not move.

Marya had seen this before. Had felt it before. In her house, so many weeks ago now, and again, when High Count Arev gave his demonstration.

It was magic.

And it was coming from Elana.

# The Tapestry

Marya was gripping Luka's hand, and he was gripping hers back, as they both watched, frozen.

Elana looked like she'd put up some kind of shimmering shield and was holding it up with all her strength.

Elana could do magic.

While she gaped, Elana kept pressing her hands against the air above her, the shimmering air a barrier. Now the dreadlings were flailing and grasping at the shield, like hungry animals desperate to feast.

But Elana was struggling. Marya could see it.

Elana needed help—she was in the middle of the main hall single-handedly holding off six dreadlings, and Marya could do nothing for her, nothing but cower with the other girls while Elana was trying to save them, all alone.

No.

No, Marya realized, she was not alone. Marya had left Elana alone before, but she would not do it again. Marya was with her; they were all there with her, all the girls of Rose Hall, and Madame Rosetti and Luka, too.

She stepped forward, pretending to be brave. "Elana! You can do this!" she called. "You're doing great! We're right here with you!"

A moment, and then Ana-Maria stepped next to her. "Elana, you're amazing! You have this!

Then Elisabet and Daria joined them. And then, of all people, Madame Rosetti stepped right next to the girls of Rose Hall and said, "We're right behind you, Elana. All of us."

There was a kind of energy there. Not magic, but something else—it didn't make the air in the room shift, it didn't rob Marya of breath, but it crackled all the same.

Still, Elana was struggling, and the dreadlings seemed to sense it. In an instant, all retreated, moving as one, and then plummeted toward her, mouths wide open, hands clawing at the air. It was no good, it was too much—

And then, with a great yell, Katya ran up next to Elana and threw her arms up—Marya stumbled to the right, as did Luka next to her, as if the floor had violently tilted. Marya and a few other girls fell to the floor.

The air above Katya and Elana filled with light. The dreadlings reeled backward. Another shifting, and then it was as if all the air in the room was being thrown upward like a weapon.

Up it went—

A crackling in the atmosphere—

A burst of light—

Some kind of explosion of energy—

And the dreadlings were gone.

Elana pitched over, like a toppled statue. Katya collapsed next to her, audibly struggling to get breath. A strangled sob came from one of the girls, or maybe it was all of them. Marya felt herself shatter into pieces.

They were alive.

After a few moments, Madame Rosetti strode across the hall and poked her head carefully out the front door.

Marya looked up, breath caught.

"They're gone," she breathed, slamming the door closed. "There's no sign of the cloud, at least none that I can see."

With that, she pressed her back against the front door and closed her eyes.

The room was filled with the sounds of panicked breathing, of relieved crying, of overwhelming relief and the release of unbearable terror. Marya could make no noise, could only hold herself tight.

They had survived.

And—

And—

Elana and Katya were in heaps, completely spent from the magic that they had not known they could work, that they did not know how to use, that had just saved everyone's life.

"Madame Rosetti?" Katya asked, holding her hands up, as if asking someone to explain what they were.

And now this.

The deputy headmistress hurried over to the two of them. "Girls, I am so, so sorry. So sorry."

"That was magic!" Katya said, her voice cracking. "I did magic!"

"You did," said Madame Rosetti. "You both did."

"How did this happen?" Elisabet asked, voice high. "What's going on?"

"I'm not mad," Elana said, cradling herself.

"You're not," said Madame Rosetti, crouching down. "I'm so sorry." She was shaking her head, as if trying to shuffle her thoughts until they fell into some kind of coherent shape. "I don't understand," she breathed.

Marya was looking around the room, taking everything in. The portraits all looked down on her, wondering if she had it in her to find the answers. If they knew, they were not telling.

They had put her in the sanitarium and told her she was mad because she would not change her story about Madame Bandu. They had arrested Madame Bandu and called her a witch, and Madame Bandu told Luka it was because she'd discovered something about the school.

The tapestry with the school crest on it hung on the landing, proclaiming:

## DRAGOMIR ACADEMY
### Established 740
## CHARACTER ABOVE ALL

And Marya found herself wandering up to it, putting her hand on the stitches as if that might connect her with Madame Bandu.

It was then that Marya saw the signature on the tapestry.

She could not read the name, but there, next to it, was a small symbol.

A crescent moon.

She had checked every tapestry in the school, except for that one. And it had been there, the whole time.

The weaver believed the school was a lie.

*But what was the lie?*

"Am I a witch?" Katya asked, voice breaking.

"No!" Elisabet exclaimed.

"You did exactly what High Count Arev did in his demonstration," Ana-Maria added, voice flat. "Exactly the same thing."

Daria blew air out of her mouth. "She's right."

Madame Rosetti had pressed her hands together and was staring at the floor, as if it had secrets to give. "Yes, Ana-Maria is right," she said, almost to herself. "I do not believe you are witches."

Elana looked up, eyes red, face streaked with tears. "We have an apprentice on the estate," she said, voice thick and exhausted. "My father mentored him for two years before his magic came in. When it did, he said it was like he felt the magic in his hands, coursing through his body, that ordinary things seemed to come alive. He expected it to come and knew what it would feel like."

*The school is a lie.*

Marya's eyes went to Luka, kicking absently, awkwardly, at the wood of the front hall floor. The council had identified him as a potential sorcerer, had come to test him, just as they did every year with a few boys across Illyria whom the sorcerers identified as having magical potential.

A few boys. Maybe about six or seven?

Had the council known about Elana? Had they known about Katya? Was that why they were there?

Was that why they were all there?

*The school is a lie.*

"Did he have nightmares?" Simona asked, hushed. Marya's gaze snapped to her.

Elana nodded. "He said he had incredibly vivid dreams."

Simona looked away. "That's what happened to me, too," she said, voice thick. "They told me I was mad for it. I saw things; I felt things."

At this, Madame Rosetti stood up and began pacing around the room.

"You too?" Elana asked.

Simona nodded.

She had had mountain madness, too. A couple of girls a year had mountain madness. . . .

"What do you remember?" Elana whispered.

"The headmaster, telling me I was mad," she said.

Elana stood up. "Yes," she said. "High Count Arev was there, too. Reciting something?"

Simona's head snapped up. "Yes," she breathed. "I thought I was dreaming!" She looked around the room. "I wasn't mad!"

At this, Madame Rosetti took a step forward. "No," she said softly, "You were not mad, Simona. Nor you, Elana."

*The school is a lie.*

No, none of them were mad.

"Madame," Marya asked, "how are we selected to come here? For the school?"

"One of the king's councils identifies you. That's all I know."

It was exactly how Luka's council visit worked.

"I thought our parents sent us!" Katya exclaimed.

"No," Madame Rosetti said. "They have nothing to do with it."

Marya looked at Luka, who raised his eyebrows. That sounded just like how Luka's test had worked.

"We're all potential sorcerers," Marya said flatly. As soon as she spoke the words, she knew they were true. "Like my brother was. The sorcerers identify us through magic. Except instead of getting council visits, we get sent here, so they can watch us."

"So," Katya said, "is it true that we're not . . . troubled?"

Madame Rosetti's jaw twitched. Her gaze went down the long hallway, where the headmaster's office was, and her eyes narrowed. "No," she said quietly. All the girls looked up at her, and she regarded each one, eyes burning. "No," she repeated, louder. "You are not troubled. None of you are. I am so sorry. I did not know. I understand if you do not believe me, but I will do everything in my power to make it up to you." Straightening, she brushed off her apron. "We need to tell someone what happened here tonight, immediately." She looked from girl to girl again, and then turned to Luka. "Young man. That is your carriage outside?"

"Yes, Madame."

"Good. Would you all excuse me for a moment?" With that, Madame Rosetti stalked down the hallway toward her office.

The girls all gazed at each other.

"I'm a sorcerer?" Katya breathed.

"We're sorcerers," Elana said, burying her head in her arms.

Marya plopped down on the step, feeling suddenly like maybe the life had been sucked out of her after all.

She was not alone. Luka leaned back against one of the walls, and the other girls all collapsed where they were.

The school was a lie.

Simona held her hands up, staring at them. "It's gone, you know," she whispered. "After I came out of the infirmary. That feeling was gone. My body . . . remembers it sometimes. Like an echo. But it's gone."

Eventually, Madame Rosetti came back into the Great Hall with a sealed letter in her hand, which she gave to Luka. "There is an estate a ninety-minute ride from here, just north of Sarabet. The estate is owned by a Count Vulpe. Tell whomever answers the door that Countess Vulpe's sister from Dragomir Academy sent you, and that it's urgent that the countess get my letter immediately. Can you do that?"

"Um"—he looked from her to Marya—"Madame, I don't want to leave Marya."

Madame Rosetti straightened. "I will not let anything happen to her. You have my word. But I cannot leave these girls. So it has to be you whom I send. They will listen to you, and they will believe you when you tell them that I sent you and the matter is urgent. Do you understand?"

Luka nodded, cheeks red.

"It's okay," Marya whispered. "You can go."

"I'll come back," he said.

"I know." There were so many Lukas. Marya had thought she knew them all, but she did not. Maybe none of the ones she'd seen before were real; maybe they were just personas he put on like clothes because he didn't know what to wear to please their parents. Just like her.

Madame Rosetti regarded the room. "Girls," she proclaimed in her best deputy-headmistress voice, "I have told my sister and her husband about the events of tonight. I believe they will be able to help us. In the meantime, I would like us all to proceed to the infirmary where Nurse Rieza—where *I* can give you something to help you rest. Tomorrow we will decide on next steps. Come with me."

She motioned to the stairway. She was not asking. All the girls stood up, except for Elana, who cast Marya a helpless glance.

"We're going to stay here for a bit," Marya said.

Madame Rosetti looked as if she was going to protest for a moment, but just a moment. "All right, Marya," she said. "I'll be waiting."

When they were all gone, Marya scooted herself next to Elana and lifted her arm up, an invitation. Elana tucked herself in, put her head down, and cried.

The two girls sat there like that for some time. Marya's brain was no longer whirling, no longer thinking anything, really. There were no words for what they had endured, just this vast nothingness.

"I remember now," Elana said, after some time. "Something that happened. I thought it might have been a dream. . . . The headmaster was sitting in my room back in that cottage—just sitting there, watching me. I woke up, and my hands felt like they were . . . almost buzzing and suddenly, the door opened. On its own. And I did it. I *knew* I made it happen. And the headmaster didn't react at all. I said, "Did you see what I just did," and he said, no, told me that he must have left it open when he came in. So then I pushed a cup off the bureau—with energy, with *magic*—and he said I didn't, that I must have knocked it over by accident. Then I fell asleep again and woke up and I couldn't remember if it even happened at all, or I'd dreamt it. And the buzzing in my hands was gone."

"Oh," Marya said, completely inadequately.

"At least, I think that's what happened. I slept so much. It must have been an enchantment. Or a potion. So I can't really tell what was a dream and what was real."

It was exactly what Simona had said.

"I still don't know what was real, even now. But this is real. Right?"

"It is," Marya said.

"You promise?"

Marya nodded.

"I don't understand any of this," she said, looking at her hands again. "I don't know how this happened. How did this happen?"

"Because," Marya said, "it was all a lie. Everything we know about Illyria. A lie."

Yes, this was the inescapable conclusion. They'd been made to believe that only men could be sorcerers. But it was all just a story, just a lie woven into a tapestry and passed down as truth.

"Why?" Elana asked. "Why would they do this to us?"

"I don't know," Marya said. "I don't know."

*Who does the story serve?* Madame Bandu would ask.

"They told me I was mad," Elana added, wrapping her arms around her chest and squeezing, as if trying to hold herself together. "They made me feel like I was mad. I can't believe they did that to me."

Marya did not say anything. What could she say?

"People are going to think we're witches, aren't they?"

"I don't know."

Elana shook her head, "I think I need to sleep now," she said, voice frayed. "I can't—I need to sleep. Do you want to come up to the infirmary?"

"I . . . can't. My brother's coming back. He won't know where we are."

"You're just going to wait down here? It could be hours!"

"Yes," Marya said.

"All right." Elana got up and stepped onto the staircase. "Marya? . . . Thank you."

"For what?"

"For trying to find me. I thought . . . I thought I was alone."

"You're not," Marya whispered.

Then Marya was by herself in the great hall, sitting on the dark wooden floor, hugging her knees to her chest. She was so small compared to the vast room, with all the giant portraits of the former trustees looking down at her sternly.

"Why?" Marya asked out loud.

They did not respond.

Marya put her head in her arms and stayed in the middle of the floor, while the portraits watched. This was the first time she'd been truly alone since she'd arrived at Dragomir.

It was the first time her heart had a chance to properly break.

So Marya folded her arms around her legs and wept. She cried for herself; she cried for her little brother; she cried for all the things she'd been ready to believe; she cried for all the things she had not done, and all the things she had lost.

And yet, as she sat alone and cried, she was also aware that she was less alone than she had been in a long, long time.

She sat there while the portraits watched her. She had so many things to say goodbye to. First, the idea that her parents would ever really have a place for her. Then the idea that they had had a part in sending her away. Because even that was better than the truth she now knew: that they'd gotten this letter, let her be taken away, and then simply went on with their lives.

And the school. She had been going back and forth between feeling like she did not belong there and that she did. It had never occurred to her to question the school itself.

Are you wicked or are you weak? Those had been her only choices.

And the sorcerers. They lied. They knew the girls who'd come through the school had the potential to wield magic, and they didn't tell them, told them instead that they were *troubled*.

Why?

"Marya," said a voice.

She popped up in a blink, startled to discover she wasn't the last person in the world.

It was the headmaster.

# The Other Monster

Marya gaped at the headmaster. She'd forgotten he
was even in the building.

But he had been. He'd been in his office the entire time,
safe under the protection of the high count's enchantment,
where he'd locked himself in after hearing the alarm.

"Is anyone else here?" he asked, looking around some-
what warily.

"No," she said definitively. And then quickly added:
"Not that I know of?"

At that, the wariness seemed to fall away, and he took a

step toward her, face a mask of concern. "And how did you get here, Marya? You were in quarantine."

Her head spun. Why wasn't he scared of the Dread? Did he think that since the school was quiet everyone must have evacuated and the Dread had followed?

"I walked here," she said.

"You walked here," he repeated. "I see. Did someone come with you?"

"No," she said. "I was alone." She added, as innocently as she could, "Who would I have come with?"

*Act like you don't know anything. Act like you think you're mad.*

"No one, I suppose," he said. "Tell me—what exactly do you remember?"

Marya had spent her time here trying to play by their rules, to prove she was not who they said she was. The only time she'd broken them was when she was trying to prove herself, to please them.

Now she needed to change the rules.

She blinked. "I woke up in a place that wasn't the school," she said carefully. "I didn't know where I was. But I was alone. And when I looked out the window, I saw Dragomir—and a cloud of Dread above it. So I headed here, in case anyone needed help."

"Ah! I should have known. You saw the Dread, so you came running here." he said. "Toward the Dread!" He laughed, the way you would laugh at a baby goat trying to make a jump her legs were too stubby for. "Do you know why you were in quarantine?"

Marya clenched her hands into tight fists. "I don't remember."

"You must have been very confused when you woke up. It was quite a scene you made in my office!"

He was lying. She knew he was lying. She had not made a scene. Madame Bandu was not a witch. Elana was not mad. It was all a lie.

"Mountain madness usually comes upon girls in the third year, but your class seems to be quite precocious. We have in the past seen it triggered by emotional distress, as happened with your classmate Elana, as you may recall." He shrugged. "Just understand that you may not be reacting rationally right now. And perhaps consider that, when you see your worst fear in the sky at a time when you are under quarantine for madness, it might not be real."

She could feel her fingernails dig into her palms. It was real. Everything had happened just as she'd seen it.

"The Dread was real," she spat.

"Yes. This time. It was real. And we managed to take

care of it without you, Marya Lupu," he said, motioning to the room around him. "You see? Everyone is safe. Say it. *Everyone is safe*." He stared at her. He meant it.

"Everyone is safe," she repeated. She knew what he was trying to do. She saw it now. There was a tiny fire that always burned inside her, because of her mother, for whom she was never doing the right thing, acting the right way. Because of her father, for whom she was an embarrassment for existing. Because of Dragomir Academy, where she could not follow the rules, where she could not do the simplest things, where she could not even play this game of elaborate pretend when the rules of it were so very clear. The headmaster saw this fire in her and was trying to throw kindling on it, to see if she would burn up.

"And, as you can see," he said, opening up his arms, "the Dread is gone. High Count Arev and I defeated it, after evacuating the students. You see, we've always had a plan in place. The students are now on their way to safety."

Marya looked up at him. "All of them?" she asked.

"Yes. All of them. Except for you." He lied with complete assurance. It was remarkable, really. But he had no idea what had happened. This was a truth that Marya took hold of, held on to tight.

That, and the most important one, the one he'd had her repeat:

Everyone was safe.

And they were safe because she and Elana had come back. Because they had decided to head toward the monster, to help the girls who had become their friends, despite everything the headmaster had done to divide them.

"As you can see, Marya," he said, "it would have been best for you to have stayed where you were, and trusted us to handle everything."

It all sounded so true. The things he said about her sounded exactly like what everyone else had always said about her, from the beginning. It sounded exactly like the thing she said about herself when it was late at night and she had nothing but her own thoughts to keep her company.

Somehow, she thought then of Madame Bandu at her loom, showing Marya the crescent moon at the bottom of the tapestry.

"Marya," the headmaster said, "have I lost you? Where did your head go? I understand this might cause you a lot of distress—"

She stared up at him.

*Who does the story serve?*

Him. He benefited if she felt like she was inept, foolish, useless, weak.

But she wasn't. She had power.

She was a troubled girl, after all.

"Headmaster, may I tell you something?" she asked, softening her voice.

"Certainly, Marya!"

"It's just . . . I had the strangest dream when I was in quarantine."

She saw something flash across his face, just for a moment. "You did?"

Her eyes widened. "Yes! I dreamed that—well, it's embarrassing—"

He took a step closer. "It's all right, Marya. You can tell me."

"I dreamed that . . . I was doing magic."

"I see," he responded, face now blank. "That does sound strange, Marya. Could you tell me more? What kind of magic were you doing?"

She blinked. "I . . . well, please don't laugh—"

"I won't. You have my word, Marya."

"It was like . . . I knew my hands had magic in them. That I could point them at something and make something happen, that I *needed* to." She looked up at him, eyes wide. "Is that what magic is like?" If years of psychological warfare with Luka had taught her anything, it was how to navigate a conversation like this.

His face was completely blank. "I myself do not know what it's like to work magic, Marya. But I would imagine your dreams are more the product of fancy than reality."

"There's something else," Marya said, keeping her eyes down. "I . . . made the bureau move. The bureau in the room where I was."

"In your dream."

"I suppose?" Marya said.

"Marya"—he cleared his throat—"I think we should get you back to quarantine as soon as we can. As soon as it's light out, we'll go back to the sanitarium."

"Is it dangerous?" she asked, holding her hands up and staring at them, as if something very odd were happening with them.

She did not have a plan. She was walking in the dark with a lantern just bright enough to show her the step ahead. That was it. But it was better than crouching in the corner.

"Headmaster!" she shouted, thrusting her hands forward.

"Marya!" He bounded toward her and grabbed her wrists, pushing her arms down. "We should get you to my office. I have something that will help."

"Am I a witch?" she asked him, eyes as big as she could make them.

"Marya, that's—"

"I am, aren't I! That's how I got out of my room! The door was locked, and I got out! It wasn't a dream at all."

"Marya—"

She let out a scream, like a girl who suddenly had magic coursing through her body and didn't understand what it was.

"Marya"—he tugged on her wrists gently—"come with me."

"No!" She wrenched her arms away. She didn't know how he'd caused her to lose consciousness abruptly, but going into his office seemed like a very bad idea. "No!" The more overwrought she acted, the more he seemed to lose his composure.

Well, he was the one who'd told her she was mad.

She stepped back. "I'm a witch!" she yelled. "What do I do?"

"Marya, Marya," he said soothingly, grabbing at her arm, "you poor girl."

"Don't touch me!" She jumped back.

He stopped. He clearly did not know what to do. But it was obvious that he was scared.

Almost like there was something frightening about being around a person whose magic was coming in when they were acting so out of control.

"Don't touch me!" she repeated, holding her hands up toward him.

"All right!" He put his palms up. "All right, Marya. You are not a witch. Not yet. But yes, that is magic you're feeling."

Her eyes rounded. She did not know what she'd been expecting, but it was not this.

"How can that be?" she breathed.

He could only see one step ahead of himself, too, she could tell. But he had his grip on a lantern now. She needed to keep hold of hers.

"Maybe you do," he said. "But as you can see, it is not something your body can contain. It is an illness. A madness."

"Mountain madness is . . . magic?"

He smiled broadly, as if delighted. "Marya!" he exclaimed. "I had a feeling you were special. This school has been open for two hundred years, and in all that time no one has ever put that together. But you, Marya Lupu, did. Incredible."

"What will happen to me?" she asked, her voice cracking

a bit. She was doing everything she could to look like the girl he thought she was.

"We simply cure you, that's all."

She started slightly. "What do you mean, *cure*?"

"Simply that we treat the magic as a disease, and draw it out of you as we would, say, poison. The sorcerers do the procedures."

"Poison?" she repeated.

"Or an infection. Metaphorically, it is helpful to think of female magic that way."

Now she just gaped at him. "Female magic?" she repeated.

"Marya, I am sure this is quite alarming. I cannot imagine you wish to become corrupted. But we will help you. Now, come with me—" He reached for her again.

"No!" she screamed, and jumped back. Her voice vibrated in the great hall, and even the portraits seemed shaken. She did not care; she was not going to go with him, anywhere, ever.

*Your anger is unseemly, Marya.*

She was not pretending anymore. She was furious, for her friends, for Simona, for all the Dragomir girls. And for herself.

And it was powerful.

"Yes, Marya. Don't you see, this magic is a curse, a burden upon you? You'll feel so much better when it's gone. And then you can finally be the kind of girl you want to be."

"What do you mean, *gone*? Where does it go?" Magic couldn't be destroyed. They had learned that.

"Ah. Yes." He considered for a moment. "The world is imperfect, Marya. Wise people understand this. A force like magic can take on a life of its own. Nonetheless, we cannot let witchcraft threaten our kingdom."

"So, by female magic, you mean witchcraft."

"Yes. Girls do not have the moral and physical constitution to handle magic. You must understand. It would be far more dangerous to let the witches have their way with Illyria."

"Far more dangerous than what?"

He did not respond.

"Than what?" she repeated. "What do you mean, magic can take on a life of its own? Do you mean—you don't mean—"

"This is the nature of female magic," he said. "It shows how evil it is. We started extracting it from the Kellian witches, and what happened?" He held his arms out.

"The Dread," she said quietly. Sorcerers had imprisoned

Kel's witches and taken their magic away, and then that uncontrolled magic had shown up in the Fantoma Forest one day, twisted and corrupted into something monstrous. Something that started attacking people. Something that has only continued to grow.

"I am afraid so," he said, sadness in his voice.

"The Dread kills people! It kills whole villages!"

"It's tragic," he said.

"The sorcerers can't control it anymore!"

"That is an unforeseen consequence. Something must have mutated. Unfortunately, that can happen. But I have faith that the sorcerers will meet this new challenge. Marya, the Guild has kept us safe for two hundred years. And if the Guild, the king, and his council feel this is the best way to protect Illyria, who are we to argue?"

Was it possible to explode from rage? If it was, then Marya was about to do just that. And then he wouldn't have to worry anymore, because all there would be left of her would be exploded bits.

But he didn't seem to want to let that happen. He was coming for her now, and no longer pretending he needed her permission. He strode toward her, staring her down, and she backed up against the wall and—

"Get away from her, you monster!"

Elana was at the top of the stairs, out of breath, Madame Rosetti right behind her. The headmaster whirled around, but before he could say anything, Elana lifted her hands and pushed them toward him, the air shimmering with power.

He flew backwards, slammed into the wall, and fell to the ground.

After Elana knocked the headmaster out cold, she, Madame Rosetti, and Marya dragged him into Madame Rosetti's office and locked the door.

"My office is not dreadproofed," said Madame Rosetti, "but it will have to do."

Not long after that, Luka burst through the front door, trailed by the Count and Countess Vulpe. The countess looked just like Madame Rosetti, only in fancier clothes. Luka ran to Marya and Elana, while Madame Rosetti took her sister and brother-in-law into one of the classrooms.

Marya perched on the stairs, Elana next to her. Luka sat on the floor, and Marya told him everything that had happened since he had left. It was not easy. The whole thing had happened so quickly, and the entire time she'd felt like she was tiptoeing on the edge of a cliff. In the dark. While a bear was chasing her. It was easier to just tell them what the headmaster had said.

"They take away magic from girls because they think girls with magic are dangerous to the kingdom," she said finally. "That's why."

Luka put his face in his hands.

"He told me this like I'd just agree: oh yeah, sure, girls need to have the magic taken from them—for the good of the kingdom!"

"So," Elana said, "the Illyrian girls that they said were witches, back in the Witching Wars, that they put in asylums, were sorcerers."

"I think so," Marya said. There was so much to think about. "I think a witch is just a female sorcerer. At least in Illyria."

Elana shook her head slowly. "My father knew. He knew when he sent me here. He knew I had magical potential, and that if I did develop magic they'd take it away."

"I'm sorry," Marya said.

"Really," Elana said quietly, "I'm not surprised at all. He wants all the power for himself."

"There's more," Marya said slowly, glancing at Elana, who gave her a small nod. Elana and Madame Rosetti had heard the part where the headmaster confessed that taking girls' magic away caused the Dread. Which was a relief, because otherwise Marya might not have believed it herself.

"How," Luka breathed, when she'd finished telling him.

"If you try to take magic from someone, magic appears somewhere else," Elana whispered. "If some raw magic appeared in the Fantoma Forest one day . . . I mean, who knows what else is in there, what it interacted with."

"They started with the Kellian witches," Marya said softly, "and girls who developed magic in Illyria. And then the Dread appeared, but they didn't stop. He said it like there was no other choice, like the Dread killing everyone was just . . . an acceptable side effect."

"I hate them," Elana whispered. "I hate them so much."

Marya nodded softly. Yes, yes. She hated them too.

She was so tired.

As for Luka, he had gotten up and was now pacing back and forth in the great hall. "I can't believe I ever wanted to be one of them," he said.

Marya shrugged. She could not respond. Anyway, it all felt so big, so impossible. "Do you really think they'll stop? They're arresting people for being witches right now. They—oh!"

She had never even told Elana about Madame Bandu.

"Luka says that she found something out, maybe about the school, and they arrested her," Marya finished.

Elana considered for a moment. "She's from Torak? In the south?"

Marya and Luka nodded.

"Well, I think my father owes me a favor, don't you?" She stood suddenly. "I'm going to write him a letter. I think I'll send it by messenger, payable on delivery."

"Did Madame Rosetti hear all of this, too?" Luka asked. "About the Dread?"

Marya and Elana nodded.

"That's good. She's probably telling the count and countess now. I got the impression they don't like the Guild much. And maybe they can—"

Just then, Madame Rosetti and her sister and brother-in-law emerged back into the great hall, all with identical expressions of grim determination. They marched over to Madame Rosetti's office, where she unlocked the door, and, a few moments later, the count emerged, leading a confused-looking Headmaster Iagar by the arm.

"... try to get the truth out of the headmaster," he finished.

The headmaster eyed Marya, Luka, and Elana as he passed. Marya went completely cold.

Elana grabbed her hand as the headmaster's gaze slid off

her, squeezed it tight. Luka put his hand on her shoulder.

When the count opened the front door and began to guide the headmaster out, Marya stood up.

"Headmaster Iagar!" she shouted.

He turned to look at her.

"I never had magic. I was faking it!"

At that, Elana cackled; Luka guffawed. Marya could see the meaning of her words settling over the headmaster's face, saw his eyes pop, and she could not help herself: she grinned.

# The Nightingale

For the next few days, it was only Madame Rosetti, the girls of Rose Hall, and Luka at Dragomir Academy. The rest of the inhabitants of the school were being housed in inns in Sarabet, and would return gradually, coachful by coachful. But, as Madame Rosetti told the Rose Hall girls, she had chosen to delay the process, given they were safe. They did not even know if there was still going to be a school.

Before the Count and Countess Vulpe had taken Headmaster Iagar back to their estate, Madame Rosetti relieved him of his keys. In his office she'd discovered the health records of the students who had been treated for mountain madness in the locked drawer in his file cabinet. (Madame Rosetti could read ancient Messapic.) They'd provided enough proof for the count to extract a confession from him about the school's activities.

The count and countess spread word of the headmaster's confession through the nobility of Illyria. In an address, the king professed outrage over the activities at Dragomir and promised a full investigation. The Sorcerers' Guild promptly arrested High Count Arev, the sorcerers responsible for identifying the girls, and a few others who were part of what they called a secret conspiracy perpetuated by a small rogue faction of the Guild.

This, then, proved to be the unspoken bargain; if the king, his councils, and the Guild would be allowed to pretend that they knew nothing of the true origins of the Dread, they would proclaim that (much to their surprise) in Illyria girls' magic was no different than sorcerers' magic. The word *sorceress* was spoken by an Illyrian king for the first time.

The girls of Rose Hall, including Simona, spent their time in the parlor, trying to pick apart all the stories they'd been told and examine the threads, trying to weave together the truth. Luka was there too; he had been pronounced an honorary Rose Hall girl. Madame Rosetti had said he could stay as long as he wished, and had found a room for him, and some clothes from the staff quarters.

Marya was glad. She had finally found him; she did not want to lose him again.

There was so much to discuss. There were so many lies. They'd been told their whole lives that being a sorcerer required years of study, but Elana and Katya both said the spell they'd cast had been instinct.

"I just knew what to do," Elana said. "I felt it."

Katya nodded. "Me too."

They'd been told witches reached into chaos to work their magic, and that sorcerers had somehow turned that chaos into order, but Elana and Katya both said it did not feel anything like order or chaos, just . . . power.

But the question that really consumed them all was: *Why?* Why not allow girls to train as sorcerers, just as boys did?

"Maybe," Katya said, "they really believed that magic in girls was evil. You know, Kel is our enemy and their queen was a witch, and so therefore girls with magic are witches."

But were magic-wielders in Kel actually witches or just sorcerers with a different name? Was there a difference in the way people used magic in Kel? And were they all only women? What was the truth?

"The sorcerers are scared," Elana said. "Scared of what would happen if women could work magic. That they wouldn't be as powerful."

As the other Rose Hall girls sat and picked at the threads each night, Marya tucked herself into a corner of the sofa, held on to one of the countess's pillows, and thought.

Who does the story serve?

Who is served by the story that magic is a learned skill that requires extensive education, mentorship from experienced sorcerers? Who is served from the story that witches are evil? That only men can be sorcerers?

It was better for her to think about these questions than about the ones that really haunted her.

A few nights after the Dread attack, the girls all gathered in the parlor talking until the fire in the fireplace was low. Marya sat in her usual spot, hugging her usual pillow, and was, as usual, watching the rest of them and turning over questions in her head. When everyone began to disperse for the night, Elana put her hand on Marya's arm.

"Can I talk to you?"

Luka, who had been heading out, stopped in the doorway, his glance falling on both of them.

"Stay, Luka," Elana added.

So Marya stayed tucked into her corner, holding her pillow close, while Elana sat next to her and Luka perched on the floor.

"I wondered," Elana asked, "if you were okay. You've just been really quiet."

Marya looked down. She could feel Luka's eyes on her.

"You know," Elana continued, "what you did with the headmaster, it was really brave."

"I didn't do anything."

Luka scoffed. "You did!"

"Marya," Elana said, putting her hand on Marya's shoulder, "you stood up to him! You confronted him, all by yourself. You got him to tell us that taking magic from girls was the cause of the Dread!" She swallowed. "The Guild takes magic from girls. Do you think anyone would really be upset about that on its own? Do you think they'd care at all?"

Marya looked down. No, no she did not.

"People believe whatever the sorcerers tell them to believe," Elana continued. "They'd just tell everyone that girls with magic are witches and they have to take away their magic for Illyria's safety. And everyone would believe them. But the Dread—that was the key. People are more scared of the Dread than anything. If you hadn't gotten the truth, we'd be back in witch asylums and the Dread would keep evolving."

She was right. Marya knew she was right. If it hadn't been for the part about the Dread, probably nothing would have changed. Except the Dread would have kept getting worse; even now the Guild still didn't know what drew the Dread to Dragomir Academy.

But it didn't exactly make her feel better. "It's not enough, though. The king, the Guild . . . they just told everyone they didn't know. Nothing's going to happen to them."

"But, Marya," Luka said, leaning forward, "they'll stop taking magic from girls. Eventually the Dread will disappear, right?"

They all looked at each other. It seemed likely, but the fact was, no one knew for sure.

At least there wouldn't be any *new* Dread. That was something.

"And they'll stop hurting girls here," Elana said. "And the king announced that Illyria has sorceresses. And that means something. Things will change. Maybe slowly, but they will."

Marya closed her eyes. An Illyria with sorceresses felt

very different, yes. But it was so hard to imagine. And still, so many people were going to get away with what they had done.

Every time Marya closed her eyes, she saw the headmaster standing over her, sneering at her, ready to hurt her. If it hadn't been for Elana—

"I just . . . ," Marya whispered. She squeezed her eyes closed again, and when she opened them, they were red. "I let him make me feel like there was something wrong with me. That I was *troubled*. Why did I let him?"

This. This was the question that kept Marya up at night. Everything he'd said to her from the moment she'd arrived at the school—the things that had made her feel useless, the things that had made her feel important, everything— had been about controlling her.

And it had been so deliberate. Everything. The headmaster had read her mail, he must have. That's the only way he could have known about Madame Bandu's apron, about Baby Pieter. He read all their mail, so he could know what their fears and weaknesses were. So he could exploit them.

He'd found her weakness: Baby Pieter. That little voice in her head that always whispered, *It's your fault.*

She was a tapestry, and the headmaster and the Guild

and the king and his councils had taken her apart and started to weave her into something else. She'd stopped them, and now she was just piles of tangled thread.

"Marya," Luka said, voice low, "it's not your fault. You didn't do anything wrong. The stuff Mama said to you— that wasn't your fault either."

*Mama.* The word hit at her heart. Maybe, someday, Marya would find words to say to her mother. She was not ready, yet. She could sort through two centuries of the kingdom's lies and the fact that the sorcerers would rather see an uncontrollable monster ravage towns than let girls have magic more easily than she could everything that had passed with her mother.

Elana sat back. "I believed them too," she said quietly. "They told me I was mad, and I believed them. I can't get over this. Why did I believe them?"

"But that's different."

"And I believed my parents sent me here because they thought I was too much trouble. I believed it so easily." Elana wrapped her arms around herself. "We all believed them. I can't sleep. I just go over it again and again. I bet everyone else feels the same way."

Marya nodded slightly. Yes. Everyone did believe them. They all thought they'd been sent there because someone thought they were troubled.

And the school had only just gotten started on them. Simona, who had been so quiet since the Dread attack, mourning what had been taken from her. Simona, who had had her edges sanded off in six years at Dragomir Academy. It must have hurt.

"What do you think is going to become of all of us?" Marya whispered then. "I don't want to go home."

Out the corner of her eye, she saw Luka nod sadly.

"I think they'll let us stay here," Elana said. "I think they have to. I mean, if people want to."

"Well, not you," Marya said. "You'll go."

Elana blinked. "Go? Where?"

"Elana," Marya said, "you're a sorceress. The sorcerers are going to want to train you."

She straightened. "I am not going anywhere."

"But they'll insist."

"Marya. I am not going to a sorcerer's estate."

"But your magic. Won't you want to learn?"

She shook her head firmly. "I can do it on my own. With Katya. With all of us. We can all work together. What the sorcerers have done with magic, how they've twisted it . . . I don't want any part of it. Besides"—she glanced away— "my friends are here."

At this, Marya released a great breath. Elana leaned in and put her head on Marya's shoulder, and Marya relaxed into her.

It turned out the rest of the girls were all lying awake at night going over everything again and again, and the rest of the girls all thought that they were alone. Maybe Marya had not noticed the way the other girls retreated into the shadows sometimes, the way they got lost in their heads, the way they carried the experience everywhere like an invisible boulder, but that did not mean it didn't happen.

It helped to talk about it. It helped to realize you were not alone.

A little more than a week after the Dread attack, a messenger arrived with a letter from the person Marya wanted to hear from most in the world. It read:

> *Dearest Marya,*
>
> *I am back with my husband and boys now. I was released on the good word of a High Count Teitler. His daughter is a friend of yours, I believe. Please thank her for me.*
>
> *I was arrested after I sent you a letter about Nadia*

Dragomir. I did some digging and discovered that she was sent to an asylum for witches. Such things existed back then for Illyrian girls and women accused of witchcraft. Her parents devoted themselves to trying to get her out. Eventually her parents made a deal with the king: Nadia would be returned to them if the family promised to leave Illyria and donated their estate for the purposes of this "school."

Now I understand that Nadia was not a witch, but a sorceress. As many of the alumnae of Dragomir should have been. I presume they took her magic from her at the asylum.

I will try to learn everything I can about the true history of Illyria. There are tapestries within tapestries.

You girls did an amazing thing. While I don't know the full story, I know with every bit of my being that you, Marya, were at the center of it all, listening to your heart and asking questions.

Remember, just because you are scared does not mean you are not brave.

Write to me, and please say hello to that brother of yours.

With love,
Lucille Bandu

And, at the bottom, a drawing:

A nightingale.

*Thresholds, a new beginning.*

She had her book back from the headmaster's office.

"I wrote my father and I said that I knew the truth," Elana said, when Marya showed her the letter. "And that I knew he knew. I told him if he did not arrange to have Madame Bandu freed, I would tell everyone that he knew about the Dread. That did it."

"Thank you," Marya said.

She read the part about Nadia Dragomir several times. She'd been right, and wrong. Nadia Dragomir had been arrested as a witch and put in an asylum. Witchcraft was Nadia's curse, or so they'd thought. But she was not a witch; rather, she was a sorceress.

"I guess," Elana said, "that the Guild realized that if the daughters of nobility were going to be among the girls who developed magical ability, they needed a more palatable solution than an asylum."

Marya shuddered. If Nadia Dragomir had not developed magic, then they might all be sitting in an asylum right now. And no one would think anything of it. And if the Countess Dragomir had not set the story down, maybe no one would have known. If someone had not saved her needlework, Marya would never have had any pieces to put together. If the villagers had not sung about Nadia's fate, if someone had not decided that their songs were worth saving, Marya would not have rushed into the headmaster's office, and everything would have been different.

This story had almost been lost. How many other stories had been lost, because no one thought they were worth saving?

All these questions were turning around in Marya's mind when Madame Rosetti came into the Rose Hall parlor to speak with the girls. She had been coming in to see them at least once a day. Her hair was still pulled back severely, her expressions all could be still described as stern, but Marya could see, now, everything that lay beneath the surface.

The girls gathered on the sofas—all seven of them fitting perfectly around the fire in a way they'd never seemed to before. Luka sat cross-legged on the floor right below Marya.

"I have news," Madame Rosetti told them. "The king has agreed to keep the school open, with me as headmaster. This academy was generously funded by the Dragomirs, so money is not an issue. But the king and the Guild have offered to add even more funds to the school's endowment, should we wish it." She gazed at the girls meaningfully.

"I'll bet," whispered Ana-Maria.

"But," she continued, "as to the purpose of the school, he has asked me for guidance. He has suggested that Dragomir be devoted to the education and refinement of all of Illyria's potential sorceresses, and that members of the Guild could come to mentor any girls who develop magic."

"No," said Elana. "We don't need them here!" Next to her, Katya nodded.

Madame Rosetti held up a hand. "I know. That is why I wanted to speak with you. What we have right now," she said carefully, "is an advantageous situation. They want to keep us happy, because we know the whole truth."

"It's power," Marya said. Reading was power; education was power; information was power. It was what Madame Bandu had been telling her all along.

"Yes," Madame Rosetti said. "We have power. We also have Illyria's first sorceresses, who can forge a path for the girls who follow—though I am sure that the Guild would prefer to forge it for them." She nodded at Elana and Katya. "So, I would like you girls to tell me what you want this school to be, and I will take that into consideration. I do not care to define your futures for you. Naturally, attendance here will no longer be compulsory, but every girl will be invited to stay if she wishes. Please discuss it, and we will talk later. All right?" With a nod to them, she headed back out the door, and then stopped. "Luka," she added, "would you come with me a moment?"

While he and Madame Rosetti headed into the hall-way, the girls all looked at each other.

What did they want the school to be? They hadn't even known for sure whether the school would stay open.

"She said 'education and refinement,'" Elisabet said. "I don't want to be refined. I don't think we need to be refined."

No. No, they did not. Marya was tired of people trying to refine her.

Elana went and got a notebook from the writing desk. "No refinement," she proclaimed. "Got it."

"No Sorcerers' Guild!" Daria called.

"Writing it down," Elana said.

"We don't need them," Katya said. "We'll figure out magic for ourselves, the way we want it to be. There will be more of us, soon."

That was true. Tereza was the only third-year to have manifested magic so far, and none of the second-years had yet. And it was conceivable that some of the rest of them might still manifest it before they finished their sixth year.

"I don't know what we'll do after this," Simona said. "The sixth-years. I do not want to work on an estate."

"And what about after us?" Daria asked. "What happens? Who comes? Is it still potential sorceresses?"

Marya stared into the fire. There were going to be new potential sorceresses every year, and the Guild would find them first. If the Dragomir girls did not take them in, the sorcerers would claim them. And who knew what they'd do?

"We can't trust the sorcerers," Elana said.

Just then, Luka came back in the room, placing himself at Marya's feet. "Madame Rosetti said I can stay as long as I want," he whispered to her. "She said I could help with the animals. I would like to stay for a while, while I figure out what I want to do. I don't—I don't think I can go home, at least not yet."

"I want you to stay," Marya said, resting a hand on his shoulder. Her other hand was stroking the embroidery on the pillow on her lap.

Luka had options. He could go home and work with Dr. Bandu, or go to school, or apprentice with someone else. He had opportunity.

And now, they had opportunity too.

It did not seem fair. She thought of the girl she'd once

been, sitting outside her family library, waiting to be invited in. She finally had that invitation, because some sorcerer had identified her as having magical potential.

How many other girls were waiting outside the door, waiting to be let into a room with books and friends and keys to opportunity? Waiting to be told they had *potential*?

"If they're going to give us all this money," Marya said quietly, "maybe we should ask them to start more schools."

Everyone looked at her at once.

"Around the kingdom," she said. "For girls. For anyone who wants to go. To give them an education."

Now all the girls were sitting up, staring at Marya. The air in the room crackled.

"We could run them," Simona said. "Those of us who wanted to. When we leave here. We could be teachers if we wanted, too." And, for the first time in a week, a smile spread across Simona's face.

Marya felt her heart lift, felt warmth and light come through her body again. She had not realized how much of her had frozen over, shut down, until she felt it all come alive again.

"We can do this," she said, eyes shining.

The other girls were grinning at her. They could do this. The Guild was still in power, the king still sat on his throne, but they could still remake the world.

There was more, so much more. Now that the doors were open, ideas were flooding into Marya's head. They could learn the embroidery language. Madame Bandu could come and teach them to weave. They needed to tell their story in as many ways as they could. They needed to send letters, tell stories, weave, and embroider. They needed to tell the truth, to record it in a way that people would keep it. They were the troubled girls of Dragomir Academy—breaking, but never broken—and they had stories to tell.

# Acknowledgments

My thanks to my readers: Swati Avasthi, Linda Urban, Kate Messner, Anne Cunningham, Sara Getzin, and Laura "More Tapestries" Ruby. To Nina LaCour and her Slow Novel Lab. To Elana K. Arnold, Tracey Baptiste, Brandy Colbert, Brita Sandstrom, Mike Jung, Will Alexander, Megan Atwood, and Megan Vossler for the right words at the right time. To my troubled girls of all genders, you know who you are. To Tina Dubois, agent and sorceress. To Dash, world's best story consultant; I'm sorry there are no evil bunnies in this book. To Jordan Brown, for everything.

Turn the page to start reading

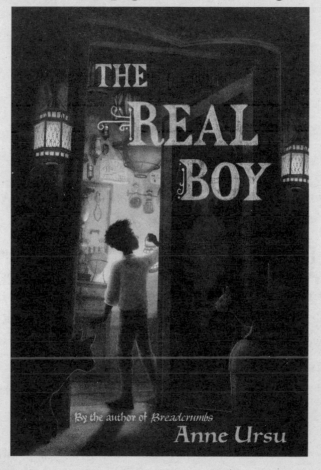

# CHAPTER ONE

# The Cellar Boy

The residents of the gleaming hilltop town of Asteri called their home, simply, the City. The residents of the Barrow—the tangle of forest and darkness that encircled the bottom of Asteri's hill like a shadowy moat—called Asteri the Shining City, and those who lived there the shining people. The Asterians didn't call themselves anything special, because when everyone else refers to you as the shining people, you really don't have to do it yourself.

Massive stone walls towered around the City, almost as tall as the great trees in the forest. And, though you could not tell by looking at them, the walls writhed with enchantments.

*For protection,* the people of the City said.

*For show,* the magic smiths of the Barrow said. After all, it was in the dark of the Barrow where the real magic lay.

And indeed, the people of Asteri streamed through the walls and down the tall hill to the shops of the Barrow marketplace, buying potions and salves, charms and wards, spells and pretty little enchanted things. They could not do any magic themselves, but they had magic smiths to do it for them. And really, wasn't that better anyway?

The Barrow even had one magic worker so skilled he called himself a magician. Master Caleb was the first magician in a generation, and he helped the Asterians shine even more brightly. He had an apprentice, like most magic smiths. But like the wizards of old, he also took on a hand—a young boy from the Children's Home—to do work too menial for a magician's apprentice.

The boy, who was called Oscar, spent most of his time underneath Caleb's shop, tucked in a small room in the cellar, grinding leaves into powders, extracting oils from plants, pouring tinctures into small vials—kept company by the quiet, the dark, the cocoon of a room, and a steady rotation of murmuring cats. It was a good fate for an orphan.

"Hey, Mouse!"

Except for one thing.

"Come out, come out, Mouse! Are you there?"

At the sound of the apprentice's voice calling down the cellar stairs, a large gray cat picked herself up from the corner and brushed softly against Oscar. "It's all right," Oscar whispered. "I'll be fine." The cat sprang up and disappeared into the dark.

The apprentice's name was Wolf, because sometimes the universe is an unsubtle place. And even now Oscar sometimes found himself expecting an actual wolf to appear in place of the boy, as if the boy were just a lie they were all telling themselves.

"Where are you, little rodent?"

Oscar put down his pestle. He was not a rodent, but that never seemed to stop Wolf from calling him one. "I'm here," he called back. Stupid Wolf. As if one could be anywhere else but *here*.

Wolf appeared in the pantry door. He was only four years older than Oscar but almost twice as tall. With his elongated frame, the apprentice seemed all bones and hollows in the lantern light. He looked around the room, dark eyes flicking across the floor.

"Where are your little cat friends, Mouse?"

"Not here," Oscar said.

Like he would tell Wolf. Only Oscar knew the cats' secrets, and he guarded them closely. He knew all their names, he knew the sound of their footfalls, he knew where each of them slept, hid, stalked, he knew which one would visit him at what time of day. The gray cat with the lantern-bright green eyes was Crow, and she liked to come into the pantry in the mornings and nestle in the parchment envelopes.

"I don't actually care," Wolf said. He turned his gaze to the towering wall of shelves behind him. "We need some raspberry leaf for a Shiner. Now."

Oscar didn't even have to look. He could see the jars on the pantry shelves just as clearly in his head. "There's none left."

Wolf narrowed his eyes but did not question Oscar. A couple of years ago the apprentice would have stalked over to the shelves himself to make sure. Except every time he did, he'd discover that Oscar was right. Then he'd get angry and kick Oscar. It worked out better for both of them this way.

Wolf scanned the room. "Well, what about that?" He pointed at a jar at Oscar's feet filled with dry, crumbled green leaves.

"That's walnut leaves!" Oscar said.

"It looks the same. Give me four packets."

"But . . . ," Oscar sputtered, chest tightening. How could Wolf think they looked the same? "That's not what they want. It won't work." In fact, the herbs were opposite—raspberry leaf was to protect a relationship and walnut leaf was to break one up. But Wolf did not like it when Oscar knew such things.

"Oh, it won't work!" Wolf exclaimed, slapping his hands on his forehead. "I had no idea! What would I, apprentice to the Barrow's only true magician, do if it weren't for the cellar mouse to tell me that it won't work!"

"Well," Oscar said, "you could always look it up in the library."

Wolf's eyes flared. Oscar flinched. He hadn't even been trying to make Wolf angry; all he'd done was answer his question.

Wolf took a step closer to Oscar. "Do you even know what a freak you are?" he asked. "There's a reason Caleb keeps you in the basement." His eyes flicked from Oscar to the doorway and back. "Anyway, who cares about the herbs? It's a Shiner. She won't know the difference."

"But . . . what if she does?" The words popped out of Oscar's mouth before he could stop them. He could not help it—they were fluttering around in his head and needed to get out.

Wolf drew himself up. "Look, Mouse," he said, voice carnivorous. "She won't. Shiners want magic to work, and so it works. If you weren't dumb as a goat, you'd know that."

Oscar smashed his lips together. If that was true, it was no magic he understood.

"You let Caleb and me worry about the customers," Wolf continued. "You can worry about the cats, and your little plants, and—"

But whatever else Oscar had to worry about would remain a mystery, for just then the magician's voice came echoing down into the cellar, calling for Wolf.

The apprentice turned, collecting his bones and hollows. "Bring the walnut leaves up as soon as you have them ready," he said as he moved out the door. "And for the love of the wizards," he added, "don't come out into the shop. We want the customers to come back."

Five minutes later Oscar was creeping into the shop's kitchen, four packets of herbs in his hands. They were not walnut leaves. He hadn't had much time, so he'd put together a package of passionflower and verbena, which at least would not cause active harm.

From his position in the doorway he could see Master Caleb leaning across the shop counter, his tree-dark eyes focused on the lady before him as if they existed for nothing but to behold her.

The shining people didn't actually shine, not like a lantern or a firefly or a crystal in the light. But they might as well have. The young lady in front of Caleb looked like all the City people did—perfectly smooth olive-touched skin, cheeks with color and flesh, hair done up in some elaborate sculpture of braids and bejeweled pins, a gleaming amulet around her neck, wearing a dress of such intricately detailed fabric it made Oscar's hands hurt just to look at it.

Wolf appeared in the kitchen and immediately grabbed the packets out of Oscar's hand. Oscar gazed steadily at Wolf's chest. *The passionflower looks like walnut leaves,* he whispered in his mind—though whether to convince himself or Wolf he was not sure.

Wolf eyed the contents and sniffed, then turned and went back into the shop. His whole body seemed to change as he walked through the door, as if he were transforming from beast to human.

Oscar let out a breath and then suddenly caught it again. Wolf was handing the packets not to the customer, but to Master Caleb. Who was expecting raspberry leaves. Oscar had never made a mistake, not with herbs anyway, not in five years.

Caleb took the packets in his hand. Oscar's heart thudded. But Caleb just smiled at the customer, his mouth spreading widely across his face the way it always did when there was a woman on the other side of the counter. He looked as though nothing had ever made him so happy as giving her what she wanted.

The lady smiled back. And her cheeks flushed, just a little.

"Four envelopes of raspberry leaves, my lady," said

Caleb. "Though"—he leaned even closer—"I don't see how a lady like you would need such a thing."

"Oh," she said, laughing like a chime, "you can never be too careful."

Caleb straightened and ran a hand slowly through his dark hair. The lady's hand flew to hers.

"I agree," Caleb said. "And that's why we're here. We in the Barrow serve at your pleasure." He leaned again, and his face grew serious. "Whatever you need."

The woman opened the package and inhaled deeply. Oscar froze. He hadn't had time to mask the smell, and surely the verbena—

"I just love the smell of raspberry," she said.

"We'll mix up some perfume for you if you want. You have such natural beauty—we could put in things that would . . . enhance it."

The lady's smile grew. "I'll come back next week," she said, and then gave a little laugh. "It's true what they say, isn't it? Everything is better here than anywhere else in the world." For a moment her eyes dropped on Oscar in the doorway and then moved away, as if they had seen nothing at all.

Wolf appeared next to Oscar and leaned in. "He's quite a master, isn't he?" the apprentice whispered, nodding in Caleb's direction.

Oscar could only nod back. Of course he was.

Wasn't that the entire point?

Just before she got to the door, the lady stopped and smelled her envelopes again. And then she turned, gave Caleb one last raspberry smile, and left.

"I don't understand," Oscar muttered.

"You don't understand anything," Wolf said. "Caleb is a genius. He makes all the old wizards look like little cellar boys."

Oscar inwardly winced. No one talked about the wizards that way. He half expected a shelf to fall on Wolf's head.

It didn't. Shelves never fell on Wolf's head when Oscar wanted them to.

"Caleb can do things no one's ever done before, incredible things." Wolf looked down at Oscar, his eyes sparkling. "I know. While you're in the cellar filling envelopes, he's teaching me everything. He's going to make magic great again, greater than it ever was in the era of the wizards, and I'm helping him. You—"

In a flash Wolf shut his mouth, turned around, and transformed into Nice Wolf. It was his best feat of magic. Master Caleb was hanging on the door frame, leaning in. Caleb was taller than Wolf, and there were no bones and hollows to him. Caleb filled everything.

"Ah, you're both here," Caleb said. "Oscar, why don't you go to the gardens this afternoon? I believe we are low on supplies . . . particularly raspberry leaves."

Oscar's stomach dropped to his feet.

Caleb turned his gaze to Wolf. "And, Wolf, why don't you stay in the kitchen the rest of the day and sort the dried herbs. It seems like the time with them would do you some good."

Wolf stiffened. Oscar gulped.

Turning back to Oscar, Caleb added, "Not bad, my boy. But next time, add some rose hips or another berry leaf for scent."

The magician raised his eyebrows slightly. Oscar's mouth hung open. Then Caleb winked, ever so quickly, before heading back into the shop.

Oscar exhaled. He could feel his mouth twitching into a smile. Caleb's words perched on his shoulders: *Not bad, my boy.*

And then the smile fled, and the words, too. Wolf turned on him, all beast. "You think you're Caleb's little pet, eh?" he snarled. "I don't know what you did, Mouse, but you will regret it."

Oscar stepped back. He didn't know what he had done, either, but Wolf was definitely right: Whatever it was, he would certainly regret it.


Oscar was out the back door of the shop and into the forest before Wolf got a chance to pounce. Some presence followed him, something soft and stealthy and entirely un-Wolflike. Oscar turned around and a smile spread across his face. "Are you going to keep me company, Crow?" he whispered.

The smoke-gray cat's eyes danced, and she slipped next to Oscar, as close as a shadow.

Oscar had been to every part of the forest, including the thin strips in the southwest and northwest that wrapped around Asteri's hill like fingers, buffering the City from the plaguelands and the sea beyond. Though hundreds of people lived in the forest's villages, and though the forest was miles wide and even more miles across, it felt as secure and familiar as Oscar's own pantry. Better, because there were only wolves, and no Wolf.

The rest of the villagers had their gardens and pastures just outside the northeast of the forest, in the swath of fertile land that separated the eastern Barrow from the plaguelands. And their barns and stables, too. No farm animals liked being in the Barrow—except for Madame Catherine's Most Spectacular Goat.

But Caleb's gardens were in the southeast. And though everyone knew of their majesty, no one would ever find them. Caleb had hidden them behind an illusion spell, so anyone who did not know what was actually there would see only a meadow. The secret belonged to Caleb, Oscar, Wolf, and the trees.

The magic of the Barrow came from its soil, and the soil birthed a half a world's worth of plants and countless species of trees—from black cherry to red mulberry, quaking aspen to weeping willow, silver maple to golden rain, persimmon to pawpaw. Plants and shrubs and flowers grew everywhere; purplish-greenish moss crawled on the rocks; improbable mushrooms sprang from the soil in tiny little groves of their own.

But nothing compared to the wizard trees. The great oak trees grew to the sky like ladders for giants or gods, and spread their twisting branches as far out over the soil below as they could.

Once upon a time, magic flourished on all of Aletheia. And for centuries, legendary wizards worked the island's magic. The wizards were so powerful that they never died—when it was time for their human life to end, they would make their way into the Barrow forest, plant their feet in the hungry soil, and transform. Their body and spirit would go, but their essence would live on forever in a majestic, thriving monument. It was the only fitting end for a wizard of Aletheia. This was the island's gift to the wizards who tended to its magic and made the island thrive. Everyone knew the story.

And the wizards had never stopped serving Aletheia. When they became trees, their magic spread down through their roots, infusing the forest earth. And that was why the Barrow was a place like no other.

At some point the last wizard of Aletheia became a tree, and some time after that the island brought forth sorcerers—not nearly as powerful, but still with the ability to work the magic for the good of the people. Gradually the sorcerers faded, too, and were replaced by magicians, and then the magicians by magic smiths. Until Caleb, that is.

The forest had exactly one hundred wizard trees, and Oscar knew every one of them. He could close his eyes and see the map of them covering the forest, watching over it, feeding it with magic. Whenever Oscar touched one, he could feel some warmth humming just beneath the surface. And whenever he passed one, anything that was buzzing or roiling inside him stilled.

When he reached the edge of the forest, Oscar stopped. He had crossed through the line of trees into the gardens countless times, and each time he had to will himself to do it. Because maybe this would be the time Oscar would step through and the gardens would be gone, and Oscar would fall into the sky.

He looked at Crow, who trilled at him. He took a deep breath. He stepped forward. The trees released him, and the ground caught him; *It's all right.*

The gardens stretched along the edge of the forest, over an area three times as big as the main courtyard in the marketplace, a small orchard, rows of bushes, and plants of all kinds spreading out everywhere. *Angelica, anise, arrowroot.* It was all perfectly organized, logical—you didn't even need to think to find what you wanted. *Basil, bay leaf, bergamot, borage.*

In the back stood Caleb's towering achievement, the greatest man-made thing in the forest. And probably the entire world.

When Caleb had begun to import plants from far-off countries, things that didn't even grow in the Barrow (*eucalyptus, wolfberry, saffron, bellflower*), he'd announced he was going to design a house to hold them all, someplace bright and lush and moist to trick the plants into thinking they were somewhere warm and wet.

The result was a great steam house—the biggest building Oscar had ever seen. Panels of glass as tall as Caleb's shop and just as wide stood proudly next to one another, embraced all around by iron. A peaked glass roof sat on top, catching the sun and cradling the plants, giving them a place that was even better than home.

Walking into the house felt like stepping into an enchantment. It was a completely different world, warmer than the real world ever was, and the air had texture and moisture and life. The flowers burst forth in colors no illustration in a book had ever been able to reproduce— they looked like birds, like bells, like butterflies. They made even the clothes of the shining people seem dull. Oscar always stepped quietly through the glass house, trying to make as little disturbance as he could. He was trespassing; this house belonged to the flowers.

Oscar took a cart from the side of the glass house and began moving it through the gardens. He scanned the pantry shelves in his mind, making a list of jars that needed filling. He worked for two hours among the green and thriving things, picking plants, trimming off leaves and flowers, plucking berries, until his cart was full. He found Crow curled up near the raspberry bushes, as if to remind him not to forget the leaves.

"It's time to go," Oscar whispered. "It will be dark soon."

Crow blinked up at him sleepily.

Oscar sighed. "You're not going to walk, are you?" The cat eyed him, as if that was a very stupid question. "All right," Oscar said, picking Crow up in his arms and putting her in a corner of the cart. She crawled onto a pile of meadowsweet and immediately curled up again. "Well," Oscar murmured, "those needed to be crushed anyway."